ONE HOLLOW LOVE

MK AHEARN

*To those who have felt broken or hidden their demons—
remember, normal is overrated.*

"It's okay to ask for help. It's okay to need help. It's okay to want help."

— UNKNOWN

TRIGGER WARNINGS

Sexually explicit content, snakes, blood, loss of a parent off-page, abusive and manipulative parent, death, OCD and panic attacks, threatened sexual assault, and torture.

AUTHOR'S NOTE

In this book, you will meet Soleil, a character near and dear to my heart. Soleil struggles with severe OCD and goes through a journey of growth trying to figure out how to manage it. Soleil's struggles were based off my own, and it was incredibly hard to put such a vulnerable piece of myself into these pages. I ask that you remember that you may not always know the struggles someone is facing and to always hold kindness and understanding in your heart.

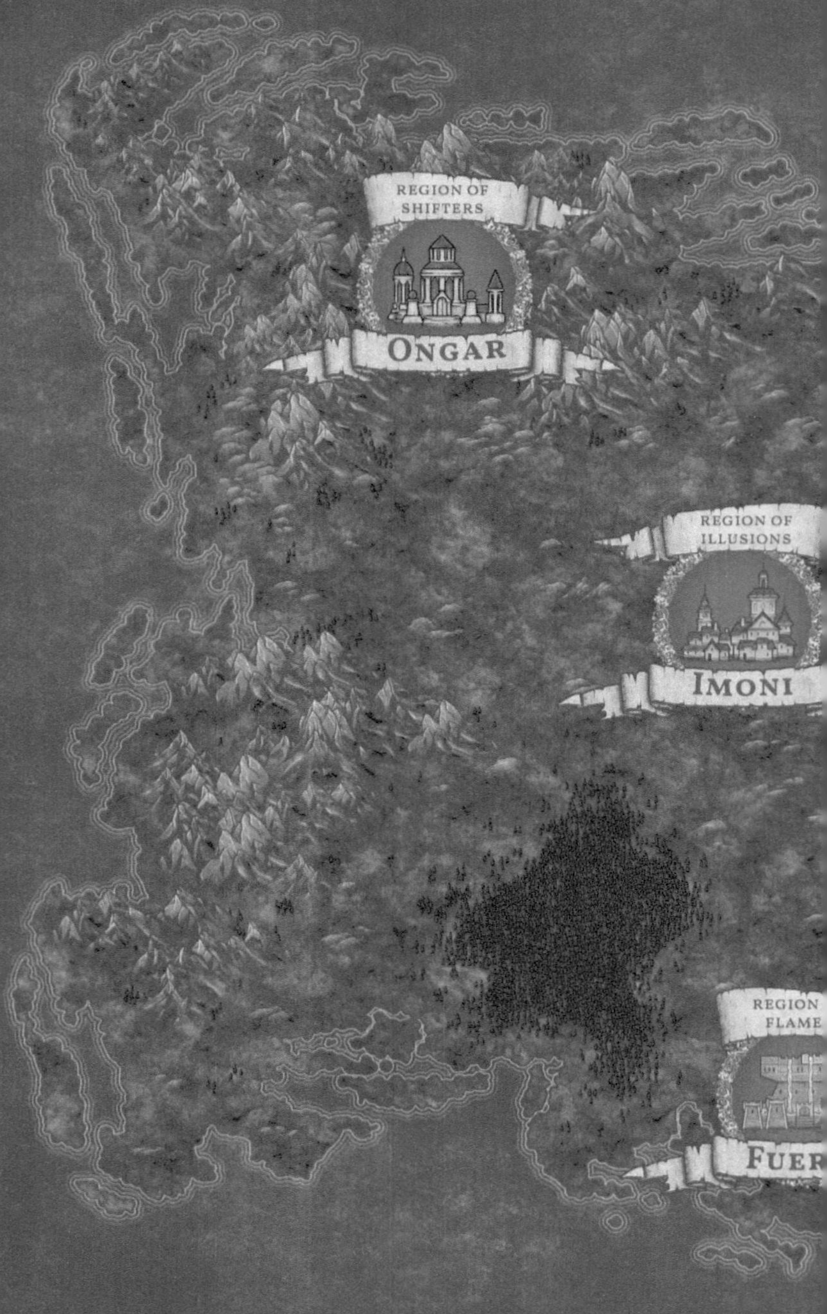

REGION OF SHIFTERS
ONGAR
REGION OF ILLUSIONS
IMONI
REGION FLAME
FUER

THE NYERA'S
TUNNEL

THE SERPENTINE
PALACE
GILDHOR

EODRATERA

REGION OF
DARKNESS
DRAZMIN

REGION OF
WATER
AUNEER

TO WEEPING VALE

To everyone still waiting for a morally grey demon king to whisk them away. Our town hopes you have a smutty Halloween.

PART ONE
SPIRITED

CHAPTER

ONE

Another Halloween, and I was locked in my room like every year before. My father had even updated the locks outside my door this year, leaving no chance for escape unless I magically conjured some heavy-duty tools.

Unfortunately, I was no witch, and I certainly didn't have any tools hidden in my room.

I pulled on the door and tried turning the knob forcefully, but nothing worked. If I tried to break the door, my father would hear and put an end to it, and I wasn't sure I would be strong enough to do any damage. Instead, I sat down on my bed, pulling my knees in close, hugging them. I rested my head on my knees, wishing I could be anywhere else.

It was for my own good, I kept telling myself, but curiosity still won my heart over.

Every year, my father did this, locking me away in my room and claiming it was the safest place for me. It was only me and him since my mother left without much explanation, just a few postcards from around the country and stray phone calls every few months. She no longer could take my father's need for control. She was free spirited, and I knew she needed to leave; I didn't blame her. Yet, here I was, stuck facing the consequences of my father's furthered paranoia.

I didn't buy his claims. What could be so horrible that I couldn't go outside? Halloween was the one night the lines between worlds blurred. All types of creatures ventured into our little town and spent a few hours roaming until midnight, when they were sent back to whatever world they came from.

Or so we were told.

There were stories of creatures that would snatch children if they weren't watched closely, of vampires looking for a quick snack who feasted on any individual they came upon. But those were just that: stories made up to scare little kids during the Halloween season.

It was also the one night of the year the community came together in celebration. The crisp fall weather, fun decor, and lots of sweet treats were irresistible to even the most sullen of individuals.

My father, however, was a believer in paranormal tales. He insisted that stories came from some fragment of the truth. Every year, he warned me about the demons roaming our world and forced me to stay inside. Creatures beyond my belief. Not that I would ever see them locked in my room.

The worst that ever happened on Halloween was some pranksters messing with our town's clock tower or kids scaring each other with ghost tales. All harmless little tricks.

I'd never known anyone in the town of Weeping Vale to run into real danger.

"Goodnight, Soleil. Tomorrow brings a new day," my father shouted through the deadbolted door in his jovial voice. I rolled my eyes. He may be ready to end his Halloween for the year, but I wasn't.

I let go of my legs and slid quietly off my bed. I carefully walked over to the door and pressed my ear to it. I didn't want my father to hear me stirring in my room; I could hear the sound of his door creaking shut.

It was only 6:00pm, but my father worked odd hours as a surgeon. This was my lucky year. This year, I would finally go out on Halloween. I had just enough time to sneak out and make it back before he woke up.

The only issue was, I had no idea how I was going to break out.

The new locks weren't going to budge. I glanced at the only other option.

The window.

There was a single window in my room, and it was just big enough for me to climb out.

My cat, Mr. Finkel, was curled up on his window-sill perch, his calico coat mirroring the colors of fall just beyond him outside. I'd rescued him only a few years ago, even after my father had protested. I needed some companion locked in this cage. With a stretch of his paws, he let out a small meow.

"Don't give me that look. You and I both know I'm not meant to be locked up in here," I said, as if he could really understand me. Was this what I was resorting to? Conversations with Mr. Finkel instead of experiencing the delights of Halloween night? It was becoming slightly pathetic.

I walked over to the window to evaluate my only escape option. My room was on the second floor of our colonial-style house. As I peered through the window, I spotted the roof to our screen porch below. If I could just hop down to the roof, I could lower myself to the ground. It wasn't a long drop, but I had no idea if the roof would support my weight. If I went crashing through, it would surely wake my father.

That would be *game over*.

No Halloween fun and almost certainly the addition of window locks for next year. That was enough to send a shiver down my spine. I seriously needed to start apartment hunting before next Halloween. If I didn't live with my father, he wouldn't be able to tell me what to do. Only issue was, I was a broke college student with a minimum wage job, barely enough to support my coffee addiction during the week, never mind a whole apartment.

Placing my palms on the window, I leaned into the glass a little, pushing up. As it slid open, it made a sound that startled Mr. Finkel.

"Damn it," I cursed. Just my luck that the window would be loud enough to potentially wake my father. Adding it mentally to my list of things to do, I noted I needed to fix this window to open easier.

I waited silently, praying I didn't hear my father stir in his bedroom. It was across the hallway from my own, only a few steps away. I could practically hear the scolding I'd receive if he found me now.

"What on Earth are you doing, Soleil? Do you want to end up

taken—or worse?" I said to Mr. Finkel in my best impression of my father.

When no sound came from his room, I did a silent celebration.

Step one of the plan was a success.

Looking down, I realized I was in my pajamas—fuzzy pumpkin pants and a loose black tank top. That wouldn't do.

Running over to my closet, I hurriedly picked out an appropriate outfit. Fall in New England was cold, but I also wanted to look the part for the night. I settled on a cute pair of ripped black jeans and a cozy tan sweater. Adding a small pumpkin pin to my sweater, I looked myself over in the mirror. I decided to add a black headband to push back my long auburn hair. I may not have a costume, but at least I looked spirited.

Before making my way to the window, I slid on my little black boots. I wasn't exactly sure if I needed to take anything with me; I had never experienced the festivities before. Was I supposed to bring treats along, or would there be treats for me to try out there?

Making up my mind, I slid my phone into my back pocket and left all my other belongings behind. I didn't have any friends to meet up with, but a small part of me would feel guilty if I didn't take my phone in case my father woke and discovered me gone.

I gave Mr. Finkel a pat on the head as I passed by my bed. He was shedding, and thin pieces of cat hair clung to my palm. The urge to run to the bathroom connected to my room to wash my hands slammed into me. It was the worst possible timing. I needed to leave before I missed my opportunity, but the growing tightness in my chest halted me. I tried to urge my feet to me move, but I was compelled in the opposite direction. The compulsion controlled me, leading me to the bathroom. I washed my hands as quickly as I could and hurried to the window.

I fit easily out the window. Sitting on its edge, I stared down at the roof below. It was only about four feet or so, but I was still nervous. I felt like those girls in the cliché movies where they sneak out to meet the boy, except I didn't have any boy to meet, and I still hadn't successfully made it out of my house.

With a deep breath, I started sliding off the edge. One last push, and I felt myself leave the safety of my window and fall for all of two seconds. I stumbled as I landed on the roof.

"Ow, fuck!" I whispered as a small jolt of pain plagued my ankle. Shaking it, I tried my best to urge the ache away. After a moment, it turned into a dull ache that was barely noticeable. Thankfully, I was fine for now, but I would be sore tomorrow.

Again, I paused, listening. This moment was crucial. If I could make it past this, then nothing would stop me.

I counted *one, two, three, four.* With each number, I tapped a finger against my thigh, waiting until the anxiety subsided and I knew I had not woken my father.

The laughter of children rung out up and down the streets, mixing with the far-off sounds of a Halloween festival, only blocks away in the town square. Even the surrounding trees seemed to whisper, their leaves crinkling as the light breeze passed through them. But there was no sign that my father had left his room.

A small meow from above caught my attention. Mr. Finkel's little head poked out the window, staring down at me.

"Stay there," I hissed at the cat. If he jumped, I would have no choice but to chase him down and put him back inside. For a moment, he seemed to debate it. Finally, he made up his mind, turning back inside, and I let out a sigh of relief. The cat may be stubborn, but thankfully, he was also lazy. Adventure wasn't for him.

My heart began to race a little with the thrill of what I'd accomplished. There was only one small leap left, and then I was free.

Closing my eyes, I let the breeze run through my hair. Small strands tickled my face as I stood on the roof. Something about the smell of a crisp fall night always brought a smile to my face. It was my favorite season of the year—the blissful scents, the cool weather, and the delicious foods that all came along with it.

Opening my eyes, I made my way over to the edge and sat down. Sliding myself down the side of the porch, I finally let go of the last bit of my home, holding me back.

As my feet hit the solid ground, I realized I had done it. I was out.

I felt a bit silly as I walked down the sidewalk. I had been nervous about nothing. Halloween was just another fall night, but possibly a bit better. I let myself wander toward the center of town. That was where everyone would be by now. Each year, the town held a festival on Halloween. There'd be a costume contest, candy, and my favorite warm cider.

I'd never seen the festivities firsthand. I only heard about them after the fact, from classmates at our community college or neighbors talking about it all. Now that I was out on Halloween, I had to see them for myself. Hurrying along, I passed children carrying their appropriately-themed buckets, bragging about who had the best candy. A small pain in my heart had me jealous. I'd missed out on these memories when I was a child. It had always been the same, spending Halloween watching the other kids out my bedroom window.

A shiver crept down my spine, and I felt like someone

was watching me. Glancing around, though, I didn't imme-diately spot anyone.

Finally, a strange man across the street caught my eye. He was watching me as I walked alone, eyeing me like I was some sort of prey. The way his eyes bore into me made my skin crawl. As he flashed a smile, I could've sworn I saw a tooth sharper than humanely possible.

He took a step in my direction. His foot left the sidewalk hitting the street, and I prepared myself to run. Was I being paranoid? Were my father's stories finally coming true?

Before I could find out, a bus pulled up between us, and I froze in place, waiting for the man to appear. When the bus finally took off, the man was gone. I must've imagined the way he'd set his gaze on me. He was likely just waiting for the bus.

Shaking my head a little, I tried to snap myself back into reality. I must just be on edge because of the stories my father filled my head with about Halloween night.

Continuing my journey, it only took me another few minutes to make it to the center of town. As I approached, more people appeared. The sidewalks were filled, and I had trouble maneuvering through the commotion.

The town festival was bigger than I'd imagined.

Blow-up Frankensteins and skeletons decorated the middle of the small park's square. The white gazebo had orange and black lights strung along the trim of it, lighting it up. The park was filled with people out on benches or in the gazebo. Jack-o'-lanterns were placed in almost every empty space around town, cut into spooky faces and spirited phrases with lit candles inside.

My eyes widened as I took it all in. It was better than my classmates had made it seem. This was a spectacle, something straight from a Halloween classic movie. The smells of warm treats wafted past my nose, cinnamon, apple, and warm nuts in the air. I let out a small noise of delight as I spun in a circle, trying to decide where I should head first.

Small booths lined the square outside the park, selling food, drinks, and other oddities. There had to be at least forty of them.

Picking a direction, I passed a booth selling old-fashioned donuts and hot coffee. As my stomach let out a small growl, I realized I hadn't brought my wallet with me. Why hadn't I thought to bring money? Of course, the festival was going to cost something. My shoulders sagged a little as my hopes of experiencing it fully slipped away.

At least I could still enjoy the sights. Although it would torture for my stomach, the decorations were enough to satisfy my curiosity. By tomorrow, there would only be remnants left from tonight's celebration.

When I was younger, I thought I could catch a glimpse of what I was missing the next day. One morning after Halloween, I woke up early and rushed off to the town center. By the time I got there, a clean-up crew was already packing away the decorations, and empty tables littered the area. It was a depressing scene. Now, I knew better than to hurt my own feelings. Stay clear of the festivities until they were fully cleaned up, as if they never even happened.

Venturing further into the festival, I paused as I recognized one of the men ahead of me. A group around my age huddled near the makeshift bar they'd set up as a booth, selling Halloween-themed cocktails. Before he could notice me, I tried to hurry in the other direction, but it was too late.

He'd turned around, spotting me.

"Soleil!" he called out, waving me over. Slowly, I obliged, trying to think of any way out of this mess. As I approached the group, I could hear their joyful laughter and chatting.

"Ben," I greeted, doing my best to plaster on a fake smile. I recognized some of the other men and women around him from our community college.

Ben and I shared a calculus class. More than that, I hooked up with him a few times. It was nothing more than casual sex, but that didn't stop him from thinking we were an item. He was constantly following me around, trying to make romantic gestures. No matter how many times I kindly denied him, he insisted. It was becoming borderline obsessive. I'd stopped hooking up with him months ago and hadn't been with anyone since.

Man, I needed to get laid—and soon.

I fidgeted uncomfortably as Ben tried to put his arm around me. "Everyone, this is Soleil!" he introduced, the alcohol on his breath filling my nose.

I gagged from the pungent smell of vodka. He was intoxicated. Pushing his arm off my shoulders, I backed away a few steps.

"Join us, Soleil!" one of the women said, her words slurred. This was not how I wanted to spend my single Halloween.

"Sorry, I really should be going," I tried. They all protested, talking over each other. I needed a better excuse if

I didn't want to spend my night with plastered college students.

"Soleil?" I heard a familiar voice call out.

Turning, I spotted my neighbor, Sandra, waving from an apple cider booth. Her family seemed to be working the booth, passing warm mugs of cider to customers. The perfect opportunity.

"I've got to go, but maybe next time," I said, trying to sound disappointed but secretly relieved.

Hurrying off to the cider booth, I suddenly was painfully reminded I had no money and wouldn't be able to buy cider. Maybe Sandra would let me pay her back tomorrow. It was worth asking, so I made my way over to the table.

"Hey, Sandra," I said a bit shyly. I was thankful she recognized me from afar.

"I don't think I've ever seen you at the Halloween celebration. Did your father finally decide we don't bite?" she joked. If only she knew.

"Something like that," I muttered. "Is that cider?" I asked, hopeful.

"The best in town," she said, holding out a mug. With the cold fall breeze nipping at my back, the drink seemed almost irresistible.

"Oh, I can't. I don't have my money with me," I said, disappointed. My smile faded as I turned down the one thing I really wanted right now.

"On the house, in celebration of your first festival." She winked, pushing the mug into my hands. A smile took over my features. Already, this night was shaping up to being one of the best of my life.

Granted, my father was always overprotective. Not allowing friends over our house. Enforcing strict curfews and constantly lecturing me about the dangers of the world. I knew he meant well, but it felt like I was slowly suffocating. This was me finally making choices for myself, and it felt damned good.

As the hot cider slipped past my lips, I let out a groan. The hint of cinnamon mixed with the apple was delightful. This was my favorite fall drink; I had never been much of a pumpkin spice girl. No matter how many times I ordered it, it never got old.

"Thank you," I managed between my greedy sips.

Turning to explore the rest of the festival, I was stopped by a massive, solid wall. My drink splashed onto my hands, burning me a bit as I stumbled a step back, realizing the wall I'd hit was no wall at all. It was a man now wiping small drops of cider off his black leather jacket.

"Are you lost?" he asked, a smirk spreading across his lips. He was *beautiful*. I couldn't help but stare at him as he asked the question. His dark hair swept to the side, and his eyes were a shade of gold. I'd never seen eyes glow the way his did. Something about them made him seem hand-picked from another realm. "You've looked like a lost puppy all night," he noted.

He'd noticed me? I hadn't even seen him around the festival. Come to think of it, I didn't even recognize him. Our town was pretty small, and I thought I'd known everyone. Was he new?

Still staring at his mesmerizingly golden eyes, I wasn't quite sure how to respond, but he let out a gruff chuckle.

"Like what you see?"

The question snapped me out of it. My cheeks grew warm as I stumbled for a response.

"Don't worry, love. You're not my type," he said, turning back to the stand.

"I don't date assholes anyway," I scoffed, trying to save some remnant of my pride. Who did he think he fucking was?

This made him pause. Maybe I shouldn't have said anything at all. I was calling too much attention to myself. The last thing I needed was word of this encounter getting back to my father. Me sneaking out was enough to give him a heart attack, never mind if he knew I'd been spotted with some cliché bad boy.

"So you do have a little flame to you," he mused, looking me over.

Why did I have to melt a bit inside at that? I could feel myself growing flustered the longer his eyes remained on me. I needed to walk away before he realized the control he had over me right now. Maybe months had been too long if I was seriously considering giving this guy a moment of my time. I didn't even know him.

Without another word, I hurried off, my feet storming through the crowds of people. Why had I let that guy get under my skin? He was probably just visiting from out of town to check out our festival. It was well loved by the surrounding towns.

I spent the next fifteen minutes wandering around. Spotting more friendly faces, I waved to neighbors or paused at their tables to say hello. I managed to avoid Ben and his friend as I finished checking out all the booths.

Eventually, I ended up sitting on one of the park benches by myself. My fun had only lasted about an hour, and already, I was considering calling it a night. If I left now, I could certainly sneak back in without my father ever knowing I was gone. I might even have time for some cuddles with Mr. Finkel before bed.

The crunching of leaves under boots behind me caught my attention. My gaze quickly fell on the man I'd run into earlier as he leaned against the back of the bench. Why couldn't I escape him? Every part of me screamed that I should get up and leave, to not even engage with him, but then, that small bit of curiosity started trouble.

"There you are," the stranger drawled. "I've been looking for you."

"Me?"

He smirked down at me, his muscular arms crossed over his chest. I rolled my eyes. He thought he was such hot shit. I knew his type—thought he could win over any girl with just the flash of a smile. Well, I wouldn't be that girl, no matter how tempting he was.

"You wouldn't know Halloween fun if it slammed into you, would you?" he accused, glancing down at me.

"Try me," I challenged, unable to stop the thrilling rush that filled my chest.

THREE

"You know, if you expect me to just blindly follow you, then you could at least tell me your name," I shouted after the man. He'd motioned for me to follow as he left the park bench, and foolishly, I had rushed a little too fast to catch up. So much for not being one of those girls.

But I couldn't help myself. I had never experienced Halloween before, and now, here was someone daring me to partake in its delights. How could I refuse that? If anything, it was for purely educational purposes.

"Jax," he said without even glancing my way. His hands were shoved into his leather jacket pockets, and his pace quickened.

"Well, Jax," I said with a slight huff, "I'm Soleil."

I had to pick up my pace to keep up with Jax. My little legs could barely maintain this speed.

"Do you think you could slow down a bit?" I tried.

Jax just grunted, and I swear, he walked faster. The

audacity of this man was infuriating. Who did he think he was? The king of Halloween? Expecting me to just go along with everything he did.

As Jax led me away from the festivities, I grew wary. Maybe this had been a terrible idea. A complete stranger was leading me off into the dark to do who knew what. I may not believe in my father's stories, but I knew plenty of horror stories of women disappearing after going off alone. Oddly, something in me said that Jax wasn't that type of threat. I felt weirdly at ease with him. I trusted my instincts and continued following.

"Where are we going?" I asked.

"You'll see," he answered.

We wandered into a small neighborhood filled with trick-or-treaters and neighbors throwing small parties. Suddenly, Jax grabbed my hand, yanking me behind a tall set of hedges. I crashed against his chest as he pulled me close.

"What are you doing?" I demanded, trying to pull away, but he held tight.

"Just wait a minute," he whispered. When I tried to fight, he pressed a gentle finger to my lips. Anger built within me. How dare he shush me? I wasn't a child, and I was getting sick of people treating me like one.

I tried to squirm away, but he wrapped his arms around me, pulling me back to his chest. I could feel the rise and fall of his breath. His arms were powerful, and his hold left no room for me to get away. My heart began racing. I could scream for help, but was I sure he was trying to hurt me?

"You're going to ruin the fun, little flame," he scolded, his mouth so close to my ear, I could feel his breath.

What was he planning? I heard a group of children approaching. From the sound of it, they were a bunch of middle school kids, laughing and joking while trying to decide which house to score candy from next.

Suddenly, the sound of rustling leaves caught my attention. There was something approaching us from the dark. By the increasing rustles, I would say multiple things were heading our way. Goosebumps ran down my arms, and I sunk a little into Jax's arms, admittedly afraid.

From the dark, three black snakes with golden eyes emerged. They slithered in sync across the ground, aiming straight for us. I jumped, a bit startled.

"They won't hurt you," Jax said with what I thought was a small reassuring squeeze. I didn't believe a word of it. As they neared, I clenched my eyes shut, trying to will them away. If Jax wouldn't let go of me, then I was stuck hoping these snakes wanted nothing to do with me.

I held my breath, and when I opened my eyes, they were gone. They'd moved right past us as if we didn't exist. The hedges rattled at the bottom as the creatures moved through them. I dared a glance at Jax's face. His eyes were piercing, even in the dark. They almost seemed to glow a brighter gold.

Grabbing my hand, he led me to the edge of the hedges. We could see the group of kids approaching, unaware of our presence only feet away. I didn't understand what Jax was playing at here. Ready to step out into the streetlights, I stopped myself when the first kid screamed.

Panic broke out in the group. The children were yelling

and tripping over each other to escape, as if they'd seen a ghost.

But it wasn't a ghost. There, in the middle of the sidewalk, three snakes chased after the group of children.

"How?" It was the only thing I could think to ask. How had Jax known the snakes would bypass us and go for the children? How had he arranged this trick? I knew tricks were a part of Halloween, but wasn't this a little cruel? Those children didn't know the snakes were harmless.

"Don't lose that flame now," Jax said, his tone a little disappointed. "It's a harmless trick. The snakes will have already disappeared by now, and trust me, I heard that same group planning to egg an old woman's house if that makes you feel any better."

Weirdly, it did. Maybe I just wasn't used to pulling pranks. I'd never really pulled my own before. My father would've grounded me if I'd tried at home. A small chuckle escaped my lips thinking about the bit of karma those kids received in a twisted way. Who was Halloween turning me into?

"There she is," Jax said, a smile curling his lips upward. Stalking toward me, he leaned in. The way his face hovered so close to mine, I thought for a second he may kiss me. My gaze dropped to his lips, distracted. "Your turn," he whispered, his words breaking me out of my trance.

"What?" It took me by surprise. What did he mean by my turn? I couldn't scare a bunch of children. It still confused me how he'd even known those snakes would be here. How would I top that?

"The next group to pass through, you're going to pull a

trick on them. Prove to me you know how to have some Halloween fun." I tried to retort, but he cut me off. "Unless you aren't up for the challenge." He shrugged. "I don't want to waste the rest of my night here."

Was I seriously going to do this? I couldn't turn down the challenge. This night was slowly shaping up to be one of the most pleasurable times I'd had in a long time. If I declined the challenge, then I'd have to head home and Jax would leave. I didn't want the night to end, and secretly, I didn't want Jax to leave just yet. As much of an asshole as he was, something about him was intriguing, beyond just his looks. I needed to stick around and find out what drew me to him.

The far-off giggles alerted me to the next group of kids approaching us. I had to make my decision. It was now or never.

"Fine," I said, pushing away from Jax. I mumbled inaudible insults as I walked away. I wouldn't let him know that this was outside of my comfort zone. I didn't want him to think I wasn't capable of Halloween fun.

Poking my head around the hedges, I could see the kids passing by the house before they'd reach us. Amongst the group, I spotted a child dressed as a vampire, a zombie, and some form of rockstar. Some of the other costumes were characters I didn't recognize.

The plan I'd been mulling over the past few seconds was coming together. I'd remain behind the hedges until they were only a few steps away. Trying for a jump scare, I hoped the dark and element of surprise would help me. Otherwise, I would just outright embarrass myself.

I held my breath as I waited for the endless minute until

they were in prime position. Their steps shuffled along the sidewalk, and their voices carried louder than before. Jax watched me with predator-like attention, waiting for me to make my move. His stare made me nervous. I wanted to impress him. It was silly.

Finally, I jumped out from the hedges, screaming like a banshee. The kids paused, staring at me. This hadn't been what I expected. There was no running or chaos like with Jax's snakes. There were just blank stares.

Then, one kid started laughing, and the other kids slowly joined in, holding their stomachs. My face turned red with embarrassment. I'd done the exact opposite of what I'd meant. These kids weren't afraid; they were amused.

Behind me, I felt a large presence step out from the hedges. A few kids gave wary looks, and some even halted their laughter. A shadowy presence grew over me, as I could sense Jax approaching. His silence had even me on edge. Some children shifted uneasily.

"I believe you may want to run," he said menacingly. I was confused. Was he going to hurt these kids? That didn't seem likely, but still, what did he mean? The children looked just as confused, some even worried. They were beginning to fear Jax.

A soft slithering sound made my skin crawl; I'd heard the same sound only minutes ago. I almost jumped out of my skin as two black snacks appeared by my feet. Holding back a scream, I stepped back, bumping into Jax.

The children's eyes fell to the ground, spotting the approaching serpents. Chaos broke out, children bumping into each other and tripping as they scrambled to run. Some let out small yelps as the snakes closed the distance between them.

Turning, I found Jax with his arms crossed, a smug satisfaction painted on his face.

"How'd you do that?" I whispered, stunned. The first time could have been a coincidence, but twice? No one could summon snakes twice to the same spot like that. My eyes found his stern face as he watched the children disappear down the street. His gaze met mine.

"What, never met a demon before?" He shrugged casually.

FOUR

"Demon?" I stuttered over the word.

Letting out a soft laugh, I searched for the crack of a smile, anything to tell me he was joking. His features remained trained, staring me down as I grasped for words, anything to make sense of what he'd said. It sounded like one of the delusional stories my father always insisted were real.

"That's impossible," I said. How could this man be a demon? Demons were supposed to be terrifying creatures, beasts of nightmares, not a normal man.

"Is it?" he asked, his eyes glowing once more.

"Demons aren't real," I said in disbelief, refusing to accept this as the truth.

"And yet I assure you, I am very much real," Jax said, taking a step closer. Brushing a strand of hair from my face, he held my gaze. He was like a magnet. I just wanted to melt into his strong arms and find out what his lips felt like. Shaking my head, I pushed those thoughts to the side.

"Fine, let's say I believed you, which I still don't. Do all demons just run around making snakes appear on command?" I demanded, backing away with my hands on my hips.

"Not unless they're part serpent demon." As he said it, the golden glow of his eyes pulled my attention again. Maybe it wasn't so unbelievable. After all, when had I ever met someone with such different features? "There're all types of demons out there. Some are worse than others, some full blooded, some only half. My mother was a witch, and my father was a serpent demon."

"I still don't believe you." I shook my head. It would take more than just his word to convince me. I needed more proof, evidence that other creatures did cross over into our world. If he was right, I owed my father a huge apology for all the years I doubted him. It didn't excuse him for caging me like an animal, but maybe I should've trusted that stories came from somewhere.

"You will when I leave at midnight," he said, starting to walk away down the sidewalk.

His back was to me now, and again, I was left with the choice of whether to follow or head home. Anyone with any common sense would probably run, trick or not. But again, I found myself drawn to Jax. I didn't care what he was. I wanted to be near him.

Trailing after him, I jogged to catch up. This night wasn't going to be all about him. I wanted to have a bit of fun too, and I had the perfect idea, another way to fulfill my Halloween fantasies.

"I think it's my turn to pick the Halloween fun," I said once I was finally beside him.

"Oh, there is zero chance that's happening," he huffed.

"Don't be such a grump. What're you afraid of? That my idea might actually be fun?" I taunted, trying to use his own tactic on him.

"There is no doubt in my mind that you and I have very different ideas of fun," he answered, a devilish look in his eyes that made my core warm.

With a small wave of confidence washing over me, I grabbed his hand and pulled him toward the town center. It wasn't until a few minutes later that I realized I was still holding onto him as I lead us the way. Immediately, I dropped his hand, a little embarrassed that I'd held it so long. He didn't seem to notice.

"Why are we back here?" he asked, glancing around the town square.

"Because there's still one thing I want to try before the night is over," I explained. "Come on."

I'd spotted the table I was aiming for earlier in the night, a small crowd near it now.

When I made it to the table, I felt overwhelmed. There were so many options. Different colors, flavors, and toppings adorned the multiple apples on sticks. Candy apples. There were too many choices to pick from. A simple caramel-covered apple sounded delicious, but then there was one covered in dark chocolate with orange sprinkles that also caught my eye. How would I ever decide?

"You look like a kid who has discovered candy for the first time," a gruff voice behind me said. Turning, I found Jax hovering, watching me make my decision. His presence made my head even more clouded. How was I expected to focus with him so close?

The stress and pressure was building, and part of me wanted to walk away with no candy apple at all, but then I'd never know what they tasted like. This would be my first time trying the sweet treat. Nowhere else sold them during fall. Only the Halloween festival had them, and every year, I had to hear about the anticipation over what flavors would be sold that year, how much someone could eat in a single night before being ill. I never once could relate.

I once tried to make my own at home, and it was a complete failure. The caramel came out as a disgusting look-ing, sticky mess that hardened before I could even dip an apple into it. Baking and cooking were not my specialty.

"We'll take two of the poison apples," Jax said to the man behind the table, handing him cash.

Money!

I'd completely forgotten again. I still didn't have my wallet with me. I couldn't even pay for the candy apple I wanted so badly. Letting out a small groan, I almost walked off until Jax held out one of the apples to me. Hesitantly, I took it. It was a simple green apple covered in a black sugar coating.

"I can't pay you back for this," I stuttered, panicked—especially if what he claimed was true, and he was about to disappear come midnight. I doubted our mailman delivered to other worlds.

"If a man ever makes you pay him back for a candy apple, run, little flame," Jax said, taking the clear wrapper that had been covering the apple from me. I was stunned. Was I mistaken, or was Jax flirting with me? I didn't know demons were capable of such a thing.

"So a half-demon and a gentleman? Consider me impressed," I said.

Surprise flashed across his face. "I promise, I am many things, but gentle is not one of them," he said in a low tone.

We held each other's gaze for a moment, neither of us making a move. Electricity seemed to pass between us until a cough from behind us pulled our attention away. An older man looked at us impatiently and gestured to the table beyond us, wanting us to move. I shuffled out of his way, allowing him to pass.

"Asshole," Jax mumbled, his golden eyes flaring. He looked like he might stick some snakes on the man—or worse. I didn't want to stick around to find out.

"Come. I want to show you something," I said, trying to usher him away before he picked a fight.

It was only a short walk to our next destination. Jax remained quiet the entire way, allowing me to lead him. We passed a small apothecary, and I tried to avoid the store as best I could. It brought too many painful memories I wasn't ready to face. It was where my mother worked before she left.

The night was becoming an entire tour of the town. While I was still in control of the adventure, I wanted to make one more stop that I'd always imagined visiting. When we came upon the giant sign right outside the attraction, I knew I'd made a good choice.

Corn Maze Ahead was painted in giant lettering on a wooden board propped against a hay bale.

It wasn't a very large maze, as it was meant for the younger children, but I'd never once seen it in person. There was no harm in going through it a few years late.

"A corn maze?" Jax asked, looking at me skeptically.

"Just trust me," I said.

The opening to the maze had a few children lined up outside. There were two entrances to choose from, allowing children to race through the maze if they wanted. Once you found the middle, it turned into one path leading out to the other side—or at least that's what the small side posted outside the entrances explained. There was only one way to truly find out.

"You're serious?" Jax said as we stepped up next in line to the maze.

"Afraid you'll lose?" I taunted. In reality, I was sure he'd win. Jax was impossibly muscular and in shape, and I was frail and hated exercise. Speed wasn't exactly my strength. If we were racing, Jax was guaranteed to win.

He just snorted a small laugh in response.

"Ready?" I asked. He gave a small nod. "Go!" I shouted, running off into my side of the maze. I giggled like a little girl, immediately getting lost in the rows of corn.

I kept finding myself at dead ends and splits, unsure which way to go. The sound of children laughing and shrieking carried throughout the maze. I startled as I almost crashed into a child rounding a corner. The kid kept running, not even slowing down. I had to be getting close to the middle. It felt like I'd been wandering forever.

There were fun pieces of Halloween décor placed throughout the maze. I passed a dancing skeleton and a giant pumpkin on my journey to finding the center. The longer I moved in circles amidst the endless corn, the more likely it seemed I would never find the center.

Finally, I found myself in a small circular opening. There was a path across from me and one directly to my right. I felt a little disappointed when I didn't find Jax here. Part of me had hoped he might wait in the middle for me so we could finish the rest of the maze together. Maybe I had misread what I thought had been flirting. He probably was already done with the entire maze.

A strong breeze picked up, blowing the stalks of corn. The rustling made me a bit uneasy. No longer could I hear the joyful giggling of earlier. It was silent. Above me, the moon shone bright and eerie, and a small chill ran down my spine. Part of me wanted to run, to hurry and get myself out of this maze and find Jax, but my feet had other plans. They remained firmly planted.

One, two, three, four.

I tapped against my leg, weighing my options.

The sound of footsteps behind me had me turning around. As I did, Jax emerged from the dark of the other path. As he stalked toward me, my heart did a little flutter. Suddenly, I felt less afraid, less alone. It was weird how this stranger could bring me such comfort.

Jax stopped only mere inches from me, staring down into my eyes. Part of me was nervous. The way he was looking at me made my skin warm. Still, I could've misread everything.

"Stop looking at me like that, or I'll be forced to do something about it, little flame," he said softly.

"What's stopping you?" I dared.

Jax moved fast. Grabbing the back of my neck, he pulled me closer and leaned in. His lips crashed into mine, kissing me fiercely. I let myself become consumed, every single piece of me on fire. This was something out of a dream. I was supposed to be the girl locked in her bedroom, and now, here I was, kissing one of the most attractive men I'd ever laid eyes on.

His tongue slid into my mouth, and I let him lead the way. Exploring each other, we remained locked in a passionate kiss. My hands grasped at his neck and chest, desperate to feel more of him, experience more with him.

Jax pulled back slightly, and I made a small noise of protest.

"I win," he whispered, kissing me one more time.

"Huh?" I asked, confused and still trying to process.

Without another word, Jax took off sprinting down the path toward the finish of the maze. I'd been so distracted, I forgot we had been racing. I sprinted after him, but it was too late. By the time I emerged from the maze, Jax was leaning against a nearby tree, a smug look of victory plastered across his face.

Stalking over, I shook my head. "You cheated!" I accused.

"I don't like losing." He shrugged, grabbing my waist and pulling me close. Kissing me again, he spun me and pinned me against the tree. His lips trailed down my neck and then back up to my lips again. "I have one last thing to accomplish tonight," he whispered.

"What's that?" I asked, drunk on the taste of his lips.

"You'll see," he answered, taking my hand and leading me off.

FIVE

Walking back in the direction of the town square, Jax led the way quickly. I had no clue where he was off to, but I followed anyway. Walking down the street, we passed fewer groups of children than had been out before. Checking my phone, I noticed it was already 9:30pm. Soon, there would be no more children out, and only the remnants of parties and celebrations would be left.

Heading down a new street, the sound of loud music hit me. As we continued, it grew louder and louder until the source became obvious. I paused, glancing up the walkway of a large house. There were people everywhere—out on the lawn, hanging out on the porch. The front door was propped open, and loud music was spilling out.

"You want to go inside?" Jax asked, pulling my attention back to him.

"No," I said a bit too quickly. In reality, I did want to. My curiosity was peaked.

Attending community college, there weren't many opportunities to attend parties. The only things I knew about them were from shows and movies I had seen. My father never would've allowed me to go to one even if I did know where one was being held.

This could be my one chance to see what they were like, but I didn't want to drag Jax inside. Was I willing to part ways with him now over a party? *Not if it meant he couldn't kiss me again.*

"Let's go," he said, stalking toward the front door. I tried to protest, but he didn't wait around to hear what I was going to say.

Approaching, I noticed everyone around me was in costume. I felt extremely out of place. My face reddened as I felt a few partygoers stare me down. I was an outcast. I didn't belong here.

"Stop worrying what they think," Jax murmured as I caught up to him.

"I'm not wearing a costume. I look so lame," I said, crossing my arms.

"Why do you even care?" he asked.

"Because you're supposed to be something for Halloween." It was the only explanation I could come up with. I still wasn't sure why I cared what these strangers thought of me. With my caged life, I would never see them again anyway.

"You are something," Jax said, looking at me with that same intense stare. "You're mine for the night, and if anyone has an issue with that, they can fuck off." His arm wrapped around me, holding me close as we entered the party, and I sunk into the comfort of it.

Inside was pure chaos. There were people everywhere, bumping into each other as they bounced through the house. The music was turned up to the point that I could barely hear Jax standing next to me. Red solo cups littered the floors, and I noticed a keg sitting in the corner of what I guessed was the living room.

"Let's get you a drink," Jax whispered, bending down so I could hear him. Grabbing my hand, he led me through the tide of people.

Finally, we found ourselves in a crowded kitchen. There were drink options and snacks spread across a counter. Cans of alcoholic seltzers sat in a tub with mostly melted ice. A bowl of questionable punch sat next to it.

"It's my secret recipe," a guy nearby said, spotting me eyeing the vibrant red liquid.

"Somehow, that doesn't sell me on it," I murmured, low enough that only Jax could hear me.

He reached over, grabbing two of the cans of seltzer and handing one to me.

"These will do," he mused.

We moved on, exploring the rooms of the house as we went. It was nothing like I expected. Mostly, it was just room after room of rowdy, drunk kids playing drinking games or making out in the corner. For some reason, I had expected dancing.

Checking my phone, I was relieved to find I had no missed texts or calls. My father still had no idea I was gone.

Hopefully, it would stay that way just a little longer. I wasn't ready to head home just yet. There was somewhere Jax still wanted to go, and I planned to see this adventure through.

As more people poured into the house, I began to feel a bit suffocated. It was becoming harder to move, and I felt like the walls were closing in with each passing moment. The seltzer in my hand was turning warm, and the alcohol wasn't helping the anxiety building in my chest.

As my breathing sped up, Jax looked over at me with worry on his face. I put a hand to my forehead, my head suddenly starting to spin. If I didn't get air soon, I was going to pass out. My heavy sweater was clinging to my arms and weighing me down.

"I feel like I can't breathe in here," I said, panic raising my voice. The blood in my ears was pounding, and the room felt like it was closing in.

"Do you want to leave?" Jax asked, wrapping an arm around me to steady me.

I could feel myself swaying, and I couldn't form words to answer. Little black dots danced in my vision, threatening to consume it. I was having an anxiety attack, and there was nothing I could do to stop it.

One, two, three, four.

I repeated it in my head, tapping my fingers against my thigh. I hoped the repetition would fix it, that I would feel some form of relief, but as I reached the last number, I knew I had to start again.

One, two, three, four.

Jax's strong arms lifted me, swooping me off the ground.

I couldn't protest; I was too focused on trying to slow my breathing. Carrying me toward the door, he paused, the path blocked by a large group trying to push their way inside. With a quick glance, he settled on the nearby staircase. His concerned eyes kept darting to me.

One, two, three, four.

Upstairs, there were significantly fewer people. Jax tried a few doors, finding them locked. As he carried me down the hallway, I spotted a white door with multiple square glass panels at the end. When he finally tried its handle, to my surprise, it opened. It led to a small balcony overlooking the side yard of the house, just big enough for two people to stand outside.

As the cold air hit my face, I immediately felt a little calmer. My shaking and sweating had already stopped, and the black dots in my vision were fading.

"Will you be okay to stand if I put you down?" Jax asked, his eyebrows pulled together.

"Yes," I said, and he seemed to consider for a moment whether he believed me.

Slowly, he lowered me, holding my arm to make sure I was steady.

"I'm alright, really. I promise," I said. "Just a little embarrassed."

I was still out of breath from the panic, and my heart rate had yet to slow down. I needed to regain my composure before I could venture back through the house to leave. Placing a hand on my chest, I could feel my heart pounding. No matter how hard I tried to take deep breaths, they still were not coming easily.

Jax placed his hand over mine, realizing exactly what I was still feeling. Taking a step closer, his firm body grazed my own. He leaned his forehead down as his hand moved over mine, placing it on his own chest.

"You feel that?" he asked, and I nodded. "Focus on my breathing and try to match it."

Closing my eyes, I imagined my own breathing slowing. Copying his pace, my breathing started to go back to normal. With each deep breath, I felt better. When I finally opened my eyes again, he tilted my chin up. With a gentle kiss, he made me feel calm, safe even.

This was a guy I had just met, and already, he knew how to make me feel taken care of. Dread filled me as I realized that soon, it would be midnight, and whether I wanted to believe it or not, he was going to disappear back to his own world.

Greedily, I kissed him back, trying to savor it, as if we had all the time in the world. Pressing me back against the railing, he gave me exactly what I wanted. My back arched a little, and I could feel my long auburn locks sway with the breeze. I didn't dare open my eyes, afraid the panic would return when I realized the drop behind me—not that I thought Jax would let me fall.

Suddenly, he pulled back, breaking the kiss. Shocked, I grabbed the railing on either side of me. I wanted him to come back. Those few minutes were not enough to satisfy my appetite.

"I don't want to stop," I protested, hoping I could convince him to stay outside a little longer.

Below us, I could hear drunk individuals stumbling

through the yard. It was growing later, and the party would die off in the next few hours. Off in the distance, the town clock tower rung out, signaling a new hour.

"Unfortunately, little flame, I have one last place I need to be tonight," he said.

CHAPTER

SIX

For the third time, I found myself standing in the town square. After we made our way out of the party, Jax led me along the streets of town once more. He was on a mission. Walking with purpose, he led me through the crowds of people. As the night grew late, parents struggled to round up their children to take them home for the night. Teens were sprawled across the park on blankets and benches, sharing treats and questionable flasks of drinks. I spotted a group of moms clinking together cups of spiked cider in celebration of another successful Halloween.

"Where are we going?" I demanded as Jax took us down a small alley off the town square.

"Can you let anything be a surprise?" he asked. I rolled my eyes in response, knowing he wouldn't tell me.

He finally halted when we reached a small wooden door. Checking the handle, Jax pulled it open. I watched as he slipped inside, disappearing. Giving a nervous glance around, I thought of following but hesitated.

"Soleil." The sound of my name startled me. I let go of the door handle and found Ben stalking toward me. I could tell he was sufficiently drunk by the way he stumbled down the alley.

I looked one more time at the door and decided not to follow until I got rid of Ben. I didn't want him ruining the rest of my night with Jax.

"Where are you going" he slurred, throwing his hands up in the air dramatically. "Why are you avoiding me?"

"I'm not," I said, annoyed.

"You left me earlier, and now you are going to leave me again." He barely managed to get the words out. He was closing in on me, and suddenly, I felt cornered.

Leaving the door, I took a few steps toward him. If I could just redirect him back to the square, I could join Jax. I tried to gently turn him the other way, but he had other plans. Ben managed to back me into the wall next to us. He was a large man, and I stood no chance trying to force him off me. His hands caged me in as he leaned on the wall.

"Why did you stop calling me?" he questioned.

I stuttered for an answer, not wanting to upset him while he was drunk and unpredictable. "I'm sorry" was the best I could come up with. There was no good excuse for why I had stopped calling him. I had just wanted him to back off. Instead, I'd made matters worse.

Leaning close to my face, he pressed a kiss to my check. I turned my head away, not wanting him to find my lips. His breath reeked; I could only imagine how much more alcohol he'd consumed since I saw him earlier.

"Stop, Ben," I said, pushing at him, but he didn't budge.

"Come on, Soleil. You liked this before."

I turned my head again, avoiding his attempts. He was clearly growing frustrated. He grabbed my chin, attempting to hold my face in place.

"I believe she asked you to stop," a low, threatening voice demanded.

"Get lost," Ben said sloppily, trying to turn back to me.

"Step away from her," Jax said, his voice almost a growl. He strode toward Ben, who finally let me free from the wall.

Ben didn't hesitate as he tried to throw a punch at Jax, but he missed by a mile. Drunkenly, he stumbled, and Jax simply looked amused. I hated watching this. I didn't want anyone fighting over me. While Ben's back was to him, Jax moved impossibly fast, grabbing his shoulder with one hand.

It stopped Ben in his tracks. I held my breath, waiting for Jax to make his move, but instead, he just help him steady, forcing him to look him in the eyes. I watched as Jax's eyes flashed that golden hue.

"Enough," he hissed. "Don't make more of a fool of yourself. Leave," he demanded. Ben tried to squirm and fight, but Jax's grip seemed to tighten.

I watched pain take over Ben's face as he let out a small gasp.

"Leave," Jax repeated, letting go.

Ben quickly stumbled back, grabbing his shoulder as he turned and ran back down the alley. I was speechless. Not only had Jax stopped Ben, but he hadn't even needed to throw a single punch.

"How did you do that?" I asked in disbelief.

"Remember? Half-demon," he said. "I'm a bit stronger than most humans. I have to imagine his shoulder will have a nasty bruise tomorrow." A smirk plastered across his lips at the thought. "Come on. No more distractions," he said, sliding back through the door.

I followed, and the door quickly shut behind me.

"Jax," I whispered into the dark.

My eyes were still trying to adjust, and I couldn't spot where he'd moved. Bumping into the corner of a piece of furniture, I let out a small curse under my breath. Shuffling slowly, I held my hands out to feel for any type of door or opening to another room.

Strong arms grasped me from behind, and I almost let out a scream until a hand over my mouth stopped me.

"Don't scream. It's just me, little flame," Jax whispered into my ear. He placed a kiss on my head, and my heart rate immediately settled. His hands grasped my waist, holding me against his body. One ventured up my side, sliding along my neck until my chin tilted up to him.

"Don't scare me like that," I chided, resisting the urge to kiss him until I had answers. "Where are we?"

"The clock tower," he answered, grabbing my hand as we ventured further inside.

I hadn't even known there was a way into the clock tower. It was one of the town's oldest structures and still worked perfectly, except for when pranksters messed with it. Is that why they were here? Did Jax want to mess with the clock this Halloween?

With ease, he led me through the endless dark space. It was like he could see perfectly even without light. Coming to a staircase, he paused, guiding my hand to the railing so I could feel where I was going.

"I'm right behind you," he encouraged. I took a step, beginning the climb.

There were more stairs than I thought there'd be. They spiraled upward forever. With each step, I found myself wanting to turn back. By the time I reached the top, I was out of breath, my thighs screaming at me. I'd be sore tomorrow.

There was a small opening to the side of the clock. Looking out, I could see almost the entire town, the moonlight illuminating the night sky, the glow of Halloween town orange and purple beneath us.

"What do you think?" Jax said, leaning against the wall beside me. His face was plastered with amusement, watching me stare out in wonder.

"It's breathtaking," I whispered in awe.

Jax moved behind the clock itself. Pulling his hands from his leather jacket pockets, he began fidgeting with some mechanisms behind the large clock face. I watched curiously as he pulled out a few parts. When he finally stepped back, the clock hands had stopped moving.

He looked oddly satisfied with the now-broken clock. I couldn't wrap my head around why he'd brought me up here just to steal a few small pieces to an old clock. Every year on Halloween, someone messed with this clock tower. I'd always seen the aftermath of the clock being out of order for the week following until new replacement parts arrived to fix it. Something clicked in my head at that moment.

"It's you every year, isn't it?"

He flashed a sad smile in my direction, shaking his head in a small nod.

"Why?" I asked.

He chuckled, as if I'd asked a silly question. Rubbing the back of his neck, I watched him search for an explanation.

"When you're part demon, you can't stay here. It doesn't matter if you're part human. This world was never meant for us. Once the blur between worlds fades at midnight, I get pulled right back into my own world."

I watched as his face saddened. He looked a bit distressed even trying to get the words out. A slight pain stabbed at my heart; I sympathized with him. I'd been locked away my whole life. I couldn't imagine being kept entirely from this world except for one night a year.

"I just like to imagine that if I could stop time, I'd never have to go back. If it never turns midnight, I can finally stay here forever," he finished.

He slid down the wall, sitting on the ground with his knees tucked up. I joined him, settling against him. I reached out to grab his hand in comfort. There wasn't anything I could do or say that would take this type of pain and longing away.

"Why did you decide to come with me tonight?" he suddenly asked.

I decided to be honest, as embarrassed as I might be. I trusted Jax already, and part of me knew he wouldn't judge me.

"My father doesn't let me out on Halloween. This is the first time I've ever experienced the holiday outside the confines of my bedroom. I just wanted to have one fun night that I would remember for a lifetime. I don't know. Part of me knew I was insane to trust a stranger, but the other part couldn't resist. I had to know for myself what it meant to experience Halloween."

I waited quietly, hoping I was right, that I wouldn't find judgement in his eyes when I glanced up again. After a minute of silence, I dared to look into his golden eyes. When I did, I was surprised to find sadness.

"I'm so sorry he did that to you," he whispered. "No one deserves to feel trapped."

"Especially not in a whole different world," I agreed, giving his hand a squeeze.

SEVEN

Jax's dark gaze raked over me as we sat side-by-side on the clock tower floor. His hand let go of mine and slowly trailed to the thigh of my bent leg. As it climbed, it settled on my waist, gripping me tight. He seemed to pause, as if awaiting my answer. If I couldn't take away Jax's pain, I wanted to at least provide him one last distraction before the night ended.

Without a second thought, I moved. Climbing into his lap, I lowered onto him as both his hands grabbed my waist, helping me settle, grinding me against him. My arms wrapped around his neck, and I didn't hold back as my lips crashed to his. I caught a glimpse of his golden eyes before I let myself slip away into pure bliss.

The kiss was anything but gentle, his desperation clear. My lips felt like they were bruising from the pure intensity. He nipped my bottom lip, and the pain sent a rush through me. A hand slid into my hair, grasping my head. Suddenly, a light tug had me tilting my head back, breaking from the kiss. My neck was exposed, and Jax got to work, trailing kisses up my bare skin and biting lightly.

A small moan escaped my mouth, and I tried to bring my head back down to his, but a tug at my hair stopped me. I let out a small wince, mainly in protest at his refusal to let me kiss him.

"I told you, little flame: I am anything but gentle," he growled in a low tone.

His words had my core on fire, aching for him. Even though every bit of my body screamed at me to demand more, I let him take as he pleased. A few more kisses led his lips right back to mine. He bit at my lower lip, and I tasted the metallic zing of blood as he left behind a small cut. That would bother me tomorrow, but right now, I didn't care. I wanted him to be as rough as he wanted. This was my one chance to experience a Halloween I would never forget.

Fuck it, I was going to live a little.

My hands grasped the bottom of my sweater, and I began to pull it over my head. The sweater got a bit stuck as it covered my head, and Jax helped me pull it off, unable to help himself. His impatience brought a grin to my face. I wasn't the only greedy one. In my head, it was going to go smoother than that, like they showed in the movies. My cheeks warmed with a little embarrassment.

I caught Jax smirking as he looked me over.

"What?" I asked, a little self-conscious now.

"Did you know you would be fucking me tonight, or is it just a coincidence you've worn a lacy red bra no demon could ever resist?"

I threw myself into him, once again finding his lips. His

tongue immediately slid into my mouth, claiming it as his. I could feel his fingers working at my bra, and as it fell off, I felt my nipples harden as my skin was exposed to the cold room.

Jax grabbed my hips again, pulling me closer so I could feel the bulge that told me just how desperately he wanted me. I ground my ass against it, teasing him, my exposed knees from rips in my jeans scraping the rough floor.

"Ouch," I murmured against Jax's mouth. Pulling away, he immediately realized the source of my pain.

"This won't do," he said, glancing around the room.

His eyes locked on a small worktable in the corner of the room. He fixed my legs to wrap around his waist and stood easily even while holding me. I was impressed with his physical strength. I didn't think it was possible for him to get any more attractive, but I was wrong.

Carrying me to the table, he used one hand to swipe the random tools and clock pieces to the floor. Then, he gently laid me back on the wooden surface. The table was cold on my back, and I shivered. Leaning over me, he placed his hands on either side of my body and got to work.

His lips made their way up my torso, finding my breasts. For a moment, he savored them, letting his teeth graze the sensitive tips of my nipples. He moved on, working his way back down until my waistband forced him to stop. His hands remained on my breasts until he was forced to let go to deal with my pesky jeans.

Without hesitating, he gave the jeans a slight tug. They were not going to come off without undoing the button and zipper. I moved quickly, trying to help him, but I was met with resistance. Immediately, he grabbed my hands, slamming them above my head.

A feral grin spread across his face, and I bit my lip, waiting for his next move.

"Don't move," he demanded. "I don't care how good it feels. I want you to keep your hands right where they are."

"You're cocky, aren't you?" I teased, knowing no matter what he did, it would be euphoric.

"I'll let you be the judge of that," he answered, tugging my pants firmly off. I caught the smirk as he saw my matching lace thong.

"That cannot stay," he said, shaking his head.

Bending down, his teeth scrapped my waist as they grabbed at the lace. He pulled them off easily using only his mouth, and my back arched as my body demanded more contact. I couldn't stand the teasing and small touches. I need all his attention.

Parting my legs, he knelt before me. I could only see the top of his head, his messy, dark hair tickling the inside of my thighs. I almost moved as his mouth found my wet core, but his hand pressed firmly on my hip, holding me in place. It was torture, perfect, pleasurable torture.

I wanted to reach down and run my fingers through his hair, but my hands remained where he put them.

My instincts took over, and I let myself arch into every delicate movement of his tongue. The way it flicked in careless circles that were somehow also intentional had me seeing stars. With every lick, I wanted to move. My body squirmed, but still, I didn't break.

"Please," I begged, needing more.

"Keep that pretty mouth shut and let me do my work," he tsked.

I listened, allowing him to have me in whatever way he pleased.

"Good girl," he praised.

Soon, I felt myself approaching the edge of that cliff. Jax's fingers slid into me, working at a rhythmic pace. The combination of his tongue and fingers working me toward an orgasm was unbearable. I couldn't take it anymore. I let myself topple over the edge, a moan escaping my lips.

Lifting my head, I found his dark gaze glued to me.

"You taste divine, little flame," Jax said, licking his fingers, savoring what he had done to me.

Sitting up, I grabbed his face. I didn't care if he wanted me on my back. I would take what I wanted first. Kissing him, I pulled at his leather jacket, and it slid easily off his body. He grabbed the hem of his and quickly pulled his shirt over his head with ease. My hands wandered the hardened muscles of his chest and abs. Was this actually happening?

I let my hands venture lower, pulling at his waistband. He pushed me back again onto my back, and I gave in. Undoing his belt and jean zipper, he pulled himself out of his boxers.

My core tensed with anticipation as his impressive cock hovered at my entrance. If he didn't move soon, I was going to have to take matters into my own hands.

"Look how wet you are for me," he said, biting his lip.

As he thrust into me, I felt every last inch of him slowly stretched me. It burned at first, as I wasn't used to taking on so much, but the more he moved, the faster that pain melted into irresistible bliss. I wanted to feel more, feel him deeper inside me.

Propping myself up onto my elbows, I made my way up to sit. Jax looked like he might protest but decided against it. Grabbing my hips, he pulled me to the very edge so he could access me. My ass was barely on the table, Jax the only thing keeping me from toppling off. I let my arms drape lazily around his neck.

As he continued to pound into me, he nipped at my neck and gripped my breasts. Again, I could feel myself approaching that edge. I didn't know how much longer I would be able to hold on.

"I want you to come for me, little flame." I could feel him losing control as he said it. The way his thrusts became feral, hurried, told me he was also approaching that same edge. Neither one of us would be able to resist soon.

"I want to know how good you feel as you come undone. Only then will I fill you," he whispered in my ear. The words were enough to give me that final push. Closing my eyes, I let go. My back arched, every feeling intensifying tenfold. I felt my body shake from the intensity of the orgasm. My heart was pounding, and I barely had time to gain my breath as Jax's hips punched into mine.

When I finally opened my eyes, I found those devastatingly mesmerizing golden irises staring into mine. Jax kissed me, and I felt him let go inside me. His hand grasped the back of my head, my hair tangling in his fingers.

I had never experienced anything like this. Nothing would ever compare. I would crave this every day for the rest of my existence.

Out of breath, I tried to gain my bearings. My head was a blur, still rushing from the ecstasy. I just stared at Jax in pure disbelief. He stood before me, buttoning his pants, his golden stare watching me intensely.

"You are a divine creature, little flame," he said, shaking his head. "If I didn't know better, I would think you were part demon yourself."

I chuckled. The idea of me being part demon was absurd. I had barely experienced life, always restricted by my father's wishes. I doubted any demon or half-demon would tolerate such a lame existence, particularly if most demons were anything like Jax. Something told me he would never tolerate being locked away.

Panic grew in my chest as I remembered why I was there. I had snuck out and would need to get back soon.

The night was growing late, and I realized I had no idea what time it actually was. Pulling out my phone, I sighed heavily. It was already 11:45pm. A small wince escaped me when I noticed Jax glancing at the screen.

"We should get going," he said.

"Where?" I asked. "You only have fifteen minutes left." I couldn't imagine what we would have time left to do in those brief remaining minutes.

"One final stop," he said, pulling me up with him as he stood.

CHAPTER

EIGHT

The park had mainly cleared, with many people heading home after the festivities for the night. Tables were being cleared off and packed up around the square. No one gave us a second glance as Jax led me to a secluded corner of the park. There was a giant tree growing in this corner. My best guess was a maple tree, by the looks of it.

Only ten minutes left before midnight, and I wasn't ready to say goodbye. It was cruel, only getting one night with Jax. One night to experience Halloween, one night to feel truly alive.

A shiver ran down my spine, as the temperature had dropped this late in the night. Noticing, Jax took off his leather jacket and wrapped it around my shoulders.

"Looks better on you anyway," he said softly before I could protest. The thick leather blocked out the blowing wind that kept kicking up leaves around us.

We stood beneath the large maple tree, the red and

orange leaves coating the ground beneath us. Under the moonlight, I could just see the warm golden glow of his eyes. They stared straight into me, right past my insecurities and worries, seeing me for who I was: a girl trapped in this life, searching for a way out, seeking freedom.

He had given me that on this fateful Halloween. If I couldn't have longer, then I was thankful for the one wild night I got.

Jax brushed a stray strand of hair out of my face, tucking it back behind my ear. I could tell he understood exactly what I was thinking. Neither of us said it, though. We weren't ready to admit the Halloween adventure had finally ended.

"You really are something different, aren't you, little flame?" he whispered.

I wasn't sure what he meant by that. All my life, I had felt less than ordinary, barely having control over my life or what I experienced. I wasn't anything to be interested in. I was just another girl, wishing for more. I couldn't give Jax more, and it pained me.

He leaned in, kissing me, pulling me away from those thoughts. As my lips grazed his, I shifted up to my tiptoes. His warm touch gently grasped me, holding me close. The wind picked up, leaves blowing around us as we remained locked in that kiss. It was pure magic. I could feel the butter-flies tumbling in my stomach, my cheeks warming a shade of pink.

All of it made me wish I was right back in that clock tower, seeing how much more we could accomplish in a single night.

Jax pulled away, and I almost let out a protest. Midnight was approaching much too quickly. I wanted to savor every last second he had. There were only minutes remaining, and the clock was ticking down too fast. Without the clock tower to tell me the time, I could only hope there was enough time to say goodbye.

"I will think of you every day in Eodratera," he said.

"Eodratera?" I asked.

"My home world. In one year, meet me here, under this tree, on Halloween night, little flame," he said, his stern gaze searching my face for my own answer. "I know it isn't fair to ask you to wait for me, but I'm going to find a way. By next Halloween, I will find a way to stay," he finished.

How would he find a way? Before tonight, I hadn't even believed in demons or other realms. Now, I wanted to know everything. Did Jax know of a way that might allow him to stay? Would I be able to have more time with him like I desperately craved?

To wait an entire year to feel this again, how would I survive? I'd never come this close to feeling truly myself before. I felt free, and already, I had to let that go another year. It was torture.

"I'll be here," I said, because I knew that a part of me would never forget the way Jax made me feel in a single night. A part of me would always ache to feel the rush of not knowing what came next and blindly following him. A part of me would always crave the way he made me feel when he fucked me on that table.

I would spend the next year learning everything about the stories my father told, doing research of my own and readying for the next Halloween. When it rolled around again, I would be prepared. Next year, Jax would come through to this world, and I would be there to help him stay. Before I could tell him my plan, a shift in the air stopped me.

The dreaded sound of the distant clock rang out in the air as midnight struck. Too bad we couldn't have stopped all the clocks in town before it was too late. I wanted more time. I needed to know where to begin my research, what Jax already knew, but it was too late.

I leaned desperately in for another kiss. Jax held tight to my waist, his firm grip trying to hold on to this world. This was our goodbye. No words, just this moment. My lips found his, and as they did, I could feel them slowly slipping away. It made my heart ache. The kiss felt lighter, and soon, I could barely feel his presence anymore.

When I opened my eyes, he was gone. Only his leather jacket remained in this world, wrapped around me like a hug.

One night was all I got. One night, and everything had changed. I had changed. There, under that tree, I realized that part of me would be hollow, always aching to be filled, until the next year, when Halloween finally came again.

CHAPTER

NINE

Well past midnight, I stood outside of my house, trying to figure out how to get back inside. I could go through the front door and let myself back into my bedroom, but my father would realize. My father had a security system installed at each of our doors, and even with the codes he would see an alert on his phone the next day for the entry. He'd also notice his locks undone on my door.

I would have to go back in the way I came out.

The window.

There was a downspout running down the side of the house, close to the screen porch. I walked over to it and gave it a tug to measure the sturdiness.

Satisfied that it wouldn't immediately fall off the house with my weight, I started scaling the side of the house. The pipe creaked in a manner that had me climbing faster.

I reached out to the rooftop the moment it was close enough to grasp. My arms ached as I pulled myself up.

I paused, waiting to see if my father had heard the ruckus I caused. A rustling behind me caught my attention, and I turned. Sandra stood in her front yard watching me, holding remnants of her table set up.

Our eyes met and neither of us spoke a word. She just gave me a small smile and a quick wink before heading to her front door.

I let out a sigh of relief.

I knew Sandra wouldn't tell my father what she saw.

The last stretch of sneaking back in was the hardest. I glanced up to the sill, the window still cracked open. If I were to have any chance of making it up, I would need a running start.

I backed up a few steps and took a deep breath in.

Running across the roof toward the side of the house, I jumped last second, reaching up. My hand narrowly missed the sill, and I landed back on the roof.

I backed up again, knowing too many attempts could wake my father.

I tried to focus, counting in my head to calm myself.

One, two, three, four.

I ran again, leaping toward the side of the house and using my foot to push off the siding and up.

I outstretched my hand and caught the sill. My fingers instantly burned, and I scrambled up the wall quickly. I pulled myself through the window, plopping inside my bedroom.

A breeze followed me in, and I shut the window.

A meow from the bed greeted me as I pulled off my clothing. I smiled at Mr. Finkel, placing Jax's leather jacket on the bed next to him.

It was late, and I knew I should head to bed, but I couldn't help myself. I sat down in my bed and grabbed my laptop that sat on my nightstand.

Opening it, I knew exactly what I needed to do.

Pulling up the browser, I typed out what had been burning in my mind since Jax disappeared.

The demon realm...

PART TWO
HAUNTED

CHAPTER

TEN

3 *64 days later*
Business Calculus was the last place I wanted to be, yet I found myself staring down a pop quiz I was having trouble completing. Professor Lutz loved being a complete nuisance. No matter how hard we worked or how long we studied, he found more ways to overwhelm us with work. Pop quizzes were his newest torture device.

At least tomorrow would be a better day. After a year of waiting, it was finally Halloween.

I couldn't help the butterflies in my stomach as I thought back to the previous year. It was completely insane to think Jax would actually wait for me, but I still planned to be under that tree come nightfall tomorrow.

It'd be the love story of a century: broken and longing girl pieced back together by the tempting demon. My father would have a heart attack if he knew. No one would believe me. Why should they? It was ludicrous thinking a man would wait a year for me—more accurately, a demon who could have anyone he pleased.

"Soleil," Professor Lutz said, snapping me out of my daydream.

Ben snickered from three rows behind me. I was stuck with him in another class. I thought I'd seen the last of him after everything that happened the previous Halloween, but I was stuck with the asshole again. After Jax had given him the fright of a life, he'd made it his goal to make me miserable. Jealousy was a poor look on him.

"Your time for the pop quiz is up. Turn it in," Professor Lutz said expectantly.

Shit.

If I hadn't been so distracted, maybe I would've finished filling in the blanks on the sheet before me. I'd completed one single problem. A quiet groan slipped from my lips, realizing the failing grade I'd receive would drop my overall grade to the border between passing and needing to re-take this class.

Somberly, I marched my almost-empty sheet to the front of the room, unable to make eye contact with my professor as I handed it to him.

"See me after class," my professor huffed at me.

I wanted to melt into my seat, away from all the eyes glancing to me. I sunk back into the plastic chair, putting my arms on my desk in front of me. Burrowing my head into my arms, I tried to pretend I was anywhere else. This was my last semester of college, and then I'd be done. I could start applying for jobs soon, leave all of these demanding professors behind.

My father also might finally let me out into the world. He couldn't keep me barred in my room forever. I had to face reality and find my place in the world.

Hopefully, that meant a place for Jax too.

It had been an entire year. Was that enough time for him to finally figure out how to stay in this world?

I'd obsessed over every book and article I could get my hands on, detailing the other realms and the myths that circled them. None had produced anything of use, but that didn't stop my fascination.

Seeing him again was everything I needed. I imagined the way his touch felt on my skin, his hands running through my hair, and-

"Soleil?" Professor Lutz asked, ruining the fantasy.

"Hmm," I answered, still only half of my attention now on him. The class was starting to file out of the room. I still had my pen in hand from my quiz and wanted nothing more than to follow them.

"Your grades are slipping," he said, his beady eyes staring down at me over the reading glasses he wore. "If you do not pass our upcoming exam, I'm afraid you will have to re-take this class."

My cheeks reddened at being singled out. I knew my grades were falling, but I hadn't expected the professor to point it out.

One, two, three, four.

I tapped my pen against my side.

"I suggest you find a tutor to help you prepare. I do not wish to have you in this class again next semester."

The insult stung, and I tried to avoid his intense stare.

One, two, three, four.

I kept repeating it in my head, trying to push away the panic creeping in. Taking another class with him was the last thing I wished to do, but none of it would matter after Halloween. Once Jax was here to stay, I would be able to throw myself into my studies again and pass the exam.

"I'll consider it," I mumbled as I gathered my belongings on my desk and shoved them into my bag.

I hurried out of the classroom, hoping to get to my car without any other disturbances. The faster I made it home, the sooner Halloween would come and I would have my demon with me once again.

The solid wooden door slammed behind me as I left the classroom, and I bumped into a solid mass before I could lift my head.

"Daydreaming again?" Ben taunted. "Are you thinking about how good it would be to have me back?" The smug look on his face made me sick. "Maybe a quick hang out in your car will remind you."

My fists clenched as I shoved my way past him.

"You wish," I muttered under my breath, hoping to escape as fast as I could. Ben didn't know when to leave well enough alone.

"You'll come crawling back to me soon enough," he grumbled after me.

Again, my mind wandered to Jax, knowing when he came back, all of this wouldn't matter. I would never have to deal with shitty men again and Ben would finally leave me alone.

Exiting the college, I found my car parked in the back of the lot. It was an old Volkswagen convertible, the light tan paint chipping away. It desperately needed a wash, but that would have to wait. I had better things to be doing with my time in the next day.

"Are you coming tomorrow?" Marielle asked, catching up to me outside. She'd been hounding me for weeks about a Halloween party, relentless ever since I met her my first semester of college.

"I don't-"

"Yes, you are," she begged, cutting me off. "Don't give me that shit about your father. I know you got out last year. You can do it again," she finished, crossing her arms. "I'm texting you the address."

I felt my phone buzz in my pocket as I watched her put away her own.

"I'll try," was the only promise I could give her. Parties were not my first priority. My mind only had one thing on it: finding my demon under that old willow tree.

It was a warm fall day, and I pulled back the roof of the car to drive home.

The radio at full volume, the song I'd been listening to when I arrived picking up again in the middle, I spotted Ben and his friends climbing into a bright red pick-up truck as I pulled out of the parking lot. With the wind blowing through my hair, I took the back roads home, taking extra time to enjoy my remnants of freedom. Soon enough, I'd be locked in my room, banned from partici-pating in anything that could be deemed Halloween festivities.

I tried not to think about it while I enjoyed my drive home. Nothing could tear me out of the dream I was living in, and nothing could stop me from meeting Jax like I promised.

DRIVING HOME, my mind swam with thoughts of Halloween. Everywhere I looked, our quaint town was decorated in orange and black. My route took me straight through the town square where everyone was already setting up for the festival.

Folded tables and chairs were splayed across the small park. Lights were half hung on the gazebo, and pumpkins were being placed strategically by some volunteers.

My house was only a few blocks away, and when I caught sight of it, I turned down the music I was blasting, hoping I had beaten my father home. If I could sneak in unnoticed, I wouldn't hear his usual speech about how the people of this town had lost their minds for celebrating Halloween.

They are asking for trouble.

I mimicked his same old line in my head, letting out a soft giggle at the absurdity of it all.

I parked my car in the driveway, covering it with the roof once more as I stepped out. The car locked behind me, and I walked along the stone pathway that led to our black front door.

"Dad?" I called out, opening it and wondering if his car had been in our garage. When I received no reply, I knew he was still at work.

A rustle from the kitchen caught my attention, and I dropped my bag by the stairs on my way.

The kitchen was perfectly clean, not a single item out of place. The room looked hardly lived in. Most nights, my father either slept at dinnertime or was at work, so it was often just me and Mr. Finkel. Admittedly, my cooking skills were well below par.

Meow.

Cat food scattered across the floor as Mr. Finkel broke into his kibble, tearing the bag open.

"Rascal," I muttered, grabbing the dustpan.

As I brushed it up, I heard the sound of the garage rumbling open and my father's loud Jaguar rolling in. I hurried to clean the mess, dumping the pebbles of cat food in the trash as my father walked in.

"Soleil, I'm glad you're home," he said, as if I had any other choice. His constant watch and control over me kept me on a tight schedule. Any deviation, and he would had the town hunting me down.

I sighed, wishing I was anywhere else. Freedom was all I ever hoped for—the ability to make my own choices, to finally live anywhere I wished.

I just had to finish school, and then I'd leave. I'd travel the world and get as far from his smothering grasp as I could.

A twinge of guilt made my chest ache, knowing my father thought he was doing what was best. He provided for me when my mother left and worked hard so we could live comfortably. Yet, his need to dictate every part of my life pushed me further and further from him. He'd never change, no matter how hard I kept trying.

It was alright to let go, I reminded myself. I couldn't keep living in misery just to serve his happiness. It didn't mean I loved him any less.

Working up the courage to ask the question that burned in the back of my mind, I leaned on the island counter as he prepared himself a hot cup of tea, pulling a mug out of one of the white wooden cabinets.

"Marielle was telling me about some of the festivities happening around town tomorrow," I started, leaving out that they included a large college party. I didn't think that information would help my case.

"Mhm," my father mumbled, filling a kettle with water from the sink. The way he kept his back to me, barely acknowledging my words, had me balling my fist. I took a deep breath, reminding myself that I would get nowhere if I didn't just ask.

"She invited me to attend with her," I blurted before I could back out.

My father ignored my words, turning on the burner as he placed the kettle on the stovetop. I huffed my annoyance, biting the inside of my cheek, trying to bite back the words I wanted to yell at him.

"Did you hear me?" I asked, furrowing my eyebrows.

"I did," he answered.

I knew I'd already failed. It was a futile effort at that point; nothing I said was going to change his already-made-up mind.

One, two, three, four.

The same four numbers played over and over in my head, a constant melody of madness. Sometimes, I couldn't form a single thought besides those four numbers. The urge to continue pushed into me until I could no longer stop it. Every day, it became harder to keep it out.

Mr. Finkel brushed against my legs, easing my growing anxiety. I took a deep breath, readying for the denial I knew would come.

"So can I go?" I asked, drawing my lips thin and tight. I was an adult, well beyond the age the world considered appropriate to make decisions for myself, yet I was still chained to the choices my father made for me. He'd found a way to always keep me needing him, putting himself in charge of my every decision.

"No," he said without turning to look at me. The blatant disregard was infuriating. My nostrils flared as I prepared my ill-fought attempt at changing his mind.

"Please. I'm not a child. I'll be safe; nothing will happen to me," I sputtered off.

"Soleil, my answer is no, and that's final. So long as you live under my roof, you follow my rules," he said sternly, pouring hot water into his mug. "You're becoming far too much like your mother, never knowing when enough is enough."

"Don't talk about her like that," I grumbled.

She may have left, but I never blamed her. She had to leave, to get away from my father's tight grasp. It didn't mean I cared any less.

"You know she started smoking again?" he accused. "She

thought she could hide it from me, but that cough came back."

I rolled my eyes. I hated when he tried to turn me on her.

"It's better than being like you," I murmured without thinking.

"Enough!" he bellowed, slamming the mug down and causing hot tea to spill over the rim. A small piece broke off the bottom edge of the mug, and he cursed under his breath.

There it was: the fiery temper I knew laid dormant, waiting for me to push back against his manipulations. I turned to leave, too tired to fight back against his narcissistic bullshit, but my father grabbed my wrist, pulling back hard.

"I wasn't finished with this conversation," he said, his voice deepening and his grasp intensifying.

"I was," I bit out, easily escaping his grasp and trying to wipe the look of horror from my face before he could spot it.

The few self-defense classes I'd convinced him to allow me to take came in handy. After my experience with Ben the past Halloween, I never wanted to feel helpless again.

My father's eyes widened, realizing his mistake. He looked down at his palms like he couldn't believe he'd actually grabbed me with those same hands. It wasn't the first instance, and it wouldn't be the last. It always came with some excuse.

"Soleil—" he started.

"I'm tired and need to study," I snapped, storming out of the kitchen and avoiding his meaningless apology. I didn't want to hear his excuses. Again, the same four numbers crept into my mind as I held tight to the comfort they provided me.

It was the one way to push out the thoughts that plagued my mind and ate away at me.

I'd known he was controlling, but this was becoming a more frequent habit, using physical strength to manipulate me.

My anxiety grew, wondering over and over, what would it be next time? If I stayed here any longer, would it only get worse?

"Soleil, please, it won't happen again," he called after me.

And part of me wanted to believe him.

It hurt not being able to, but I knew if I pushed back hard enough, it would only get worse.

Mr. Finkel trailed closely behind me, the feline following me everywhere.

One, two, three, four.

I counted each step until I reached the top, finishing my third circuit of the numbers in my head.

My steps were heavy as I stormed to my room, loud enough to echo through the house. I heard the clatter of my father's mug being added to the dishwasher as he moved on from our conversation.

I locked myself in my room and fell back into my plush bed. Wrapping the pale green comforter around me, I gazed up at the blank white ceiling long enough to think the shadows on it were moving. My eyes burned, aching for sleep and a new day to forget the shitty one that was today.

I needed to get out. I'd done it last year. I could do it again.

SATURDAY WAS the ideal day for Halloween. Most individuals had Sunday off from work and could spend the night out without worry. Even the children had time off from school to fully indulge in the celebrations.

Regardless of the day, I was always forced to watch from my window.

This year was no exception. What he didn't know, though, was that my plan was already in motion, and there would be no stopping me once it started. I refused to spend another day under his suffocating supervision.

I hurried to the kitchen to grab a waffle for breakfast before rushing back upstairs, determined to avoid my father. I had no desire to speak to him after what transpired the previous night. If I could avoid him straight through Halloween, I would do so.

Unfortunately, that wasn't the case. A knock came to my door only half an hour later, startling my cat as I finished cleaning the crumbs that fell onto my little white desk. Turning in my desk chair, I waited for him to enter. Mr. Finkel watched the door with his intense stare.

The door slowly creaked open, and I saw the mug in his hand before I saw my father.

"I brought this for you," he said, holding out the coffee-turned-olive-branch. I hesitantly accepted, knowing I'd regret denying myself the caffeine. The rich scent of the freshly-brewed coffee and vanilla creamer wafted past my nose as I grabbed the outstretched mug.

Shifting my gaze from the mug to my father, I waited to hear what he'd come for.

"I'm sorry for yesterday," he started, and I placed my mug on the desk to better cross my arms. "I never should've grabbed you or said those things."

A spark of hope grabbed hold of me, blinding me from his empty apology. Was this his way of saying he'd changed his mind?

"Does this mean I can go tonight?' I asked, a smile growing on my lips.

"I think it would be best if you stayed here all day today," he said, crushing my dreams faster than I could create them.

"I can't stay here," I pleaded, hoping he'd finally see the insanity and hypocrisy of locking me away. "Please, I need to go. I made commitments to friends," I tried, attempting to win him over with a new form of guilt. Maybe if he thought there were others relying on me and expecting me, he'd give in.

"You're going nowhere, Soleil," he said firmly, already backing toward my door.

Pulling out a key, he began closing the door while he slipped out. I'm not sure at what point he'd become my captor instead of my father, but my room was becoming a cage, and I was its prisoner.

I needed to face the threats of the world head on and learn for myself, but instead, I was confined to the four walls of my bedroom, no larger than a few paces in each direction.

"What're you—" Before I could finish, the door shut, and I heard the lock clicking into place. "It isn't even night yet!" I yelled after him in protest.

"You need to learn to listen, Soleil," he called out through the door. "You'll be going nowhere today, and I am taking no chances. You have everything you need in there, and I will bring you lunch soon," he shouted, already heading down the stairs.

Luckily, I had a small bathroom attached to my room and all the entertainment I could need, with a television mounted to my wall and a bookcase filled with novels. I made my way to the shelves, running my fingers along the spines of the books. I settled on a Halloween romance, deciding if I couldn't spend the day celebrating, I would at least lose myself in a world that was.

After hours and hours, one food delivery, and endless cuddles from Mr. Finkle, I heard my father making his way back up the stairs.

"Goodnight, Soleil," he called out, turning in for the night. My silence was answer enough to communicate my rage with his decision.

He was heading to bed early, and I could only guess work played a role in that. I had been lucky two Halloweens in a row with his schedule. It seemed almost impossible, but I gave a little thanks to whatever higher power wove fate to my favor.

Once again faced with breaking out on Halloween night, I stared out my bedroom window. My father never found out about my adventures the year before. It was lucky that he barely had time to be friendly with our neighbors. There was no opportunity for them to reveal how I'd spent last Halloween.

I could see the children starting to wander down the

sidewalk in their costumes. I checked the window lock and easily flipped it to face the opposite direction. My father thought he was clever, but not clever enough.

I grabbed the leather jacket I'd held onto for the past year and slipped it on quickly. It matched my band t-shirt I'd been wearing already. I walked to the window, catching Mr. Finkel's attention as I did. The cat studied my movement before resting his head back onto my bed.

I slipped out the window the same as I had the year before to the roof of our sunroom. I made quick work of finding my way off the roof.

When my feet hit the ground, the front light flickered on. I paused, watching as the front door flung open.

"Soleil!" my father bellowed, loud enough that the group of children passing by picked up their pace.

I started back away from the house, my eyes wide as they met my father's. I'd never meant for him to find out like this. I wanted to find Jax, and once I knew he was here to stay, I would've introduced him to my father without him ever realizing how we'd truly met. It would've taken awhile, but I knew I could've won my father over.

Now, all of that was ruined. No matter what I did, I knew he'd blame Jax for this now.

"Soleil." His darkened tone threatened punishment for my defiance. I'd been lucky to attend college and sometimes see friends; now, I couldn't imagine leaving my room ever again if I gave in.

"I'm sorry," I whispered and took off.

CHAPTER

ELEVEN

ouses passed me in a blur as the urge to keep going and never stop washed over me. I didn't stop running until I heard the growing sound of music. Without thinking, I'd taken myself straight to the Halloween party Marielle had begged me to attend.

It was a large white house, and I know it was the correct party as a few girls from one of my classes passed by.

I hesitated in front of the house, weighing whether to go inside.

"Come on," two drunk men said as they passed me. One carried a bottle of brown liquor, and the other had his arm merrily wrapped around his friend's shoulder.

With a deep breath, I walked across the lawn already littered with cups and Halloween décor. An orange streamer caught on my ankle, and I quickly plucked it off.

The steps to the house were short, and already, I found myself pushing the red front door open. The pounding music slammed into me like a brick wall. My ears were ringing, and

80

I could barely hear my own thoughts. Everywhere I looked, men and women were dancing, their Halloween costumes on full display. I could already spot at least three women dressed as black cats, their tight bodysuits clinging to their curves. I hadn't even thought to throw together a makeshift costume before leaving.

I glanced down at my cut-off jean shorts and baggy band t-shirt under my jacket, realizing I stuck out amongst everyone today. My cheeks warmed, and I tried to hurry through the crowd, hoping to stay unnoticed.

I scoured the party for Marielle, but with the loud music and strobing lights, it was almost impossible to wade through the people. The Halloween costumes didn't help. Many of the partygoers were dressed in masks, face paint, or accessories that shrouded their identity and made it impossible for me to tell who hid beneath.

A man in a black mask brushed by me, his large frame towering over me, and I had to slow my breathing so as not to retreat into a full panic. I was beginning to feel closed in, my skin turning clammy. I wanted to leave, to find Jax, but I needed to find Marielle first. I'd hate to see the disappointment on her face the next day if I didn't show my face for at least a second. Yet, the anticipation of finding Jax was starting to eat away at my patience and desire to be at the party even a moment longer.

Another person passing by handed me a cup of some vibrant red liquid.

"Here, have a bloody margarita," he insisted. I glanced down into the cup and my stomach turned, realizing whatever concoction they'd put into this was no margarita I'd ever drink. Nor would I be putting my lips on any open drink a stranger passed me. I may be fearless, but I wasn't naive enough to think there weren't predators among my own kind.

I placed the cup down on a nearby table I passed and continued my hunt for my friend. If the party was this lively, there was no way she'd be missing it. I just had to push further in.

Eventually, I found the kitchen, which was full of punch bowls and kegs. I spotted a large jug of the red liquid someone had pawned on me and, watching another woman fill her cup with it, I wanted to gag. The smell of potent alcohol wafted past my nose, and I crinkled the bridge of it as I inhaled.

A familiar voice caught my attention from the far end of the kitchen, near a folding table set up for a drinking game. I pushed past a group of men trying to convince each other to drink straight from the keg and made my way over to Marielle. As I approached, I could hear her arguing with her girlfriend, who had her hands placed on each hip.

Their matching costumes did not go unnoticed, and I admired the delicate black corsets and fake blood they wore. A pair of matching vampires.

"I am not cheating. I am just very talented at this game," Marielle insisted, slurring the last word.

"Marielle, you're drunk and very clearly cheating," Lyla retorted. "I just watched you flip the cup over using your entire hand instead of two fingers."

"You doubt my ability to flip this with two fingers? I

happen to be very skilled with these two fingers," she said, stepping closer to Lyla.

I could already see her frustrations fading, traded for a mischievous grin.

"Oh, I know exactly how talented you are with them," she said, her voice sultry.

"Get a room," I teased, interrupting the pair. Marielle's dark eyes flashed to me, and a wild smile grew on her lips.

She threw her arms around me in pure delight, the smell of her vanilla perfume slamming into me. A smudge of fake blood wiped onto my neck, and I could feel the thickness of it coating my skin.

"You came," she squealed.

"I came, but I can't stay long. I actually came to find you and then head out," I admitted.

"What? No!" she pouted.

"I promised I would meet someone tonight," I admitted, holding back bits of the truth.

I promised to meet a demon I met a year ago.

The idea sounded insane in my head; out loud, it would be even worse. Marielle's eyebrows shot up, and she gave me a knowing glance.

"Who is he?" she cooed in a sing-song tone.

"No one you would know," I answered, wanting to get out of the conversation as fast as I could. Coming to the party had been a major mistake, but when I saw the look on my father's face, I had fled without thinking. My feet had just carried me, and never once did I stop to think about where they were taking me.

Now that I had gotten myself into this entanglement, I

needed to find a way out, and fast. Time was running out, and Halloween night would not last forever. I wanted to savor the time I would have with Jax.

"I'm sorry, but I really should get going. I don't want to keep him waiting," I tried.

Marielle curled her lower lip, sighing. "Fine, but we are coming too. This party is lame, and I want to see the man who has you so on edge," she said, looking me up and down.

Was it that apparent?

"No-"

"Don't even try to argue with her," Lyla warned. "You know she'll never listen, especially not after three bloody margaritas," she laughed.

I let out a defeated sigh and a light chuckle. "Fine, but you only glimpse him from afar. I don't want you scaring off my date," I teased.

"Deal," Marielle said, her eyes lighting with wonder.

We pushed our way through the crowd back toward the door. There were more people pouring into the rooms, which I had assumed could hold no more individuals, but I was wrong. The night was still early, and I had a feeling this party would only grow more rampant throughout the night.

"Why is it so loud?" I complained, strobing lights blinding me as I tried to follow Marielle.

"It's a party, Soleil," Marielle huffed. "What kind of party would it be without music?"

I thought back to the last party I went to. Jax had pulled me out of the crowd, carrying me to a balcony. Suddenly, the feeling of suffocation crept back in, remembering the way I'd felt that night, anxiety rearing its ugly head at me.

"What's wrong? You look pale," Marielle slurred, glancing from me to Lyla and back.

I tapped the tip of my thumb against each of my other fingertips.

One, two, three, four.

One two, three, four.

It barely soothed the growing anxiety and need to flee.

"I need to get out of here," I said, my vision dancing with black specks and my heart racing.

I hurried through the crowd without a care for how many people I had to push aside to make it through. Their sweaty bodies bumped into me, and I tried to keep my mind on Jax. He'd tell me to breathe and give me peace of mind if he was at the party, but I was alone. I didn't have him, and my mind was shutting down, replacing every happy thought of him with intrusive fears.

I made it to the door, Marielle and Lyla close behind me, and stumbled into the yard. Holding my chest and hunching over, I slowed my breathing and regained my bearings.

"You alright?" Lyla asked, concern creeping into her features.

"Yeah," I said, standing upright again. "Let's just get far away from this place," I added.

"Where'd you say this man was meeting you?" Marielle slurred, tripping on a crack in the sidewalk and barely catching herself.

"The town square," I answered, my strides picking up in pace. I almost tripped on the untied lace of one of my black Converse. There was no time to fix it; I needed to get to that tree and find Jax. I already spent far too much time at the party, and I was worried he may have already left. Or maybe he wouldn't show at all. I tried not to let myself think of the possibility.

One, two, three, four.

I counted each damned crack in the sidewalk, avoiding stepping on each one. The last thing I needed was bad luck. I may not be superstitious, but I knew better than to tempt fate on such an important night.

We waded through hoards of children trick-or-treating up and down the length of the neighborhood. It took longer than usual to reach the square, but soon, I could see the large tree where I'd left Jax last year.

All year long, I had to pass by the tree every time I ventured in the direction of town. It was a painful reminder of everything I couldn't have with him. I had been given one night, and it had left me feeling hollow inside for an entire year. Nothing compared to the fire Jax had awoken inside me that night.

We approached the square, and I felt my fingers automatically begin tapping at my side. It was impossible to control the compulsion.

I couldn't see into the branches of the willow this far back, but each step I took, I felt my heart beat a bit faster. I gave a nervous glance to Marielle and Lyla, and the pair paused at the edge of the square. I knew I had to continue the rest of the distance on my own.

They had no clue what I was walking into. The pair was there to catch a glimpse of the mystery man who pulled me out of my prison of a house on Halloween. Marielle knew I wouldn't leave for just anything; it had to be something big.

The tree was the same as I had left it the prior year when I had to exit the safety of the hidden world beneath it, leaving Jax as only a memory. I felt my pace quicken the closer I got. Marielle and Lyla waited back on the sidewalk, affording me my space.

Butterflies fluttered in my stomach, the anticipation building as I finally passed through the branches. The leaves brushed against my skin, tickling me and sending a shiver down my spin.

"Hey!" someone shrieked, catching me by surprise.

A couple by the trunk looked at me wide eyed, the girl's strap to her little black dress falling. A witch's hat sat on the ground beside her, and her hair was slightly messy.

The man glared at me, expecting me to leave. Part of me wanted to outright protest. This was where I was to meet Jax, the spot I'd clung to for a year now. Yet, the involuntary tapping of my fingers protested, forcing me to retreat into myself, all confidence disappearing.

"I'm sorry," I murmured, knowing the couple was hiding out here for privacy. The last place I'd choose was the public square, but Halloween made people do wild things.

Had Jax already come through here and found the same?

I hurried outside of the branches, looking around the square, hoping to spot him. Wishing I'd see him walking toward me, a hot cup of cider in hand, I scanned every last corner of the square before rushing back toward my friends.

The longer I searched the bustling square, the more my hopes began to fall. Marielle and Lyla helped, unsure of whom or what they were even searching for. Their drunken giggles only fed into my panic, and another feeling starting to sink its fangs into me.

Jealousy.

The more their affection hung in the air, the worse it grew. I wanted what they had. I hadn't realized it before, but it was abundantly clear the missing demon was splitting my heart in two. Had he completely blown me off? I knew the idea of him being at the tree was a far-off hope, but I'd let myself become a dreamer over the past year.

I knew there was little chance he'd come, but part of me had held tight to the possibility. It was the only thing that had got me through the year, making life in this small town more bearable.

My heart had a stabbing pain pulsing through it, and I sunk to my knees on the soft grass beside me. My entire delusional dream was crashing down around me. The one lifeline I had clung to throughout the year, the only thing that made life bearable in this small town, was torn away in an instant.

"No," I whispered, placing my head in my hands, not caring who saw me. The world continued around me, the square bustling with festivities. Not a single soul aware I was fading into the darkness of the night, all my dreams gone.

I'd placed all my hopes and wishes into this one night. There was nothing more for me here. I'd burned every bridge and met my limit. I couldn't stay locked away in my father's house another instant. I was done sitting through pointless classes when I knew my father would never loosen his hold on me.

What good was studying if I'd never step foot far enough to apply it?

Everything came crashing down on me at once, and I didn't realize I was crying until I felt the tear drip down my cheek.

"Soleil…" Marielle's gentle hand was on my shoulder.

"Not now," I started, knowing I couldn't handle the optimistic words and contagious smile Marielle always carried.

"Soleil, I think that guy is staring at you," she said, concern lacing every word.

My gaze flew up, searching the square, my hopes returning for only a moment until my eyes settled on a tall man with dark brown skin with warm undertones watching me. His hair was as black as midnight, and he wore a similar leather jacket to the one I had last seen Jax in.

He started approaching, his hands tucked into his pockets, and for a minute, I contemplated running and dragging Lyla and Marielle with me. His intense stare unsettled me, and a lump formed in my throat.

"Soleil?' he asked, only feet from me. I was on my feet once more, and I stepped in front of my friends, hoping to offer some barrier of protection

"What's it to you?" I snapped harshly, trying to put on a brave mask. The moving fingers against my side told a different story, the same thought repeating in my head.

Run. Run. Run. Run.

My feet remained firmly planted, failing to oblige the repeating warning my mind was firing off.

"This is for you," he said firmly, holding out a folded parchment.

I stared at it, tilting my head. The man raised his brows, raising the parchment a little to invite me to grab it. My shaking hand took it from him, opening it slowly. He was already turning to leave as I read the words scribbled.

I'm sorry. -J

The small parchment in my hand shattered my heart.

"Why?" was all I managed to say to the man before me as his eyes flashed that familiar gold. He was no man at all—he was a demon in a man's body.

"He's rather tied up," the demon said hesitantly. I could tell he was holding back.

"What do you mean?" I begged, needing more answers. Marielle and Lyla just stood silently behind me.

"It's better if you stop asking questions and move on," the demon said, turning again to leave.

"Wait—" I called after him. "Please," I pleaded.

The demon paused, glancing me over and giving me a look of sympathy.

"He wanted to come, he truly did," he said before stalking off.

My heart well and truly shattered, the pieces so small, I struggled to grasp for them, trying to keep my composure. If I broke down now, I'd never find out why Jax didn't come. Something in my gut told me to keep pushing, to find the answers. I would spend all night before the line between worlds solidified again searching for a reason why he would stay away.

He'd promised to be here, and although it was a year ago,

I knew from just that night that Jax was not the type of man —or demon—to break his word. He'd been so raw and open with me when he'd admitted his struggle to find a way to stay in my realm. That type of emotion was not the type one could fake so easily.

The night was still early, and there was still time left to find Jax.

A wild idea formed in my head, and my hope once again began crawling back in. If Jax could not journey to my realm, then there was only one other way I would find and see him again: I would find a way to cross into his world while the line between us was thin.

TWELVE

"You're going to do what?" Marielle shrieked.

"I'm going to the demon realm," I said firmly for the hundredth time as we walked the square.

"She's joking, right?" Marielle asked, turning to Lyla. "Even you are not that crazy. Plus, that's not a real place. It's a made-up story to scare children," she accused.

"I don't think she's joking," Lyla murmured, her face unconvinced.

"So, explain this to me again," Marielle demanded, her drunken daze fading with every minute, the reality of my words finally sinking in.

"I met Jax last Halloween," I said, searching the bustling crowds for the demon who had slipped away from us. I'd been too slow to stop him before. Had he already gone back to his realm? Something told me he hadn't, but with each minute spent searching, I was starting to doubt myself.

"And he's a demon?" she asked. "Like an actual demon, not just dressed as one for the occasion?"

"He's an actual demon. You don't have to believe me, but the sooner you wrap your head around it, the easier it will be to find this guy."

"Who is also a demon?"

"Yes," I ground out between my clenched teeth.

"So what's your plan then when we find him?" she asked, taking Lyla's hand. "That guy didn't seem willing to help you before, so why would he now?"

"Because I'm going to give him no choice," I said. In all honesty, I was still working out my plan, but my mind was set. He wouldn't leave my sights until he agreed to give me what I wanted.

We pushed into the crowds in the streets that had been blocked off for the night. Children ran around, chasing each other with pretend swords and light up wands. I heard one little girl calling out a pretend spell, waving her wand over her friend's head.

The joy they displayed crushed me. I wanted that blissful feeling of soaking in the magic of Halloween. Yet here I was, sulking through town on the hunt for a demon.

One who was doing a fantastic job of blending in with the residents of Weeping Vale.

The chime of the clock tower pulled my attention from my fruitless search, and I listened as it chimed out ten bells. The night was growing late, and I only had two hours before I'd be stuck here without finding the demon I yearned for.

A distant memory tugged at me as my eyes remained on the clock tower, nagging me to remember. That was one of the last places I'd seen Jax, one of the few peaceful places in town, away from watchful eyes.

If there was anywhere to avoid humans and blend in with the night, it would be the room that sat atop the tower.

"I know where he is," I said firmly, my gaze locked on the clock.

"Huh?" Marielle asked, following my gaze.

"Just trust me," I said, already heading toward the alley I knew held the entrance.

The pair shrugged, exchanging wary glances, and followed me. It didn't matter whether they believed me or not. I'd do this on my own if I had to, but I appreciated their willingness to help.

I just hoped it wasn't for nothing.

I led my friends to the dark alley void of any of the celebrations we had passed through only moments before. The door to the clock tower opened easily, creaking as I pulled it. Inside, there was no light besides the moon shining through a single window.

I found the stairs, grabbing Marielle's free hand and tugging her to follow. She still held tight to her girlfriend.

Our steps echoed up the never-ending stairs, and I clutched my chest, trying to catch my breath from the quick pace I'd set.

The burn in my thighs was nothing compared to the ache relentlessly stabbing at my heart.

One, two, three, four.

I counted the steps over and over until we reached the top, and the anxiety subsided for a second.

I spotted the demon immediately, peering out the cracks of the clock tower to the town below.

"So he brought you here," he said without turning around.

I swallowed, stepping forward and searching for the right words.

"Yes," I admitted.

A breeze slipped through the cracks, and I felt it run down my spine, blowing small pieces of hair that tickled my cheeks. Another step forward, and the boards beneath me creaked loudly. The demon turned, cocking his head at me and letting his golden eyes show.

"You shouldn't have come. I have nothing more for you."

"Please, take me with you. I need to see him again," I pleaded, the words sounding too desperate and too raw.

My lungs ached from the climb, and my heartbeat picked up awaiting his answer.

"I cannot," he stated, tucking his hands into his jacket. "It is not what he wants."

"Screw what he wants," I said a little too quickly. I saw the demon's eyebrow raise. "What about what I want? Don't I have a say too?" I asked.

Marielle and Lyla remained quiet; I had almost forgotten their presence until Marielle's arm brushed mine as she moved closer.

"You don't know what you're asking for. I can't give you what you want. He would never allow it, and I can't disobey his orders."

I didn't understand. I couldn't see the reason behind his words. If Jax had wanted to come, why couldn't I go to him? Was the demon realm really that terrible of a place?

It could be no worse than this life I was currently living,

locked away every day by the one person who was supposed to care for me. I knew I had Marielle, but it wasn't enough. I wanted to live, I wanted to love, and I wanted to know what it would be like to be free. If I didn't have that, what was the point of living?

"Please, you have to take me back with you," I begged.

"I'm sorry, but I can't do that. It's better if you just forget about him and the demon realm."

I felt Marielle shudder beside me as his voice raked across the room.

"Maybe we should go," Lyla suggested. "There's still time to go back to the party. I promise you can have fun with us."

But her offer fell short. I knew it's not what I wanted. I knew I would never be satisfied if I just gave up. If this demon wouldn't take me, then I would find someone who would.

"Don't do it," he warned. "I can see what you're thinking. I know that you're going to try to find another way, and I'm going to tell you there isn't one. You need to let the idea go. It is not safe for you, and it's not safe for your friends. He's trying to protect you, not hurt you. Just let him do that one thing."

The demon cocked his head, studying my features. I clenched my fists, frustrated by my inability to make any progress with him.

Damn his protection and damn this demon's demands. I could make my own choices. Someone else had been making them for me all my life, and I was sick of it.

"What are you to him?" I asked.

Why had the demon come in place of Jax? Why had he not come himself?

"I am a friend," the demon answered. "I am a friend and a loyal subject. I will never betray his orders, and right now, his orders are to ensure that you stay safely in this world, that you don't go looking for him."

"Are you a serpent demon like him?"

The demon gave a light chuckle. "No, I'm nothing like him."

"Then what are you?"

"Something of nightmares."

His words made me shiver, and a breeze ran across my skin, the hairs on my arm standing up.

"I'm going to find a way," I said, crossing my arms, Loose curls fell over my shoulders, and I could feel them brush against my exposed skin.

"Just drop it," the demon growled. "Do not make me have to do something I don't want to do."

"You don't even know me. Why are you trying to protect me?"

"I told you: it's what Jax wants."

"And I told you it's not what I want."

The demon's jaw tensed, realizing the conversation was going nowhere. He saw the sheer determination in my eyes and knew I was not going to be stopped.

"You'll never find someone to help you," he said.

"We'll see about that," I said as I grabbed my friends, dragging them back to the staircase.

"Slow down, Soleil," Marielle begged. "Maybe you should listen to this guy and not go looking for trouble."

"So you believe me about the demon realm?" I asked.

"I just think regardless of who this guy is, it sounds like he's bad news. I'm worried about you, Soleil. You're making a rash decision. You barely know Jax."

"I know him enough," I said, unable to explain it. My heart knew deep down I was supposed to be with him. Even if I'd had one night with him, it felt like I'd known him for an eternity.

I LEFT the clock tower without a single plan, but one goal in sight: I was going to find a way into the demon realm, no matter what it took. My determination would guide me, and my heart knew it was the right decision. I couldn't go back to the bleak house that held me prisoner. There was nothing more for me there, just an eternity of misery locked away and a father who cared more about the idea of a perfect and safe world than his daughter withering away before him.

The more I thought about it, the more I came to realize how unhappy I was becoming. I spent an entire year obsessing over the idea of Jax, and I was too blind to see that my life around me was crumbling. Without Jax, I had nothing left.

I had minimal friends, and even then, the friendships were surface level. It was impossible to feel close to someone when my father kept me away. It drove every potential friendship, every potential love, away.

I stalked through the town square with my friends close

behind me. There was no destination in sight, but I knew this was the best place to begin my hunt.

If the demon in the tower wouldn't help me, then I'd find one who would.

A cauldron on a nearby table boiled over, two women working behind it wearing witch hats. Not demons. There was a group of adults near the hot chocolate stand, wearing white sheets with holes cut in the face for their eyes. An attempt at ghost costumes, but still not what I was searching for.

"Seriously, Soleil," Marielle pleaded. "Let's just go back to the party. Or we can even grab pizza from Albert's down the street. Greasy pizza sounds fantastic," she offered.

Although I appreciated a good slice of cheese pizza from Albert's, it still was the last place I wanted to be right now.

"I can't, but you guys can go without me," I said, catching the worried glance Lyla gave Marielle.

"She's right, Soleil," Lyla added. "Obsessing over this isn't going to do you much good. There's still plenty of night to turn this around. I know you're disappointed, but you still have us."

A twinge of guilt hit me. The offer was generous, but I needed to see this through. Even in their company, I knew I'd still have that lonely ache eating at me every second.

It was like something was pulling me straight to the demon realm. All year, that small thread connected us and kept me steady, and now, I could feel the pull from the other end drawing me closer. Soon, the thread would become so taut, I feared it'd snap.

"I appreciate it guys, but this is something I really need

to do," I said. "I don't know how to explain it, but I can't go home right now, and I am not in much of a mood to party or get pizza."

Marielle gave me a knowing look. If anyone knew the reality of my life, it was her. She was the closest thing I'd ever had to a true friend. Multiple times, I had to bail on her and our plans or make excuses for her to leave my home early because of my father. I'd never told her outright about his controlling nature, but it wasn't hard to guess.

"Then we'll keep helping you," Marielle said, looking to Lyla for reassurance.

Lyla nodded.

"You don't have-"

"Oh shush," Marielle said, waving a hand playfully at me. "You know you are never getting rid of us, no matter what you say."

She linked her arm through mine, pulling me back into the crowds of the square. A little ember of hope reignited in my heart. With their help, I might be able to pull it off. I knew if anyone could find a way to the demon realm, it was Marielle. That woman could talk her way into anywhere and was smarter than most gave her credit for. She might look like a party girl on the outside, but she was more cunning than most people I met.

Lyla took Marielle's other arm, joining us.

A Halloween jingle broke through the air, played through some small speaker at one of the tables. Its abrupt start pulled my attention in the direction. A man passing the table wiped at his face, and something about the movement held my gaze.

I spotted exactly what I'd been searching for. The blood dripping from the man's lips told me exactly what I needed to know. Even fake blood couldn't look that real. The red on his lips was a stark contrast to the fake blood smeared on Marielle and Lyla, which was already fading away. The vampire licked his lips, scanning the crowd for his next meal. I watched as he followed a woman heading for a side road alone, until her friends caught up and he paused.

"You really won't change your mind?" Marielle asked, snapping my attention back to the pair.

"I can't," I said, my adamance flashing in my eyes. "And I know exactly who is going to help us."

The pair followed my gaze, spotting the man.

"And how is that guy supposed to help?" Marielle asked warily.

"He's a vampire," I explained. "And he's going to tell me exactly what I want to know."

Any other day of the year, I would've hesitated, letting my anxiety control me. Yet, even as I repeated the four numbers that brought me so much comfort, I felt confident in my decision. Maybe I was drunk on the rush of it all, or maybe I was just finally losing my mind after years without a voice, but I knew this was what I needed to do.

"Let's catch ourselves a demon," I said, narrowing my eyes.

THIRTEEN

It took another ten minutes to convince Marielle and Lyla that vampires truly existed and the demon realm was not a made-up fantasy.

"So, the demon realm-" Marielle started.

"Eodratera," I added.

"Eodratera," she repeated, nodding. "So this world is where Jax is. And it's the same realm from all the folklore this town dredges up at Halloween?"

"Yes, but all those stories are true. The ones we thought silly as children are all true."

We slowly walked toward the table we'd seen the vampire pass. I didn't want him to notice us just yet, but I also didn't want to lose sight of im.

"You know, this is still really hard to wrap my mind around," Marielle said.

"I still don't know if I even believe it," Lyla said, eyeing us skeptically.

"I wish I had more time to prove it to you, but the line

between worlds returns at midnight. If I don't find my answers before then-" I didn't even want to consider the possibility. The idea of Jax slipping away for another miserably long year was too painful to think about.

"We'll still help you," Marielle assured me. "Whether or not we believe everything about Eodratera is to be decided." She gave me a small smile.

"Thank you," I said, and I truly meant it. I knew I hadn't always been the most present friend to her, and she was still spending her Halloween helping me with a task they weren't fully convinced was even real. Every part of me yearned to be with Jax again, the thought of it plaguing me. I felt empty without him, and I couldn't stop mulling over the possibility that this may not work.

I tapped at my side with my fingers to distract myself.

Chasing away then obsessive thoughts, I focused back on the vampire. He still watched the crowd, pretending to look at trinkets strewn across the table in front of him. A woman wearing a sweater with a giant pumpkin on it tried to speak to him, making friendly conversation, but he brushed her off. His only focus was his next prey.

"How are we supposed to corner him?" Marielle asked. "If he's truly a vampire, doesn't that make him dangerous?"

"I don't know," I admitted.

"I'll be bait," she suggested, not an ounce of fear in her voice. "I'll go down that alley alone and see if he follows. You two can follow right behind me and come up behind him. Three on one; there's no way he can escape that."

"No, I'm not going to offer you up to a vampire. You could die," I said, rejecting the idea.

I'd find another way. These creatures had to have more than one weakness. Blood could not be the only thing that blinded their reason.

"Don't be silly," she said, waving her hand in dismissal. "There's no time."

She had a point. Midnight was approaching far too quickly.

"Fine, but no unnecessary risks. If it seems too dangerous, we abort all together and call it a night," I said warily.

It only took us a few seconds to get close enough where we needed to split up. Lyla and I pretended to look at a table about two booths away.

"You know the plan?" I asked, afraid the alcohol could cloud Marielle's judgment. "No risks."

"I know," she said, rolling her eyes.

I worried she still didn't comprehend the threat she faced. The pair indulged my stories, but that didn't mean they were sold on the idea of Eodratera existing.

I picked up a small piece of obsidian from the table in front of me, turning it in my palm. The black reminded me of the black leather jacket Jax had left. A few others stuck out to me, but I didn't have the luxury to browse as Marielle made her way down the alley.

The moment she disappeared from view, my heart sped up. I watched as the vampire did exactly what we expected: he followed her down the alley. The gleam in his eyes was primal, a predator stalking its prey. That prey happened to be my friend, and I felt my hands shake as worry plagued me.

The alley wasn't very long, and the moment we came to its head, I spotted Marielle pretending to text, like she didn't notice the man creeping up behind her. His beady eyes were stuck to her, and he didn't notice our added presence. He was too focused on Marielle.

She glanced up, feigning surprise. The vampire rushed her, pushing her back against the wall. The shock on her face this time was genuine. I saw the flash of white as his fangs were exposed. Before he could sink them into Marielle, Lyla and I ran, each grabbing an arm and pulling him back.

I kicked the back of his knee, causing him to crumple. It was another technique I'd learned in self-defense class. I knew if we kept him down, we'd stand a better chance.

I expected the vampire to be faster and stronger, but it turned out he was no more than a man with a lust for blood. He writhed in our grasp, trying to escape, but my determined grip tightened.

"You're going to answer some questions for my friend," Marielle said, placing her hands on her hips. Her scowl at the vampire made him screw his in displeasure.

"And if I don't?"

She huffed a slight laugh. "You don't want to find out," she warned. Even I was taken aback by her threat. The steel in her eyes backed her words, and I feared using her as bait had shaken her more than she expected.

THE VAMPIRE STAYED silent during our rounds of questions. No matter what we asked, he refused to answer.

I was growing tired of his games and frustrated with the

little remaining time I had. The moon was high in the sky and provided light in the dim alleyway. I caught a glimpse at the vampire's face. He was surprisingly handsome, with his blond hair pushed back and vibrant blue eyes that followed Marielle's every movement.

He was still stalking his prey, looking for a new approach to attack and claim his meal.

"Keep eyeing me like that, and you'll lose an eye," Marielle growled at him.

He averted his eyes to the ground, but I could feel his muscles tense beneath our grasp.

"Just answer our questions," I pleaded.

He remained silent.

"How can a human cross into the demon world?" I asked for what felt like the hundredth time.

Silence.

My hands held tight to the vampire's arm, and I feared loosening my grip to even tap my fingers. Anxiety built in my chest, and I could feel it taking hold. It threatened to be my demise, ruining everything I'd worked for.

I pushed it away, repeatedly tapping my foot as my impatience grew. I pulled his arm further back, the vampire grunting in discomfort. I knew the position was uncomfortable enough to cause minor pain but no major injuries.

"Just answer the question and you can go."

"You can't keep me like this," the vampire said instead. "Someone will eventually notice, and how do you think that will look?"

I swallowed, realizing he had point. My morals didn't keep me from holding him here and forcing him to face our interrogations, though. I knew the longer we kept him here, the fewer victims he'd find tonight. Yet, to any other person, it would look like the three of us were beating on this helpless man.

"I know where you can find endless blood," Marielle taunted suddenly.

This peaked the vampire's interest. A low hiss escaped his lips as he writhed against our grip again.

"There's a blood bank not far from here. They keep lots of blood locked up. I used to work there and know the passcode," she said.

The vampire seemed to debate the validity of her words. He tried to glance between me and Lyla but struggled to strain his neck. He grumbled as his knees scrapped against the pavement.

"Fine," he agreed through gritted teeth. "Passcode."

"Answers first, demon," I warned.

"I am no demon," he snapped.

"Are you not from the demon realm, Eodratera?" I asked.

"I am, but that world is full of more than you know," he hissed. "You would do best to stay away."

"I didn't ask for your opinion. Answer the question," I said, losing my patience. He was playing games, biding his time. I knew he was waiting for someone to find us.

"You need a witch if you want to go," the vampire explained, giving in. His lust for blood won. "Without a witch, I'm afraid you're out of luck," he grumbled, struggling to break free.

"And a witch will help me venture to your realm?" I asked.

"For the right price," he said, baring his fangs at me.

My frustration built, and it took everything in me not to lash out. As human as he appeared, I knew his soul was different. Deep down, he was consumed by a darkness, one that drove him to crave blood and prey on helpless humans.

I narrowed my eyes down at him.

"And I don't suppose you would know where to find a witch?" I asked.

The vampire let out a dark laugh. "I think you already know," he said.

Surprisingly, he was right. Everyone in town knew where to find a witch, and it just so happened, my mother used to work with her.

The town's apothecary was run by Serafeen, an irritable old woman who had no desire to deal with anyone's antics. Rumors ran rampant about her witch heritage and the spells she'd place if you weren't careful in your dealings with her.

My stomach turned, knowing where I had to go. Marielle gave me a sympathetic glance, knowing my hesitation.

I hadn't been back there since my mother left, and I knew Serafeen would be less than likely to help us.

A pit formed in my stomach, and I felt my chest rise and fall heavily as my breathing sped up.

I tried to calm myself, tapping my thigh. Over and over, the word rang through my mind.

Witch. Witch. Witch. Witch.

I tapped to the beat of the word echoing through my thoughts. Every second, I learned something new of the two worlds. Demons, vampires, and now witches filled my reality.

"Hey!" a man shouted from the top of the alley. I immediately recognized him. Ben's unwelcome presence set me on edge. His gaze settled on me, realization dawning, and a slimy grin curled his lips.

"We need help over her!" he shouted. "These girls are attacking this poor man."

I saw the revenge in his eyes. Satisfaction spread across his face as he crossed his arms, waiting for more people to hustle over to the alley.

"We need to go," Lyla said, wide-eyed.

"2673," Marielle, spouted at the vampire.

He rose to his feet the second we loosened our grips. Ben's shouting had gathered attention, drawing the police to the alley. I glanced both ways weighing our options. The other direction was a dead end with a fence. It was low enough to climb up and over, but we risked the officers at the entrance to the alley easily catching up to us.

Marielle saw my gaze and nodded to me. It was our only option. The vampire backed away from us toward the officers. He had nothing to fear. He was the one they thought was being held hostage. Without another thought, I took off, hoping my friends would follow. I ran as fast as I could toward the fence, and the officers sprang into action, chasing us.

Lyla and Marielle were barely a step behind me. We threw ourselves at the metal fence, climbing as fast as we could.

I risked a glance back at the officers as they paused, distracted by something else in the alley. In a dumpster to my left, a fire had sprung to life. I hadn't noticed it before.

The flames must've started small and built into a full-scale fire while we had been questioning the vampire.

I could've sworn I saw embers trail behind me before the fire grew larger. The vampire stared at it, bewildered, glancing to the fire and back to me again. The police paused their pursuit to deal with the new issue, allowing us the time we needed to escape their custody.

I thanked the higher powers that this coincidence saved our asses. I was determined, but I wasn't so sure I could outrun the law. Sooner or later, they would've caught up to us in this small town.

FOURTEEN

"That blood bank closed last year," I said to Marielle as we walked down any empty street. We were close to the apothecary now, and the unsettled feeling in my stomach grew worse with each step.

I tried to push away the repeating thoughts, reminding myself this was once a place I loved. Serafeen had always been good to me as a child. She had a soft spot for me then, and maybe she still would now.

"I know," Marielle said, smirking. "But we will be long gone before he realizes that."

I let out a laugh, tossing my head back and letting my red hair fall down the length of my back. My father always said it reminded him of the colors of fall. An autumn baby, born in September, with hair the color of beautiful leaves. I liked to think it was more like the flames that burned deep down, keeping me going and preventing me from fading away to darkness.

We approached the tiny apothecary, the outside covered

in vines. A sign hung on it that read 'Open'. I twisted the doorknob, and as I pushed it open, a small chime signaled our arrival.

I heard shuffling in the back of the store, the counter out front empty.

My eyes wandered the room, taking in all the herbs, bottled mixtures, and candles. There were other items like soaps and tonics mixed in on the shelves, advertised as cures to every health ailment. I spotted a bottle that boasted helping migraines. Another near it was for colds.

"I'm not handing out candy, if that's what your after," the old woman yelled as she shuffled her way to the storefront.

"We're not children," I shouted back.

Her slim face appeared in the doorway, wrinkled skin aging her. She wore a long black dress with a purple celestial design. If she didn't appreciate the town calling her a witch, she wasn't doing anything to help it. She looked like she'd stepped straight out of a Halloween movie. She was only missing the hat.

"Soleil," she crooned. "What a lovely surprise."

My nerves calmed for a moment, relieved that the woman still found a soft spot in her heart for me. She'd always been kind to my mother.

"What brings you here?" she asked, toying with a bottle, trying to pry the cork lid off. After a moment, she gave up and moved to a new bottle.

"I need help I think only you can give me," I started. "I need to go to Eodratera."

Her eyes widened at my mention of the demon world,

proving she knew more than most. Maybe all the accusations weren't entirely false. I'd already seen proof of demons and vampires; the reality that witches were real wasn't a far off idea anymore.

"So it's true, then. It is real and it can be done?" I asked, partially hoping she'd confirm the answers my friends had been yearning to hear all night. I wasn't crazy, and this wasn't all for nothing. I felt Marielle shift nervously beside me.

"Yes," she whispered. "But it is not a place humans belong. Does your mother know you're asking around about this stuff?"

I hesitated. I hadn't spoken to my mother in months. The last call I'd received, she told me about some new job she was pursuing and that she promised to visit soon. She never did. I partially blamed my father. I knew she would fear returning and falling under his grasp again.

"No," I offered, embarrassed to admit to the old woman that my relationship with my mother was not the same.

She shook her head, fiddling with the glass bottles before her. They were filled with vibrant concoctions.

"Please, I need to go. I need to help—"

What was he to me? We'd only spent one fateful night together. Would he even remember me? Something in my heart told me things weren't right. I knew Jax wouldn't miss this night for no reason. It was all he'd dreamed about, coming into this world and living a new life.

I'd hoped it'd be one with me, but maybe that was a childish fantasy.

Still, that thread kept tugging at me, telling me to follow

my heart. Something in Eodratera called to me, and I needed to find out what it was.

"I need to help Jax." Serafeen just cocked her head, studying me. I could've sworn I saw a flash of understanding across her face.

"Traveling to the demon realm is no easy feat," she stated carefully. "If I help you, then you need to be sure this is what you want."

My fists clenched, and I gave a firm nod. All night, I had been a bundle of anxiety and nerves, unsure if my night would end in disappointment and failure. There was nothing I was surer of than this one thing. I would give anything to see Jax just one more time. My soul was incomplete without his presence. For one night, I felt complete until it was ripped from me. I couldn't continue that way.

"There is only one way a human can cross to that world, and it has a steep price," she said warily. Her beady eyes looked me over as she placed the glasses on the counter.

I moved closer to the counter, my feet moving without a second thought. The woman pulled out a pen, placing it down on the countertop. She picked up the bottle, placing it on one side of the pen.

"This is you in our world, and this pen is the line between the two," she explained, meeting my gaze.

Marielle and Lyla remain silent and tense, consuming every word the woman said.

"You cannot just cross over to the other side. If you did, your soul would be called right back to this world with nothing to keep you there. It's why at midnight tonight, the demons will be drawn back to their world. Even they do not have the power to tie themselves here. There are only two ways to bind yourself to the other side: be a witch who can pass through as they please or have a witch do it for you."

I listened carefully, taking care not to miss a single word. All I needed was a witch willing to help me. They could bind me to the other world, allowing me the ability to stay and find Jax.

"It isn't that simple," Serafeen continued, reading my mind. "Even if a witch is willing to do it for you, the cost is steep."

"I'm willing to pay," I said, trying to move things along. Midnight was creeping up on us.

"Are you sure? You have not even heard the price," the old woman accused.

"No price is too great," I insisted.

"Do you value your life so little?" she asked. "Do not be naïve; there are demons out there who will take advantage of you and cling to every word you say as truth. They will play your words against you and lure you into promises and deals you cannot undo."

I swallowed hard. Placing my hands on the counter, I tapped my fingers.

Again, thoughts plagued me, playing over and over in my mind. Could I do this? Everything inside me screamed to go to Eodratera, but then what? I knew nothing of the world, as Serafeen had now proven.

"I need to go," I insisted, partially for myself.

"To keep yourself there, you need to bind your very soul to the world," she said.

A sigh of relief escaped from me. At least the price was not death.

"It would mean you could never return here," she said.

I tensed, hearing the small gasp that left Marielle. Never returning to this world meant I'd never be able to return to my old life. I'd have to leave my friends behind, never finishing school or moving out. Yet, there was that little spark of hope. It was also a way out. I could finally leave the life I felt trapped in, end the cycle of control and manipulation.

Before I could respond, Marielle placed a gentle hand on my shoulder. "Listen, it's never been my place to push, but I can see how unhappy you are here," Marielle said. "If this truly is a fresh start for you, then you should take it."

Her soft smile comforted my nerves. It was all I needed to hear to know what decision was right.

"I want to go," I said firmly.

Serafeen's eyes widened. "Are you sure?" she cautioned.

I nodded, trying to shove away any doubts.

"Then we shall begin," she said. She pushed back the long sleeves of her black dress, cracking her knuckles. I saw her flick her hands, murmuring words I didn't recognize under her breath. At first, it seemed as though nothing had changed. There was no blinding light or sparkles floating in the room. That was until the binding stabbed into me with blinding pain.

"What did you do?" I asked, my voice barely a whisper, trying to breathe through it.

"I tethered your soul to Eodratera. You will forever be chained to that world, the same as I am chained here."

I didn't imagine it would feel any different, but I could feel my soul slipping away. It ached where an empty cavern was left within me. Every part of me was restless, yearning to reunite with it. I could already feel the other world calling to me. It was like a magnet, impossible to escape the tug of. Every part of my body ached.

Had I made a terrible mistake? Already, dread filled every inch of me. These were my last moments in this world, and I could barely think straight. My hands shook, finding Marielle and Lyla staring at me like I'd disappear any second. I could tell they were taking in every last detail of me, a memory to last a lifetime.

It hit, suddenly and rapidly. I was no longer in the apothecary, and the pain was subsiding. All I could see was darkness, but not the kind one experiences when they step into the night. This was the darkness of nightmares, the kind that consumed you, that left you in a void with nothing to save you. There was no world, no sound, nothing to tell me if I was alive or dead. Had the binding killed me in the process?

It vanished, dropping me into a world that was no longer my own. I fell over as my wobbly legs found purchase. Closing my eyes, I shielded them from the dust kicked up around me as my body hit solid ground. When I opened them, I found a world I never expected.

PART THREE
BEWITCHED

CHAPTER

FIFTEEN

The journey to the other realm took no more than a few seconds. Everything blurred, my world turning black before once more, a world came to view.

I was no longer surrounded by the familiar apothecary. Its walls were replaced with a vast land, the ground dust and dirt. There were no familiar plants or signs of life; instead, I saw a group of trees, their trunks a deep black. The leaves were blood red; not the warm color of autumn, but rather, the bleeding color that promised death.

This world was different than my own. It was darker somehow, like the sky has been traded for gray. There were no red and orange trees I had left behind, not a single soul wandering around. The silence sent a shiver down my spine. Was this what the demon realm was like? Desolate and bare, not a single soul to be spotted?

A meow beside me caught my attention, and I glanced down, cursing under my breath.

"Mr. Finkel? What're you doing here?" My question was panicked. The creature blinked at me with its typical intrigued stare. Had he followed me to the apothecary?

"Ugh, what am I supposed to do with you? We're stuck here, you know," I groaned.

"Come on, let's see if we can find anything," I said, as if the creature could understand me.

I wandered with the cat for another ten minutes without spotting a single demon. As we walked, our feet kicked up dust. My white Converse were now a dull shade of gray.

Was this truly where Jax lived?

The dust now coating my ankles made me cringe. I wanted to find the nearest water source and wash up, but there did not seem to be anything besides dirt and rocks. We were in barren land, lost.

I pushed on, determined to find Jax. I wasn't sure where I was wandering, but I could still feel that thread between us, tugging me forward. It didn't matter where I was—I could always feel that pull.

The scenery soon changed. In the distance, I could see small hills rising, spread in a small patch, made of stone. No longer was our path only dirt. The closer I got, I realized they were not hills—they were entrances. Each of them led down to narrow tunnels that I assumed were interconnected under the surface.

I walked around the entrances for a few minutes. I couldn't find anything special about them from first glance. There was still no signs of demons, and I could tell night was approaching in Eodratera.

The sky was growing darker, and a faint red orb started growing in the sky. It was like the moon I used to gaze up at from my bedroom window, but this one looked like it was bloodstained.

A rumble in the distance pulled my attention from the sky. I glanced behind me, spotting a large cloud rolling across the flat land. It was a plume of dust barreling toward my cat and me. The dust kicked up everywhere it touched, and I quickly realized we were about to be caught in the middle of a sandstorm.

We needed to take shelter and fast. The only places to find safety from the storm were the tunnels beside us. My stomach sunk, knowing I would have to venture down into them. I imagined all the beasts and creatures that could dwell within.

My confidence wavered as I wandered over to a cave. The sandstorm threatened to consume me if I waited another moment, and still, I hesitated. I could hear the intense wind picking up at my back, my hair starting to catch the breeze building. The tunnel leading down was dark, and I couldn't see the end. There was no way to know what awaited us once we entered.

I hurried inside, trying to shove aside my fears. The howling winds echoed behind me as the storm passed the cave. I was already far enough inside to escape the fine grains of sand carried by the storm. Mr. Finkel followed close beside me.

The further I pushed inward, the more the silence grew, no signs of any other creatures yet.

I tapped my fingertips against my thumb, hoping to bring myself comfort, but the further I walked, the worse the growing anxiety became.

VENTURING INTO THE TUNNELS, I realized just how endless they actually were. The further I went, the harder it became to see, and the air became colder. The walls of the cave felt almost damp as I ran my fingers along the smooth stone.

Mr. Finkel followed me into the caves, pushing deeper with every step we took. His soft fur brushed against my ankles as he kept close.

The hair on my arm stood up as I thought I heard a something echo in the distance.

"It's probably nothing, right?" I asked the cat, as if he would give me a response.

Maybe I had gone insane, leaving behind my own world for a demon world and talking to a cat. I could only imagine what my father would say right now: the disappointment would hang on his shoulders, and that look in his eye would build a guilt that would eat away at me. I tried to push those thoughts aside as the tunnel opened into a small cavern with nothing inside.

The dirt looked scuffled, as if something had passed through not long before. I listened, hoping I hadn't stumbled onto a demon's den, but there was nothing.

"This will have to do until the storm passes," I told the cat.

I walked the length of the cavern, running my hands along the wall until they brushed over a small divot in the smooth stone. I paused, looking over the wall. I realized there were lines etched into the stone, and the closer I looked, the more apparent it became that these were tally marks of some sort, as if someone had been counting the days down here.

My heart raced, and my stomach sunk—whoever had made these marks had not been here by their own free will. I tapped my fingers against the wall in a rhythmic beat. I counted them.

One, two, three, four.

Repeating it three times, I finished, my finger still hovering over the last mark. This person had been stuck down here twelve days.

Were days even the same in this realm? Were the nights longer or shorter here?

I realized I didn't know the answers. I didn't have any of the answers I needed to survive this realm. I'd come here without any knowledge of the world I was stepping into. Maybe that demon had been right. Maybe this place wasn't safe for me.

A small echo drew my attention away from the wall. It was the first sound I'd heard since arriving in this world that I knew was not a figment of my imagination, the first real sign of life.

It sounded like claws raking against the stone, coming my way. The louder it got, the more my heart pounded. It was getting closer and closer, louder and louder. I tried to slow my breathing, counting in my head, trying to soothe myself, but it wasn't working. The nearer sound drew, the more panicked I grew.

I knew I should flea, but my feet were firmly planted on the ground. I was terrified of whatever was approaching.

Mr. Finkel raised his back, his hair standing up as he hissed. The cat let out a low growl in the direction of the tunnel we'd come from.

Something else had found shelter here.

There was another tunnel that led out of the cavern, but I was afraid if I ventured down it, I'd become lost in the tunnels.

If this was this creature's home, it knew these tunnels better than I did. I did not want to become prey, stuck in a labyrinth underground. I'd fight my way out if I had to. I took a defensive position, ready to fight, unsure if the demons here were anything like humans in my world.

Would my hands be of any use?

I got my answer as a large black mass entered the cavern. Its thin, prickly legs carried its almost too big body. I counted six legs with thorn-like appendages. The creature was abhorrent to look at. It reeked of death.

The moment it entered the space, I crinkled my nose, its scent stunning me. Everything in me told me to flee, to run down that other tunnel as fast as I could. Its glowing red eyes locked on me, and a low chuckle escaped the beast.

"And what do we have here?" the creature asked, its voice like nails on a chalkboard.

A shiver ran down my spine and froze me with fear. I was ill prepared for this world. Demons and vampires were one thing, but this was a monster out of nightmares.

I took one step back, afraid that the movement might cause the creature to lunge. It moved slowly, its six legs moving much like a spider. I held my breath, waiting for it to make a move. I didn't want to be trapped down here for days with this beast.

What had it done to the last person?

My eyes glanced to the other tunnel once more and then back to the one I came from as I sucked in a breath.

"There's no escape, little human," it said.

I let out my breath.

"I can smell you. I know you're human. You're not from this world," it continued. "You reek."

"And what are you?" I dared to ask. Maybe if I could keep the thing distracted, I'd find an opening to be able to run. I stepped to the side, putting myself between the creature and my cat. If anything, at least one of us might escape. Part of me felt overly protective of the feline. He had been there for me at my best and worst, and here he was, still by my side, a loyal creature to the end.

"Go," I whispered to the cat, hoping it would run off down the other tunnel and find a way out. I tried, but the cat remained by my side.

"And you brought a familiar with you. How interesting," the creature crooned.

I didn't have time to consider what that meant, why the beast thought my cat was a familiar. I'd never heard the term before.

"What do you want?" I asked, watching the creature carefully.

"Your soul, of course." The answer sent panic through me. I knew it wasn't lying.

"What else would I want?" it asked, cocking its head and glancing me over. "Your soul from your body. I want to know what it tastes like. Are human souls as rich as I remember them?"

I felt my soul leave me for a moment when I was tied to the realm. The pain was unbearable, and I didn't want to know that pain again.

The creature took three steps forward, and I took one more back. I could feel the wall of the cavern dangerously close to my back. There was no easy path out.

"This is my maze. You may have found your way in, but you will not leave," it warned.

I realized it was ready to pounce. I knew it was coming, and a heartbeat later, it lunged. I kicked the ground, dirt flying at the beast, straight for its eyes. Its head was bent forward as its appendages reached out for me. I hit my mark as it retracted in pain, screeching and using its two front legs to paw at its face.

I took that as my chance, running, praying that my cat would follow. A moment later, I was relieved to find the feline close beside me. We ran as fast as we could, but I could hear the beast gaining on us. Pushing further into the labyrinth of tunnels, I came to a fork.

I paused for a second then decided to push right. Mr. Finkel and I ran faster, weaving through the curves and turns of the cavernous tunnel system. After a few minutes, my heart sank when I rounded a corner. The wall at the end trapped us. My heart raced as I looked for a new way out.

Turning, I made to head back the way we came. We'd have to retrace our steps.

"I can smell you, human." The raspy voice drifted down the tunnel.

I stopped in my tracks, knowing the beast had us cornered.

SIXTEEN

I saw the beast's shadow before the creature itself. It crept around the corner, its thin legs carrying a thick black body. I could hear the scuttling sound as it crawled closer on each of its spider-like legs.

My hands turned clammy, and I wiped sweat from my brow from exhaustion and nerves. If I didn't come up with something soon, I would find myself trapped down here forever.

As it crawled closer, I remained still, my eyes never leaving the beast.

"There you are. I knew I could smell you down here," the creature said.

"You never answered my question. What exactly are you?" I asked, trying to buy myself more time.

"I am your nightmare, dear human. I am the Nyera, the collector of souls."

The way its eyes settled on me had my hair standing up on end. My cat huddled closer to my legs, wrapping itself around them in a protective manner. I took a step forward, placing myself between the beast and the cat almost instinctively.

"Human, there's no use. You've run out of places to run."

There were no weapons down in the tunnels. The only things I had were dirt, sand, and rocks. Faster than I expected, it jumped forward, and I narrowly missed it rolling off to the side. The beast rebounded fast, regaining its balance, turning on me once more.

"Go," I demanded of the cat.

The feline stared at me with worry and hesitation. I worried for a moment that it didn't understand what I meant. The beast prepared for another attack, and I wasn't sure I could protect us both. After a moment, the cat sprinted toward the tunnel opening, giving in to my command. The creature's eyes followed the feline but settled back on me, allowing him to escape. A sigh of relief escaped my lips knowing at least Mr. Finkel would make it.

The beast jumped again, its two front legs aimed directly for me. I shuddered thinking of what those sharp appendages would feel like raking over my skin. The end of the beast's legs was pointed, and I imagined it spearing through me with minimal effort.

Again, I dodged the creature, its large mass narrowly missing me. I spotted something to my left and realized it was a large chunk of stone that had broken off the wall. It was jagged and rough and exactly what I needed. Unfortunately, the creature also saw it. It threw itself in that direction, and I reacted, praying I reached the stone first. I slid on the dirt right as the beast landed almost directly on top of me. My outstretched hand grabbed the stone, and the beast leaned forward to sink jagged brown teeth into me. I slammed the rock as hard as I could into its head, and the beast staggered backward, stunned and writhing in pain.

It let out an awful sounding growl. I tried to run through the opening of the tunnel. I had no more tricks, and the beast was clearly more powerful than I was.

I thought I had made it, a small relief lifting from my shoulders, but my shirt caught on something. One of the beast's legs snagged on my shirt, pulling me back toward it. It was still moaning in pain, but it had a firm grip on me. I tried to wiggle loose, but it was no use. It wrapped its leg around my body as I tried to hit it with my hands.

I looked down at the palm of my hand that was now bleeding and realized that the thorny appendages were just as sharp as they appeared. My hysteria had blinded my senses, allowing my quick lapse in judgment.

"Your soul is mine. You should give up now," it drawled.

My heart felt like it was shattering, my hope running out. I squeezed my eyes shut as the beast moved its head inward, as if it was going to take a bite from me. Preparing myself for the teeth to sink into my neck, thoughts swam through my mind. Would it be like a vampire feeding on a human? My soul would once more no longer belong to me. It would be torn for my very being and handed over to this creature.

I waited for the agony of which fate would be worse. Would I die immediately from the blood loss, or would I live and suffer through miserable days until I could no longer stand the pain, losing my soul?

My eyes held shut, and my fist clenched as I finally gave up.

Before the creature could sink its teeth into me, I heard it let out another growl, loosening its grip on me then tightening once more. It let out another ferocious screech, the sound ringing through my ears. I threw my hands up over them, covering the awful, high-pitched tone.

The beast would not stop yelling in agony, and I opened my eyes as it dropped me. With my feet on solid ground, I watched as the beast recoiled, as if something had burnt it.

I wasted not a single moment waiting for the beast to attack again. I ran down the tunnel, hoping I was fast enough to escape its grasp this time. I found myself losing track of the turns I took, playing the event over and over in my head.

Maybe it had been the stone after all, the effects from me hitting it in the head finally catching up with the beast. I didn't think too hard about it. I wanted to forget the entire experience. Instead, I pushed on through the winding maze of tunnels, hoping to spot the entrance and my feline.

Adrenaline guided me, carrying my legs and forcing me to continue as growls echoed off the stone walls behind me.

CHAPTER

SEVENTEEN

Running through the tunnel, I could hear the beast's angry growls. Mr. Finkel had run far ahead, and relief washed over me knowing at least the cat would get away unharmed.

It was gaining on me, fast. My legs were tired, and the bottoms of my feet burned in the thin sneakers. At this pace, the demon would capture me in a matter of moments.

I couldn't outrun it.

I'd have to outsmart it.

Stopping, I turned to face the tunnel, waiting for the creature's ugly, distorted face to appear.

I saw its shadow before the actual creature. Its spider-like body barreled through the tunnel, awkwardly moving faster than I'd thought possible.

I planted my feet firmly, bracing myself for the demon's attack. My hands were ready in front of me, waiting to accept the demon and fight back. As it lunged, I instinctively withdrew, knowing the pain that would follow.

One moment, I was cowered, closing my eyes, and the next, the demon was hissing its retreat, limping away. It was the same high-pitched screech I'd heard before. I swore I saw a bright light before I could open my eyes. It seemed to emanate from me, but that was impossible.

A trick of the mind is what I told myself. Perhaps the demon changed its mind, decided I wasn't worth the effort.

I didn't push my luck, hurrying out of the tunnel, not willing to spend another moment sitting around. The demon could change its mind as quickly as it did before.

As I burst out of the tunnel, I spotted the red moon above. The sky had grown dark, and there were no clouds in sight. I spotted a few lights burning in the sky like stars.

I tapped my fingers over and over getting into my usual, repetitive motion soothing me.

One, two, three, four.

It was the only comfort I had in this unknown world. The soothing, repetitive act calmed my nerves and brought me a sense of familiarity. I paused as something brushed my ankles. Looking down at my feet, I found Mr. Finkel and gave a small smile.

"Let's go," I said, knowing we couldn't stay put any longer. I feared the beast would follow us, eventually venturing out of its cave. We needed to move, and we needed to find shelter, fast.

"Come on," I said sleepily, pushing on in the same direction we had been traveling.

Our scenery began to change not long after we began walking. I spotted more and more trees and shrubbery as we ventured. Trees here were nothing like back home. Dark trunks grew, with sharp gray leaves attached to the thin branches. I dared to take a step closer to one. Reaching a hand up, I touched one of the leaves, recoiling as it pricked me and drew blood from my fingertip.

I shook my hand, hoping the pain would reside. I walked around the base of the tree, wondering how its roots grew in such infertile soil. The ground below us was dry and dusty. Not many plants in my own world would be able to survive such conditions. The shrubs were no different, just as vile and dangerous.

The temperature was like my own world, a cool breeze blowing my hair back from my face. It was like a crisp, autumn night back home.

I was finally free, but for what? I still hadn't found Jax, and I still had no idea where I was as we walked for another hour or so.

I spotted a structure in the distance and had to squint in the dark to try and make out the features of it. It looked like a small shack, and as I inched closer, I noticed it was made of wood, weathered and worn. The door was cracked open, and there were no lights inside.

I tried to walk the perimeter, glancing into open windows to see if I could spot any creatures within.

I couldn't hear anything nor sense anything off, everything in me telling me this place was abandoned. Yet, I had thought the same thing of the tunnels before entering. Could demons mask their presence to humans?

Glancing around, I realized I had no other options left. Sleeping outside in the open only made me more of a target.

Having a roof over my head at least helped hide. It was a risk I would need to take.

I made full circle around the shack and found myself at the front door once more. Looking to my cat, I shrugged and pushed the door open a little wider, the space inside empty. It was a single room with a small sink-like structure in the corner. A table with a single chair sat on the other side of the room, and there was no bed or fireplace, no cabinets to hold food.

What was this place?

I wondered if this once had been someone's home.

We had no other choice but to rest. Closing the door behind us, I made my way to one of the empty corners. I pressed against the wall and sat down on the floor, sliding my back down until I hit solid ground. Slowly, I lowered myself to lie on it. It was freezing as it pressed against my bare skin. I removed my jacket and placed it over myself like a blanket.

Luckily, Jax was bigger than me, so it was already over-sized but left a bunch of my body exposed. A shiver ran down my spine as the cool ground embraced me. Every decision leading to this moment played over in my head like an obsession I couldn't let go of. If I had just made one different choice, would I be in this predicament?

I tucked my knees in as tightly as I could, trying to fit them under the jacket. Mr. Finkel cuddled in tight to me, his soft, small body pressing to my chest. Even though the jacket barely covered me, I moved it so it was draped over us both, and I could feel the cat's purr of gratitude rattling against me.

I didn't want to let my guard down, but I knew I needed rest. I couldn't take another step forward without a little bit of sleep, so I let myself drift. Closing my eyes and giving in to the heavy weight that pressed down on me, I let my first day in the demon world melt away.

CHAPTER

EIGHTEEN

I woke to the sound of creaking floorboards and the smell of lavender.

Why was I on the floor of my room? The cold, hard ground pulled me from my sleepy haze.

Blinking away the drowsiness, I sat up, and the black jacket slid from me. I quickly realized I was still in my clothing from the day before, and as I glanced around, sheer panic took over. My heart raced, and a lump formed in my throat when I recognized the small shack around me.

This was not my house nor my room. Pushing off the ground, I stood, which woke Mr. Finkel from his own deep slumber. The cat let out a sleepy purr, rubbing against my legs.

Suddenly, the feline startled, tensing. He hissed in the direction of a wall, but no one was there. I glanced around, confused. The wind must've picked up outside, spooking him. I didn't hear any sounds or signs of creatures outside the small cabin. A slight chill ran down my spine.

"Lost?" a dark voice called out from behind me.

I turned quickly, putting my hands up in front of myself, ready to defend. My nerves still hadn't fully settled from the Nyera, and my hands were trembling. I only hoped the tall, mysterious man now across from me didn't notice.

He took a few steps closer, looking me over with his deep purple eyes. My eyes trailed up to meet his gaze. The demon was rather handsome, especially compared to the vile creature I had faced the prior night. He had short blond hair and tan skin. He reminded me of the men you'd see in a rom-com movie where the girl goes on a beach vacation and falls for the surfer.

"Human," he stated more than asked.

"How'd you know?" I asked, keeping my guard up. I grit my teeth as he again took another step toward me. There was nowhere to run, my back against a wall.

"Relax. I am not going to kill you or steal your soul, unlike the beast that lives in that cave." A smile grew on his lips as I cocked my head in confusion. "You didn't try very hard to hide where you came from."

Worry grew in my chest, realizing the demon was correct. I had been so sleep-deprived and exhausted, I had just pushed onward until I found this place to rest. I hadn't thought to cover my tracks or worry about anyone following me.

"Is this your house?" I asked, confused why the demon would be here.

"You could say that," he drawled, crossing his arms. "Think of it like a temporary home I utilize on special occasions."

I took a step back as his menacing gaze raked over me, resting finally on my face. His brows furrowed and eyes narrowed, watching me slowly recoil.

"If I wanted you dead, you would already be dead, human," he sneered at me. I tried to let the words bring me comfort, but somehow, I only felt more unsettled. What did he want?

I checked each of my options for escape, noting the door and a small window only steps away from me. The demon's eyes never left me for a second, and I knew he could tell I was evaluating how I would free myself from the shack. I'd already been trapped by one demon in this realm; I refused to be the hostage of another.

In a split-second decision, I bolted for the door, my cat following. Before I could open it or throw myself through it, I slammed into a solid mass. I fell to the floor, thrown back by the sheer force of my collision.

My head stung where it had collided with what felt like an invisible wall of concrete. I rubbed at my forehead, anticipating a lump to swell, but luckily, I was only met with another wave of pain.

"What the-" I started.

"An illusion, m'dear."

The demon waved a hand, and the room melted into a new scene. Where I had once thought the door was, it moved about two feet away. In front of me was a wooden wall. I glanced between the wall and the demon, my eyes narrowing on him.

"How?" I demanded, sick of the tricks of this new world.

The pain in my head, combined with my sheer annoyance, pushed away any anxieties, giving me a few moments of pure bravery to confront the demon.

"What do you want?" I grumbled, wanting to get on my way.

"What does any demon want?" the demon inquired.

"Death, chaos, my soul…" I muttered under my breath, rolling my eyes.

"No, human," the demon stated, glaring down at me.

I tried to scramble to my feet, brushing dust off my exposed legs. I met the demon's gaze and held it, waiting for an explanation.

"You'll soon learn," he said with a shrug. "Come."

My heart pounded at the demand. There was no room for arguing, and I didn't wish to wait around and find out what other demon may stumble upon us in the shack.

I grabbed the leather jacket from where it still sat on the ground and followed the demon out the door. He'd already stalked well ahead of me, heading in the same direction I had been traveling. A quick glance down told me my cat still followed along.

We walked for miles, passing new scenery. I spotted more plants I did not recognize, a nearby pool of water ahead of us. I quickly looked to the demon for approval, who nodded. Hurrying over to the water, I scooped some into my cupped hands and splashed it on to my face. I wanted to test it against my skin before consuming it. Even with the demon's approval, I didn't fully trust him. At any time, he could change his mind on helping me.

I sipped a bit of the water, and it slid blissfully down my throat.

It was a long trek before the demon uttered more than a single word to me. Admittedly, I knew my judgement was not at its best, following a demon I had just met. Yet, he had every chance to kill me and hadn't, which raised a little of the curiosity within me. Another part of me knew I was too cowardly and anxious to keep venturing through Eodratera alone.

At least with this demon by my side, I stood a chance of making it through this vast land alive. It could buy me enough time to finally find Jax. Without that guidance, I considered myself as good as dead out in these lands. I'd already made two grave mistakes that could have led to my untimely demise.

Both times, I had let my guard down. I now built it like a wall of stone around me. No one would break through again. Every step I took to follow the demon was made with a sense of wariness. A small laugh accidentally escaped my lips as I imagined what Marielle would say in this situation.

"How crazy are you? You'll get yourself killed trusting a demon."

Her familiar voice rang through my head. I caught the demon ahead of me casting a scowl in my direction when I realized the laugh had carried up to him.

"What?" I asked when his eyes remained settled on me.

"Why are you in the demon realm?" he asked, pausing. The question was simple, yet somehow, it still felt personal. I didn't want to share everything with this demon, so I settled for a plain answer.

"I'm searching for someone," I said.

"And how exactly did you get here?" he questioned,

raising a brow. His features seemed to soften as he recognized my hesitance. "The line between worlds is not easy for a human to cross, so you must have had help."

I gave a firm nod, but nothing more. He let out a chuckle, an amused look taking over his features.

"What?" I demanded, sick of his allusiveness.

"It was stupid of you to come here," he stated, his words holding no compassion or understanding. I strode past him, not willing to deal with his judgement. I wanted more than anything to find Jax, and I was done blindly following this demon without any answers in return.

I stormed toward what appeared to be a field of flowers in the distance. Finally, something that wasn't grey and bleak growing in this world. I moved a few strides ahead of the demon when I heard him call out to me.

"I wouldn't go through there," he warned cryptically.

I ignored the warning and continued at the quick pace I set. Mr. Finkel gave a worried meow down near my feet, but again, I ignored the concern. I was set on finding Jax, and that invisible string was tugging at me again. I could feel it pulling me in the direction I was walking, like a strong magnetic force was drawing me in. My other senses were dulled, my judgement nonexistent. Only that thread existed, and I would find the end of it.

I approached the flowers, their deep navy the first pop of color I'd seen in this world. Footsteps approached from behind me, but I ignored them. If this demon wanted to stop me, he'd have to try harder.

The pungent scent of the flowers hit my nose first, alerting me to the erroneous choice I had made. One of the flowers physically extended its stem, coming to life. The large navy bloom itself snapped at me like a hungry, wild animal. This close, I spotted the sharp edges now visible on each petal. I pulled back quickly before the flower was able to grab hold of me. It was like an oversized Venus fly trap, and I was the fly.

The jerking motion caused me to stumble, and I fell back.

I plopped onto the ground, not caring that my shorts would be covered in dirt as the dust kicked up around me. After the past day, my mind was far too concerned with other problems. Usually, I would obsess over the cleanliness of my clothing, and although my mind came to peace with this instance, I couldn't help but feel unsettled.

I'd traded one obsession for the next.

It was never as simple as getting over the constant thoughts that plagued my mind. The compulsions were endless, and I constantly felt like I had no control over some of my actions. The compulsions weren't an excuse, more of a hinderance to my daily life.

"I just wanted to find Jax," I huffed into my forearm as I wrapped my arms around my knees, pulling them closer.

At the mention of Jax, the demon's eyes widened in recognition.

"You know of him?" I asked skeptically.

"Serpent demon, similar in height to me, slightly less handsome?" he asked, and I frowned at the first joke the demon had made.

I nodded slowly, hopeful it truly was my Jax.

"As a matter of fact, I do," he said, a grin curling his lips. "It just so happens he lives where I am taking you."

My heart skipped a beat. I was finally getting somewhere.

"Let's make a bargain," he said, those lavender eyes studying me predatorily.

"I think I've had enough bargains for a lifetime," I murmured. "The last deal I made ended with me binding my soul eternally to this realm."

"But that is our way. That is what all demons want. To get ahead, to hold the advantage. If you wish to be taken to your Jax, a bargain is the cost. You will find that most demons here would rather kill you than make a bargain, because a bargain with a human is almost always useless," he said, raising an eyebrow.

"What is the cost?" I asked, crossing my arms. The hairs on my forearm raised as he glanced me up and down, as if deciding my worth.

"On a day of my choosing, you will visit my home," he said.

"Your home?" I asked, surprise making my voice waver.

"Yes, I think you will find the region I come from is quite pleasing. I'd like to show it to you," he said.

"But you don't know me," I stuttered, running over every possible underlying benefit he could gain from this.

My mind came up empty. I tapped nervously at my knee.

One, two, three, four.

"Let's just say I find you fascinating. It is not often a human finds their way to our realm and survives. I'd like to find out why that is," he said. "A single visit is my price."

I paused, again trying to find another motive and failing. "You have a deal," I said firmly, making up my mind.

A searing pain crossed my forearm, a crescent moon appearing where my skin was once a blank canvas.

"What is this?" I asked, rubbing my fingers over the black mark that now marred me.

"The mark of a bargain," he shrugged. "It will disappear when it is fulfilled."

I wrinkled my brows, studying the mark. My heart sped up, fearing I'd made a terrible mistake trusting this demon. Seeing the mark made it all too binding. There was no backing out now.

"And if it is not fulfilled?" I dared to ask.

"Then you will die," he said, walking off.

We continued our journey, and another hour passed before I found the nerve to prod at the demon again. The blush on my cheeks was finally subsiding after my embarrassing error with the flowers.

"Why are you helping me?" I asked, daring a glance at the demon's face.

He was handsome, his features human-like. His lavender eyes flashed as he cocked his head to meet my stare. "I have my reasons," he said.

"What type of demon are you?" I asked, unable to stop my curiosity again. The more I learned of the demon, the more I was able to convince myself that maybe this bargain wasn't so bad. It was getting me to Jax, and without the demon's help, the chances of me making it alive grew slimmer.

Jax had been able to summon snakes, and I wondered if this demon could do something similar.

"Why do you ask?"

Cryptic again. I wasn't going to receive a single straightforward answer from him. The thought crept into my mind that it was possible his intentions were not as pure as he had stated. This could all be an elaborate façade, and I could be walking into another trap.

I kicked a pebble, watching it bounce ahead of us. The path was completely soil, and again, there were minimal trees and shrubs around us. Ahead, I spotted what looked to be the end of our journey. A cliff was rapidly approaching, and I shuddered at the thought of what I would find at the bottom of it.

My palms felt slick with sweat, and I glanced around weighing my options.

"It's just that Jax was part serpent demon and part human, and you also look human. I just was wondering if you're only half-demon too?"

"I assure you, I am full demon. And Jax may not be everything he appears to be," the demon scoffed.

We finally stopped at the edge of the cliff, and my breath caught. The view was stunning, a new stretch of land laid out before us.

In the distance, I could just make out the outline of a palace, the black shape of it looming like a shadow over its kingdom. It was more extravagant than anything I had come across in Eodratera, a faint picture of a city before me. To the right, I noticed a winding path leading down toward the city.

"Is this your capital?" I asked, curious if this realm was like my own in that aspect. My excitement built, and I felt anxious to continue moving. The faster I got down into that city, the sooner I would locate Jax. The invisible thread between us tugged at my soul again.

"It is. Welcome to Gildhor."

CHAPTER

NINETEEN

The demon insisted on resting for the night before making the trek to the city. After a short sleep, we finally continued down to Gildhor.

I could see what the demon referred to as the Serpentine Palace, its black spires rising into the sky. The early morning sun cast pinkish hues across the sky. By the time we made it to the city outskirts, it was beginning to fade.

The black palace loomed over the rest of the city, its presence like midnight washing over the sky. I could tell it was meant to keep outsiders away, yet I felt drawn to it. A large serpent statue wrapped around one of the tall spires, and I knew I had found what I was looking for.

A palace of serpent demons. Jax had to be here.

"If this is Gildhor, what are the other regions?" I asked.

"Fuerya, the region of fire, lies to the west. To the north are Imoni, the region of illusions, and Auneer, the region of water. Even further north lies Ongar, the region of shifters,

150

and Drazmin, the region of darkness. I suggest if you value your life, you never visit the last one."

A shudder ran down my spine, and I didn't push for more answers.

The demon guided me through the streets of Gildhor, which reminded me of those in the human world. The streets were surprisingly lively. The souls filling the streets were the biggest difference between the realms. I spotted demons who looked eerily like humans and those who could never pass for one. One demon had pink skin and two small horns that curled back from her head. She was engaged in conversation with a vampire, who had their fangs on full display. I shuddered, remembering my own encounter with a vampire on Halloween. The occurrence felt distant already, and a twinge of pain struck my chest.

I played with a stray thread on my jeans, twirling it around my finger.

One, two, three, four.

I almost bumped into another demon, letting my eyes wander the streets.

"My bad," I said quietly, meeting his gaze.

As I did, I realized his eyes were blood red. A sickly-sweet grin grew on his lips. His black teeth were showing, and I almost recoiled back from him. My heart pounded hard enough, it felt like it echoed through my own hearing.

"Why don't I buy you a drink?" he asked, motioning to a little outdoor booth set up like a bar. Candles were carefully placed across the small bar top, and other patrons shared in glasses of alcohol and conversation. The drinks they served were vibrant, and some had steam pouring over the edges.

"She's with me," the demon I traveled with said, stepping in and ushering me away from the demon.

"Careful," he whispered. "Some demons will recognize a human a mile away, and none of their intentions will be pure.". Again, I found myself thankful for the help. I still barely knew anything of him, and he had saved my life countless times.

"Why do you care so much about my wellbeing if every other demon wishes me harm?" I asked.

He tapped his chin, pausing to look at me.

"Do I need a reason besides not wanting you to die? It would be unfortunate if our bargain was to end," he said, watching the other demon walk away.

I watched as children played in the streets, their laughter ringing through the air. There were small shops selling trinkets and baked goods. I spotted varieties of demons and noted them in my head with each one I passed. I wanted to know everything these demons had to offer. I wanted to know what they were like, everything about their world.

The demon watched me with interest as I took in my surroundings. A shiver ran across my exposed skin and down my spine, his eyes raking over me while I walked down the cobblestone road. I was thankful for his help and guidance, but I did not forget that we were only here because of a bargain. His kindness would only go so far.

The closer we got to the palace, the more I noticed the black embellishments throughout the streets, the shops closest to the palace resembling small stretches of it. I spotted a few serpents worked into stone walls and statues placed carefully outside of shops.

Another sign that I was finally where I belonged.

I noticed many of the demons in this section of the city were dressed in clothes resembling finery, the male demons in clothing comparable to suits and many of the females in fancy dresses and skirts made of exquisite fabrics. I spotted jewels lining one woman's arm, the red rubies catching the light of the moon.

There were fewer children running through the roads, and the interactions I witnessed were more formal. I gave a curious glance in the direction of my guide, wondering why the atmosphere had become such a blatant opposite from where we were before. The demon just returned my pleading look with a stern nod of his head to the palace and no explanation.

After a few minutes, when the streets around us were clear, the demon finally spoke.

"This is where the upper-class lives," he answered. "Even in this world, there is a hierarchy. It is much like your own, and you will find that the demons who live in this section will be even less likely to accept your presence here," he said.

I couldn't help but get the feeling that part of him didn't agree with my presence either. Either way, his eyes never left me, making me feel like prey under his watchful case.

"When will you be returning for this bargain?" I asked, wondering how long I had to wait to find out what he wanted with me.

"What fun would it be if I told you that?" he questioned, tilting his head. "No rush. Your soul is tethered here. You are stuck in this world. I will at least let you get used to it before I return."

Pushing through the last stretch of the streets took us longer than I expected. The palace gates were large, towering over me. The black metal was adorned with a silver serpent crawling up the walls that extended from the gates. The palace was a fortress contained within a bustling city, and I was about to knock on its front door.

IT FELT like an eternity had passed, and I had yet to move in front of the gates to the palace. I held my breath, staring at them, unsure of what was holding me back. The demon behind me let out an impatient breath. My eyes automatically glanced beneath me for the comfort of Mr. Finkel, but I found no feline.

Panic set in, realizing that along the way, the cat and I had been separated. How long had he been gone? How had I been so distracted that I hadn't noticed until now?

Sheer alarm pulsed through me, pulling my attention away from the towering black walls. My head swiveled wildly, hoping to find the cat nearby.

Before I could inquire for the demon's help, he tapped the gate, a small burst of dark purple magic trickling along it.

"That will get their attention, trust me," he said, annoyance dripping from each word.

"My cat-" I started, but he cut me off.

"He'll find you," the demon said.

"How do you know?" I insisted, my chest feeling tight.

"Trust me, creatures like that are terribly *familiar* with the people they are loyal to," he said.

There that word was again. *Familiar.*

I didn't have time to ask before he turned away, his hands in his trouser pockets. There were no goodbye or formalities. He had served his purpose of leading me here, and now, I was held to a bargain I wasn't quite sure I wanted to fulfill.

"You never told me your name," I said. I watched as he paused, his hand stroking the stubble on his chin, debating the answer he'd give.

A devilish grin crossed his lips. "Seri," he answered. "My name is Seri."

"Thank you, Seri," I said, but already, he'd vanished into thin air.

I glanced around wildly but didn't see the demon anywhere. The gate before me creaked open, only enough to allow a person or creature through. A small, stout demon stood before me, arms crossed.

"You dare use magic on the Serpentine Gates?" it asked.

"Uh—" I stuttered. "I need to see Jax. I was told I could find him here." I rattled off the words nervously, half expecting the demon before me to laugh at the insanity of my ask.

The demon's eyes narrowed on me. It glanced me over and sniffed the air.

"Human?" it asked, its lip curling in disgust.

I gave a slow nod, realizing there was no use in lying. If it could scent me somehow, it already knew the answer.

"Follow me," it answered, turning around, the gates

already slowly shutting. Before I could second guess myself, I took three large steps forward. Already, the gates dragged shut.

The moment they closed, trapping me inside, demons appeared, grabbing my arms and seizing me. I struggled against their grip, but it was no use. Dread filled me head to toe. This was not the welcome I had expected at the Serpentine Palace.

CHAPTER

TWENTY

The demon's tight grip burned against my skin as he dragged me forward. I kicked my legs in protest, but it was no use. We approached the front doors, and before I could say a word, I was dragged through them.

The main entry was grand and lavish. The black marble tile was polished enough that I thought I could see my reflection in its shine, but my head hung in defeat. A grand staircase led to what I imagined to be the main floor of the palace. Each black step was wide enough to fit multiple demons at once. Two serpent statues sat on either side, their eyes made of obsidian and their bodies of stone.

I shuddered as I felt the eyes follow me as I passed. The two demons pulled me forward, my legs dragging on the steps as we finally reached them.

"Please, let me go," I said. "I'm looking for Jax. The demon who brought me here said this is where he'd be," I pleaded, sounding more pathetic than I imagined I would.

My ask was absurd, and I didn't blame the demons for ignoring me.

"And who exactly would that demon be?" one of the demons asked. "There was no one in sight when you arrived at our front gates."

"I bet she's a spy," the other demon chimed in. "The king will be pleased with us for catching one."

A spy? I was in over my head. I knew how spies were treated. A lump formed in my throat, making it hard to swallow. I could already feel the noose around my neck if my suspicions came true.

The demon on my right side, who had spoke second, had dark black skin that was wrinkled the way a human's would be if they spent too much time in the sun. His red eyes continually glanced at me, and I caught him reaching up to stroke one of his two light red horns spiraling out of his head. During my struggle to regain my freedom, I caught sight of what looked to be a barbed tail trailing from his back. It flicked up with each step we took, avoiding snagging on the black carpet that cover each of the steps.

The other demon was a stark contrast. His skin was a pale cream, and the closer I looked, the more I noticed it had an iridescent shine to it and tiny little scales. The chandelier above us cast a vibrant light into the room that illuminated each of the scales. The scales trailed along parts of his body; the ones I noticed were by his elbows, and I caught sight of more trailing up his neck.

I wiggled in protest, unsure of what I would do if I broke free. A small twinge of sadness hit my chest as I realized that these demons were going to take me prisoner. I'd traded one cage for another.

My feet found the steps as the demons forced me up them, and I tried my best not to trip. I counted them over and over as we made our way up, my same comforting pattern.

One, two, three, four. One, two, three, four.

The more I counted, the more distracted I became until we finally reached the top. There were twenty-four steps total. Just twenty-four steps lead me to my new fate.

"Let go of me," I demanded. "I'm not a spy!" Even as the words left my lips, they felt unconvincing. Could I really say I wasn't being used as a spy? A demon had led me here all too willingly, and now, I owed him a bargain. A low groan left my mouth, grasping my mistake.

Both demons just let out low chuckles. Their dark raspy voices raked through me, and I knew it was no use. I'd have to face wherever they were taking me.

I noticed a few other demons had gathered at the top of the steps to find the source of commotion as I protested against the demons' grasps.

With each turn we took, I spotted more serpents woven into the architecture of the palace. It didn't surprise me that a half-serpent demon would work here.

Was Jax also some type of guard like the pair of demons dragging me?

As soon as I found him, this would all be sorted. I repeated it in my head over and over to comfort myself. I wouldn't lose my life today, even if they deemed me a spy.

Jax would find me. He would sort this whole mess, and I'd finally be able to settle.

The demon with black leather skin dug his nails into me the more I squirmed in his grasp. At the top of the landing, I found prodding eyes watching me, anticipating my demise —the foolish human who dared knock on the Serpentine Palace gates.

I was pulled down a long, narrow hall. The further we went, the more my arms stung from fighting against it.

"Please, just find the demon who brought me here. He couldn't have gotten far," I explained. "It was only moments before you found me."

Large silver doors sat at the end of the hall, and I knew that whatever lay behind it would be my fate. There were two guards posted outside the doors, one of whom opened them when he saw us approaching.

We passed by, and I caught a snicker about the spy who wouldn't live long. Beads of sweat formed on my forehead, and I swallowed hard, preparing myself for the punishment that would be inflicted on me if I didn't find Jax.

I imagined all the ways demons could torture humans. My mind wandered back to the caves with the soul collector —would there be another creature as such that here? I fought harder, no longer wishing to wait to find out, but it was no use. They were much stronger than me, and their hands tightened around my upper arms as they dragged me forward. Halfway across the room, they threw me to the ground, and I lifted my head on my hands and knees as I realized slowly that we were in the throne room.

The heart of the palace.

A silver throne sat atop a dais at the far end of the room. My eyes raised to find the arms carved with serpents. The closer I looked, I realized a large python sat partially on top the throne, its long, thick body trailing down the side. Its dark eyes settled on me, and I heard the small hiss that escaped as its tongue rattled. My heart raced, and I felt the palms of my hands growing slick with sweat.

I tried to stand, my knees wobbling and my hands trembling, threatening my consciousness. My anxiety growing and my ears ringing, I steadied myself, standing tall. The same plaguing thoughts passed through my mind, bombarding me until I felt like I couldn't breathe.

I counted the seconds that passed. The room held its breath as I did.

One, two, three, four.

My eyes started around the room, and I noticed it was different from the rest of the palace. The black tiles from before were gone, the floor here a dark gray. The walls were cream color, with white pillars lining both sides, demons hugging them tight, trying to blend into the background of the room. High up on the walls, there were circular windows set a few feet apart from each other, allowing the sun to illuminate the room.

I wiped my forehead, nervously awaiting whoever appeared to deliver my punishment.

Had the demon who led me here set me up? Did Seri know this would be the consequence of leaving me at those gates? He warned me that most demons would rather see me dead; maybe this had been his plan all along.

I tried to push the thought away, unable to comprehend

what the demon would stand to gain if I was to lose my life. The bargain would be rendered useless if I was dead. Something deep down told me the demon was not the type of being who would strike a hopeless bargain. The entire day I'd known him, everything he had done had been for his own gain, meticulously calculated.

The room fell still, silence ringing through the air as a door behind the throne opened. All the demons in the room bowed their heads, and I heard the sound of serpents slithering into the room, hissing to announce their presence.

I saw those creatures first.

Two snakes slithered in front of the throne, moving to rest on either side. The python on top barely moved to acknowledge the new serpent's presence. Footsteps echoed as a demon walked across the dais.

"King Jaxilien, son of Resnix, Controller of Serpents," one of the demons announced.

I tensed as Jax appeared atop the dais, a black crown tilted on his head. I realized his crown was formed by woven metal serpents.

"I caught one of his spies, Your Majesty," a demon said, kicking the back of my knee, forcing me to kneel. "She claimed she knew you." My head dropped before he could get a glance of my face.

The demons in the room broke into snickers and laughter at my poor attempt to stand, forcing my shaky legs to straighten.

"Enough," Jax demanded, his eyes narrowing as he took a seat in the throne. His hand stroked the long body of the python draped over it.

My hair hung in front of my face, shielding me from his view. I lifted my face to meet his stare, and his eyes widened.

"No," he whispered, his lips dipping into a frown. "How are you—" He stumbled on the words, his face paling like he'd seen a ghost. I supposed I was just that: a ghost from his past. Had I made a mistake coming here?

"Leave us," he commanded of the room.

The demons stared blankly at him, their laughter having turned to silence.

"Do I need to repeat myself? Kasius," Jax growled from tightened lips, his gaze snapping to the demon behind me with the iridescent scales. "No one disturbs us."

The demons scrambled, abandoning their posts.

I took slow shaky steps towards the throne. His dark gaze never left me, and I held his stare, no matter how nervous I felt. His black button-down shirt's sleeves were pushed back, and I could see his muscular arms covered in the ink: a snake with an open mouth and sharp fangs that trailed up across his arm to his neck.

"I told you not to come here," he said in a low tone. His eyes raked hungrily over me, and I could tell I hadn't been wrong to come. That desire still hung there, and I could tell he still longed for me the way I did for him.

As I took a few more steps up to the throne, he waved the serpents at his feet away. They slithered off just as quickly as they had appeared, and I could feel my muscles relaxing the closer I got to him. This was everything I had dreamed of this past year.

I finally found Jax again.

"I told Drakor not to allow you into this realm," he

growled. "Why am I not surprised that you still found a way here, little flame?" His hand stretched out for my waist, and I let him pull me closer.

I was standing mere inches from him, glancing down at his golden eyes. I held my breath as I waited to see what he would do, wanting to melt into his touch.

His strong hands guided me down into his lap, and I let out a shaky breath as he pulled me back into him. His breath tickled my skin as he whispered, "You shouldn't have come here."

"And yet, I'm here," I whispered.

"Why?" he asked again, stopping inches from me. His hand grazed my cheek, and he tilted my face up to meet his stare.

"You don't want me here?" I asked, avoiding the questions I knew would follow if I answered him.

"There is nothing I wouldn't give to have you here, little flame," he said, his gaze turning primal. "But it shouldn't be possible."

"I made a trade with a witch, tethering my soul to this world," I explained as his thumb brushed against my cheek.

"No," he said, his eyes widening.

"It can't be undone. I've already made my choice," I stated firmly.

"Why would you do that, Soleil? You have no idea what you've done." The way his words shifted to anger, his look boring into me, had my heart racing.

"I told you not to come here for this very reason," Jax growled, his hand snaking up my neck. The feeling elicited tiny butterflies in my stomach, the kind that grew until you desperately needed more.

"I don't answer to you," I dared.

His face was hovering by my ear, his hot breath running down my neck as my face turned to the rest of the empty throne room.

"Say that again," he demanded, his voice low and full of desire.

"I don't answer to you, and if you want to punish me for defying your order, so be it." I spun around, meeting his deadly stare, his dark eyes promising the most sinful things. I shifted from sitting on his lap, climbing to face him. I let my legs straddle him. They were open just enough for him to run his hand wrapped around the back of my thigh along the inside.

"You didn't come like you promised," was all that escaped my lips. I could smell the scent of pine clinging to his skin. I recognized those calm, deep breaths as his chest rose and fell.

"You still have this?" he asked, his freehand tugging at my leather jacket. He was avoiding the question.

"Why did you send that other demon?" I continued instead.

"Because I knew you would never stop looking if I didn't send someone, little flame," Jax said. "Clearly, I was right about your adamance."

I felt a surge of frustration and let out a puff of air.

His calloused fingers rubbed circles on the exposed skin of my upper thigh. The cutoff shorts I wore felt like a pesky barrier from what I wanted now.

My legs trembled, begging and inviting at the same time.

A loose thread on the edge of my shorts caught his attention, his finger leaving my skin to twirl it. A half-second later, his hands moved at lightning speed as impossible demon strength grabbed the denim and tore it. The large rip up the inside of the shorts exposed my black lace underwear.

"I've missed this," he said, his finger trailing the edge of the lace. "And these," he said, slowly sliding his hands up my torso to cup my breasts.

I frowned, hoping I was more than just someone for him to fuck.

"And most importantly," he added, finally moving a hand to cup my cheek. "I have missed you, little flame," he said, closing the distance and kissing me hard.

I lost any composure I had left, kissing him back with just as much passion.

My body and soul needed him as much as it needed air.

My hips moved into his touch as he grabbed them.

They slowly moved down my body, back to the rip that welcomed him to my core. I pushed against his hand that hovered so close to where I desperately wanted it. I needed him inside me, to feel his fingers satisfy me again. Thoughts of this exact moment had plagued me for a year, and now that it had finally come, it was more than I could've prayed for.

When his fingers slipped under the lace fabric, my heart skipped as he breathed, "Slick and ready for me."

I kissed him in a desperate attempt for more. The teasing was building to a point where I didn't know if I could hold back any longer.

"Are you sure?" he asked, and I nodded.

A moan escaped my lips as two fingers parted my core and slid inside. I let my knees slide apart further as I lowered myself into his touch, his fingers pumping in and out in a rhythmic pattern. My breath hitched, and each passing second led me closer to climax.

I felt a small shudder as Jax let out a soft chuckle. "You feel delightful, little flame," he said in a low voice.

My head felt light as my lungs begged for gasps of air between intense kisses and my mind begged for more. I could barely hold on, the year without any form of pleasure catching up to me.

Satisfaction flowed through me like a tidal wave, coursing through every inch of me, wringing pleasure everywhere it traveled.

"Fuck," Jax moaned, moving his hand from between my thighs to my face. His thumb raked across my lip, and I glanced up at him through my lashes.

"What?" I asked.

"If you make that little noise again, I think it might just be my undoing," he said.

A smirk grew on my lips. "I can think of a few more things that might undo the demon king himself," I said teasingly. My hand traveled down his chest toward his waist. His own hand covered mine, guiding me.

When my hand was at his waistband, he paused, as something caught his eye. I froze, following where his gaze had landed on the crescent tattooed to my skin. My chest heaved in anxious breaths.

One, two, three, four.

His hand was wrapped around my forearm, keeping it straight before I could pull it back in.

"What is this?" The hurt in his voice struck me like a bullet. His grip tightened, and I winced in pain before I could respond.

I immediately felt him relax, letting go of my arm. His eyes remained narrowed, and I caught a flash of annoyance in his eyes as they moved between the mark and my stare.

"It's a bargain," I began hesitantly. I withdrew my arm, pulling it close to my body, rubbing the stinging skin where his grip had been too firm.

"I know," he growled. I could feel the heat rolling off him, his temper rising. I watched his fists clench, his eyes still glued to the tattoo that marked my arm. "How did you get it?"

"The demon who brought me here struck a bargain with me. I was out of options, and I had no idea how to navigate this realm-"

Shadows filled the room, enveloping us in darkness. My breathing quickened, my words cutting off when I saw the fury behind his eyes.

"I'll kill him," he said. "I'll kill him for this, daring to lay a finger on you."

"Who?" I asked, confused. "You know the demon who did this. How?"

"Vileer," Jax sneered, his lip curling as he did. "He is the demon who rules the region of illusions, Imoni. The moment you spoke my name to him, he saw an opportunity and seized it. He has been searching for a way into this palace for years, and now he has one, a direct invitation through this bargain. He wants nothing more than to claim this throne."

My stomach sunk as I realized my mistake. I led someone who threatened his reign straight into the heart of the palace, into the heart of Gildhor. The words to apologize started to form, but I couldn't quite get them out. Panic rose in my gut, and I found myself tapping my fingers against my thigh, trying to bring back comfort. The usual rhythmic taps failed, and every possible repetitive thought plagued me, only worsening my growing panic.

Jax saw the way I was slowly losing my composure. His shadows disappeared in seconds, and he wrapped his arms around me, pulling me tight against him. I felt him press a light kiss to the top of my head.

"You didn't know. I will find a way out of this, I promise."

As much as I wanted to believe him, I knew he was only saying it for my sake. I hated myself for allowing this to happen. I should've known better. Trusting a demon had been a grave mistake. He would come back to claim what was rightfully his. I owed him the bargain, and there was no getting out of it. The only way out was death.

"This is why I did not wish for you to come. Spies are being found more often, and the other regions are growing restless. Vileer continues to stir conflict, and I have a duty to protect the demons in this realm. I am not the demon you met in your world here. You may not like what you find," he said, barely meeting my eyes.

"I don't care. Nothing I see here could convince me I made the wrong choice," I assured him. My heart knew I was meant to be here. It was like a piece I'd been missing finally fell into place.

"I'm a monster," he whispered, finally meeting my gaze. "I have to maintain fear of my power and rule. Otherwise the others will come, the same as Vileer."

"Others?" I asked, unsure what he meant.

"The other rulers," he explained, his tone softening.

"There are more of you?" I asked. "Are they your brothers?"

He laughed quietly, brushing a quick hand across my cheek.

"No, little flame. This world is not like your own."

"I don't understand."

"In this world, power is claimed by strength and loyalty. There have been five demon families who have resided over the regions of our world, with one throne to rule over them all. They keep power due to pure strength, not familial ties. Each family has always vied for more than they have, biding their time to make a claim for my throne. Any sign of weakness, and one may make their move. It is a brutal system and always has been."

I listened, trying to absorb all the information. It was a lot to take in all at once, and a wave of overwhelming anxiety fell over me. Jax cocked his head, watching as I tried to train my face to neutral again.

He brushed my hair from my face, a small smile gracing his lips.

Calling one of the demons back into the throne room, his voice bellowed through the space, causing me to jump. One of the demons appeared, bowing his head and waving in Jax's direction.

"You need rest," he said gently. "Go for now, and I will see you soon."

"But-" I started, but I felt the exhaustion catching up to me. With my adrenaline fading, my body was sore, and I could feel the intense need for sleep.

"You will take her to my chambers, and then you will direct Althea to find me," he commanded the demon named Kasius.

The demon's eyes whipped to me before he turned toward the door. I gave a nervous glance to Jax, who nodded. That reassurance was all I needed. I followed the demon out the door.

TWENTY-ONE

"I understand why you did it," I said, hoping to break the silence as I followed Kasius through the halls.

"I would do anything to protect my kingdom and His Majesty," he answered. "Your presence here is a threat."

I shuddered at the last part, knowing every word spoken was the truth. I'd given Vileer a way into this palace; he could come claim the bargain, and no one would be able to stop him. The only way out was death or fulfillment, and I was willing to bet many of the demons within the palace walls were willing to kill me to protect Jax.

I didn't blame them. I was a human who had disrupted their peace and protection, and that made me their largest threat now.

"I would do anything to protect him," I said, knowing Kasius knew who I meant.

"Are you willing to die for him?" he asked, raising a brow as I caught up to walk beside him.

My hesitation spoke loud enough. The demon scoffed, picking up the pace ahead of me once more.

"That's what I thought, selfish human," he muttered.

It wasn't as easy as a simple yes or no. I had only just broken free of my cage; was I willing to give that freedom up so soon? Even with that tug continually pulling me back to Jax, I wasn't sure what my heart wanted or how I truly felt about the demon king. Even though I had said nothing would change my mind, I still didn't know this side of Jax. No longer was he the demon wishing to stay in my own realm. He had a whole kingdom to look after.

I didn't understand why he would want to leave the realm. His loyalty to the demons he ruled was clear; I'd seen the genuine concern for their well being only moments before. How could he leave them?

Kasius didn't say another word and his tensed muscles never relaxed.

He opened the door for me but did not follow as I walked in. I stole a quick glance back at him, and he gave me an encouraging nod, but his face remained stoic.

"If you need something, ask a guard. Don't wander. Wait for His Majesty here," he ordered.

He let the door close, and I ventured further into the room. The chambers were spacious, a large bed with four posts set against the center of one wall. Across from the bed on the other wall was a fireplace. It was empty of flame, but I could see the remnants of the last fire coating the walls of it. There were minimal items set on the mantle, but I spotted a familiar one, a small snow globe with Weeping Vale displayed inside, the town name written on the base.

A warm smile grew across my lips, recognizing my little town, a souvenir from one of Jax's trips to the human world. My heart ached a bit, remembering the town I'd grown up in and would never see again.

I walked around the room, taking in every detail. An hour passed as I explored the room and rested before I decided to venture further. A washroom was attached, and inside, I found a luxurious bath. The slight echoing of water into the tub called my attention.

Drip, drip, drip, drip.

The sound echoed in my own mind, mesmerizing me. I'd let my head empty of worries, lulled by the sound. My eyes felt heavy, and for a moment, I considered crawling into the bed.

A sound from the room drew my attention back and snapped me out of the daze. My heart sped up, hoping I would find Jax had returned.

I made my way back into the chambers, finding a woman standing in the center.

Not demon.

The thought popped into my head the moment my eyes settled on her. Even with her back to me, her long blonde hair shielding her face, I could feel she was something else. Everything in me screamed that I should know who she was. It was like electricity coursing through my veins, trying to shock me into remembering.

She had opened a nearby wardrobe, filling it with a few dresses on hangers.

"What are you doing?" I asked.

The woman startled, and a slight chuckle escaped her lips, realizing there was no threat in the room.

"The king has ordered me to bring these clothes for you," she explained. "I am here to help you dress for dinner."

"I can dress myself," I answered without thinking. The woman's eyebrows rose before she shook her head.

Turning back to the wardrobe, she pulled out a long black dress. It was simple but elegant, thin straps holding it on the hanger as she held it up.

"The king insisted I help you. I cannot disobey his orders," she explained. "I am happy to help you; it's part of my job here."

I realized it was no use, remembering back to the town square and the demon Jax sent to my world. I knew a loyal subject wouldn't disobey his orders.

I cocked my head. "What are you?" I was still not convinced she was any form of demon, but something told me she wasn't human either.

"What do you mean?" she asked. Long fingers fiddled with the hanger.

"I didn't mean to be rude. I just meant that you don't look like the demons here. You are like Jax—you appear human," I said, eyeing her. "Yet you are not human either, are you?"

"Observant," she noted. "That is because I'm not a demon. I'm a witch."

I started twisting the ring on my finger anxiously. I turned it back and forth, repeating the comforting motion. This was the second witch I'd met. The first had been the one to tether my soul to Eodratera. The idea of the magic this person possessed made me take a step back.

"Come," she said, waving me over, but I didn't move.

"Most of the demons in this palace want me dead," I said.

"And I am not a demon," she reminded me.

"You possess magic that could kill me if you wished," I noted.

She nodded firmly. "I am loyal to Jax. If he commands that you remain alive, then you are safe in my presence."

"And I'm just supposed to trust that?" I asked, crossing my arms.

"You have no other choice," she said, growing impatient with me.

I thought for a moment, realizing she was right. If I ran to the door, her magic would catch me first. Even if I made it out, the other demons wanted me dead, and I didn't know who else to trust besides Jax.

"Fine," I murmured, deciding this was my best option.

She undid the corset back of the dress, staring at me expectantly.

"What?" I asked.

"Undress. You can't wear those to dinner," she stated, nodding to my dirty and ripped clothing. I blushed a bit, remembering the tear in my pants. Quickly, I pulled off the disgusting clothing.

She sighed, placing the dress on the bed. "Let's go," she said, walking past me.

"Where?" I asked, unwilling to go far in just my undergarments.

She didn't answer, entering the washroom. Only a moment later, I heard running water. I hurried to the room, watching as her magic controlled the flow of water from a spout, pulling it out faster than a normal tub would fill.

"Quicker this way," she said with a warm smile. "Jax expects you soon. Now, wash up, and I will prepare everything else for you."

She hurried from the room, and right before she stepped out, I worked up the courage to murmur, "Thank you."

A slight smile formed before she disappeared.

I hurried into the tub, sliding into the warm water. It felt blissful against my tired and sore muscles. Dirt easily washed from my skin, as I scrubbed the rest of the filth from my body. My long, wet hair felt heavy against my back, and I ran my fingers through it, trying to work out the knots.

I wrapped a towel I found around my dripping body and padded back to the woman.

I stood in front of a mirror beside the wardrobe, the witch behind me. She quickly gathered my wet hair, twirling it into a tight bun. She helped me into the black dress she'd left out for me, the black fabric feeling like the perfect fit.

My nerves grew thinking about dinner with Jax. I was anxious to see him again, but his words still stuck with me.

I'm a monster.

A chill ran down my spine. Jax was no monster. He'd shown me love and freedom. I needed to push the thoughts out, fast. I blurted out the first thing that came to mind.

"What's your name?" I asked, realizing I knew nothing more of the witch.

"Althea," she said, and I recognized the name. It was who Jax had commanded Kasius to find.

Althea laced up the back of the dress, tying the ribbons tightly at the bottom. It no longer felt like the perfect fit. A breath escaped my lips, my lungs constrained by the gown. My chest felt tight, and I couldn't tell if it was my nerves or the gown itself. Its long, flowing fabric was made of satin, the shape simple, and as I glanced in the mirror, I noticed how elegant it looked on.

The witch took a step back, admiring me. Before I could thank her, she pulled a pin from her own neatly gathered hair and secured it into mine. I caught a glance in the mirror, noticing the tiny little gems on it.

"He won't be able to take his eyes off you," she noted.

The thought turned my cheeks pink.

"Someone will come soon to lead you to dinner," she added before turning to leave.

"Will I see you again?" I asked, hopeful. Something about Althea drew me in. Maybe it was because this was the first kindness I had genuinely received in Eodratera, but it didn't matter. I knew I needed to see her again.

"Of course," she answered, smiling. "If you need me, just send a guard for me, and I will come."

I nodded before she left.

I sat on the bed, waiting for my escort to dinner. The sky had grown dark, and I spotted the red moon already casting a glow outside. A set of glass doors led out to a balcony, and the red light poured into the room through them.

A meow out on the balcony caught my attention. I raced from the bed and threw open the doors to check if I had imagined it, but no—sitting outside on the large circle of a balcony was Mr. Finkel. The cat looked up at me with those big green eyes, cocking its head as it let out another soft meow.

I glanced around, unsure how my cat had found a way up this high. How had the cat made it through the palace gates? Regardless, I was thankful the feline had found his way back to me.

I ushered the cat inside and closed the doors from the cold winds of the night. Mr. Finkel made his way to the large bed, hopping on before he curled up into a small ball. A smile grew across my face, realizing the ridiculousness of the situation. I could only imagine what the king of serpents would say when he found a tiny little cat curled up in his bed. A soft laugh escaped my lips, and it was the first time since I left home that I finally felt some comfort.

Before I could join the cat, a knock sounded from the door, and I was thrust back into reality.

CHAPTER

TWENTY-TWO

I instantly recognized the demon at my door: the one who told me Jax was not coming on Halloween. Rather than his black jacket and jeans, he was now dressed in all black, his button-down shirt neatly tucked into his slacks.

"You," I said, narrowing my eyes.

"You made it after all," he observed, darkness flickering in his.

I scoffed. "No thanks to you," I muttered, folding my arms across my chest.

"I was following orders. It was nothing personal, I assure you," he said, scowling.

I knew this, yet every time I looked at him, I saw an obstacle to my happiness, to finding Jax. The thought brought a frown to my face.

"Why are you here?" I asked, biting out the words.

"Jax sent me to escort you to dinner," he said, holding out an arm to lead me. Instead, I brushed by him and started down the hallway. A dark chuckle followed me, almost mocking. "You may want to try heading the other direction."

Ugh.

One, two, three, four.

I counted as I took a deep breath, restraining myself from letting out all my irritation.

"You're insufferable," I muttered, passing by him once more.

"Better get used to it, human. I suspect you will be here for awhile," he laughed, and I rolled my eyes.

I quickly admitted defeat, conceding the lead to the demon as I found myself lost, searching for the dining room. For a few minutes, the demon let me wander; I was too stubborn to ask for help.

"A right," he murmured under his breath as we approached the end of a hallway that split off in two directions.

I raised a brow, looking back at him. I knew he meant well, but I had yet to forgive him for keeping me away from Jax. I needed time to settle into my new life, time to process the role he'd played. No matter how loyal he was to Jax, my heart wouldn't accept that as an explanation.

I continued my determined strides, hoping I would find the dining room soon. I needed to rid myself of the demon following me before I let him dampen my mood further.

An expectant cough forced me to pause. I turned, finding the demon with his arms crossed, glancing between me and a door beside him. I rolled my eyes, realizing I had passed right by my destination. To assume the dining room would be more obviously marked or placed had been naive. What had I expected—a flashing sign or Jax to intercept me along the way?

I brushed past him, placing a palm on the wood that separated me and the demon king. Before I could push open the door, the demon grabbed my arm. His touch was gentle, hesitant to hurt me. I glanced back and found pleading in the demon's eyes.

"I never meant to keep you apart. I was only following orders," he said, and I could hear his desperation for me to believe him.

"Why does it matter?" I asked.

"I'm just trying to say I'm glad you made it," he said.

I raised my eyebrows, at a loss for words. There was no possibility I heard him correctly. This was the demon who warned me against trying to find my way to Eodratera.

"I haven't seen him this happy in years," he said, his features softening. His hand slipped away from my wrist, taking a step back.

A flicker of black shadows crossed his vision, and in the blink of an eye, it was gone. I tilted my head, waiting to catch a glimpse of it again, but instead, I found his mouth dipping into a frown.

"Your eyes," I found myself saying. "How?"

"Some things are better left unknown," he said, a grim look crossing his face.

"But—" I started, but I paused, realizing the longer I argued, the less time I'd spend with Jax.

I turned again toward the door, accepting his cryptic answer. My palm pushed against the door, cracking it open.

Before I could step through, I heard the demon begin to walk off.

"Drakor," he whispered. "My name is Drakor."

I paused glancing back, but already, the demon was gone. Rather than dwell, I continued into the dining room. I would have an eternity to figure out the enigma that was Jax's subjects.

The dining room was long, a wooden table lined with wooden chairs taking up the majority of the space. The table was set for two at the end nearest to me, a plate with utensils and a wine glass at each spot. Jax had not arrived yet.

I sat on the corner, leaving the head of the table for Jax. As I sat, the dress was pulled tighter around my body, constraining my breathing even more. I writhed in my seat to make the fabric more comfortable, wiggling around as the wooden chair rattled.

"Careful, little flame. If you're going to make so much noise, it should at least be from pleasure," Jax whispered in my ear. I never heard him enter the room and I watched, my cheeks turning pink, as he took a seat across from me, his outfit matching mine.

"I could hear you from down the hall," Jax explained as my curious gaze watched him.

"Sorry," I said meekly.

"There's no need to apologize, little flame."

Three palace workers ran into the room carrying glass bottles of wine.

"We will take the red," Jax said, and the workers placed a singular glass bottle on the table, hurrying off.

I went to grab the wine but was interrupted.

"That is potent," Jax said, a daring look in his eyes. Part of me felt like the warning was a challenge.

Even with the word of caution, I still poured myself a full glass. After the few days I had, the way wine made my muscles relax had me eager to take a sip.

I sipped it quickly, unaware of any differences between this wine and that of my own world. If there were any, I would find out sooner rather than later. I placed the glass back down on the table, and Jax reached a hand over, covering my own.

"You look..." Jax paused to think over his words carefully. "Divine."

My core warmed at the compliment. I shifted in my seat, hoping the demon couldn't sense my clear desire. I could make it through one dinner without giving in to those wants.

They felt more like needs.

I took a deep breath, my fingers curling into the cloth covering the table.

One, two, three, four.

I let my mind fixate on the repetition rather than the handsome demon. I barely knew Jax, and this dinner was the first opportunity I had to become acquainted with the demon I sold my soul for. That thought opened a flood of tumultuous feelings.

I let my fingers relax, tapping them as I waited for the effects of the wine to take hold. I needed to chase away the plaguing thoughts before they sunk their claws into me and ruined the night.

The palace workers appeared once more, carrying trays

of food. I wondered if there was any difference between the food of this world and the food of my own. Was there a warning that came with eating this, the way Jax had cautioned me of the wine?

Casual amusement crossed Jax's face as he watched me serve myself tentatively. He sank back into his chair, relaxing, his hands on each of the arms.

"What?" I asked as he studied me.

"I just can't believe you're actually here. I dreamed every night of seeing you again, but when this year came and I knew I couldn't go, I was crushed. Now that you are sitting in my court, eating at my table, I'm wondering if I'm trapped in some illusion."

"I'm real," I whispered, knowing the feeling. I still felt like I was trapped in a dream, one I would soon awake from to find myself locked in that same room I had wasted so much of my life in.

I fidgeted in my seat once more, not used to the gown. The material was unforgiving, and already, I could feel it tightening against my skin as my meal settled in my stomach.

One, two, three, four.

I tried counting as I toyed with the skirt.

"What's with the fancy attire? Were my normal clothes not good enough?" I asked, letting annoyance slip into my tone.

"You could wear anything, little flame, and I'd still be completely and utterly obsessed with you," Jax answered, and I watched as his hungry gaze raked over me.

"Then why is my wardrobe all this finery now?"

"As much as I hate it, appearances make a difference here, and if you are to stay, then I need these demons to accept you. I can't be everywhere at once, and plenty of demons out there would take the opportunity to move against me by harming you."

He sat forward in his seat, placing his clasped hands on the table.

"I know this world is unlike your own, and there are still many rules and customs for you to learn. I promise I will teach you, but for now, just relax and enjoy yourself. We are celebrating. Let's not ruin that."

Remembering a few of those less enjoyable parts from my own journey to find him, I didn't argue as he changed the subject.

"You met Drakor," he stated, and I couldn't discern if he was asking me or telling me. "I sent him to escort you earlier. He is Hand to the King," he added, catching the confused look on my face.

I gave a slight nod.

"If you need anything here, he will help you. If I am ever unreachable, send for him. I trust him with my life, and so can you," he explained.

I scoffed at the last bit. I trusted no other demon with my life, and especially not that one. I'd faced trials in getting to Gildhor, but nothing I had faced had been as dangerous as he made the world sound.

He let out a sigh. "You are going to have to learn to trust him if you are to navigate this world," he said, studying me.

"I don't want to trust him. Why can't I trust someone else?" I asked. "Anyone else."

"He is my closest adviser, extremely loyal. I would not trust anyone else to look after you in my absence," he started.

"What about Althea?" I interrupted. I'd spent time with the witch already, and something about her felt familiar. Maybe it was just that she was a witch like Serafeen. The familiar magic and mystery surrounding her provided a sense of home.

"I suppose-" Jax started.

"Please," I added, hoping he'd drop his determination to convince me to trust Drakor.

"Fine," he conceded.

His golden eyes found me, and I soaked in the rich, unique color. I picked up my chalice, taking the last sip of the wine in the glass. I weigh the consequences of pouring another glass. I'd always held back if I made it out of my home without my father knowing, but here, I didn't have to worry. I felt safe in Jax's presence.

"What happened to your parents?" I asked, realizing I hadn't heard about either since arriving.

"My father died a few years ago. He was killed in his sleep by a spy. It is only luck that kept my mother and I alive. Since that day, my mother has lived in hiding while I took the throne. I have diligently rooted out spies and will do anything to prevent it from happening again," he explained.

"I'm so sorry," I whispered, unable to comprehend the pain Jax must feel.

"It's alright. Here, little flame," Jax said, sliding the bottle of wine closer to me.

"Thank you," I said softly.

Pouring the wine, I placed the bottle back between us and watched Jax pour himself another glass.

I spotted a painting on the wall. "Who is that?" I asked, taking in every detail of the painting.

"My last love," he answered, his smile dipping to a frown as my face changed from passive to shock. "You look surprised."

"I just—"

What was I to say? That I didn't expect him to have other lovers?

Nothing felt right to voice. Instead, I stumbled for the right words to convey my guilt.

"It's okay, little flame," he said, crossing the room to my side of the table. He stood behind my chair, brushing a strand of hair from my face. "I didn't expect you to know."

"I'm sorry," I said, knowing it truly wasn't enough. My apology could never account for my ignorance.

"You have nothing to apologize for. You didn't know. I never shared this part of me with you," he insisted. I knew it was to comfort me from the guilt eating at my heart.

"What was he like?" I asked, and a sad smile spread across his lips.

"Seri was light in the darkness," he said.

My heart dropped at the name.

"What?" Jax asked, towering over me. I felt his hands grasp my shoulders, slowly massaging them.

"Seri is the name Vileer gave me before I knew who he was."

Jax froze. "Seri was killed at Vileer's hands," he said, his eyes glazing over with deadly rage. My heart raced, and shame crept through me. I'd spent hours wandering with the demon who cauesd the agony I recognized on Jax's face.

"I'm sorry-" I started, reaching out for his hand.

"It was a long time ago," he answered, cutting me short. "It was not your fault; you didn't know who Vileer was."

Once again, he read my thoughts.

I shifted uncomfortably in my seat, bile rising in my throat. I abhorred the idea of everything Vileer stood for. He could never be allowed to succeed.

I would be dead before Vileer ever took the throne, but even as a human, I would do everything in my power to protect Jax and his crown.

"What's wrong, little flame?" Jax asked before I realized I was still squirming in my seat.

"I can barely breathe in this dress," I admitted, still eyeing the dark red wine I'd poured.

"Let's fix that," he breathed into my ear. The tickle of his breath along my neck had the little hairs on my arm standing as I felt the ribbon of the corset pulling loose.

"We don't have to," I whispered.

His hand gently pushed me forward, leaning me over the table.

"Be still," he commanded, trailing kisses along my neck and peeling off the long gown.

"Jax, seriously," I insisted. "We don't have to do this right now if you don't wish to."

"I waited an entire year for you. I will not spend another moment waiting. This is the distraction I am choosing from my issues with Vileer. Those can wait," he answered, trailing a slow finger down my shoulder. The light touch sent a whisper of a shiver crawling down my spine.

"If this isn't what you want..." he started, pausing his exploration of my body.

"It's everything I want," I answered.

The gown dropped to the floor, the thick material gathering into a pile. My breasts were exposed, the thin lace underwear the only thing left on my body.

The demon king pressed against me, brushing against my ass as his strong hands gripped my hips. I felt his cock harden the moment it brushed against my backside. That ache in my core grew, and I whimpered as his lips grazed my neck.

I desperately wanted him inside me.

Not only did I want it, I needed it, the same way I needed air to breathe. The urge to turn around and beg him to thrust into me increased tenfold.

I knew he'd never give it to me.

Jax liked his fun, and he'd have his way with me first.

His wandering hands moved to my opening, slick and ready for him. I arched my back, hoping his fingers would push inside. Instead, he moved them in lazy circles, teasing me.

"Jax," I moaned.

"Little flame," he growled in my ear. His low voice rattled through me, awakening some primal need deep down.

I turned, grabbing his cock through his pants. He froze, his dark gaze meeting mine. I let my hand stroke his length, feeling its response to my touch, feeding my insatiable desires.

"Is this what you want?" I asked, giving him a devilish grin.

"Yes, little flame," he barely whispered. "You have no idea."

He threw himself into me, kissing me hard.

The teasing movements resumed as his fingers once more found my center. His thumb circled my clit, moving faster the more I arched into his touch.

I needed more.

I could feel how desperately he wanted me through his affectionate strokes. Every inch of me needed to feel him.

"Jax," I murmured.

"Yes, my flame?" he whispered, never pausing his circling.

"Please," I whimpered, unable to hide my desperation. He was driving me insane, my body slowly approaching release.

I was able to find the button of Jax's pants, fumbling to undo it. I made quick work of the zipper, and Jax used a free hand to tug the pants and his undergarments off. Spinning me around, he found my hips again, this time tugging my underwear down. They fell to the ground, and I felt his hardened cock graze my center.

My legs spread enough to allow Jax to find my opening as I bent over the table, my fists clinging to the maroon tablecloth.

Jax took me against the table. I had to adjust and hold tight to ensure my hips didn't slam into the edge. As he slid into me, I winced slightly. It had been a whole year without sex, without Jax. I had almost forgotten how good it felt as he pumped in and out of me.

I adjusted to the size of him quickly, and a moan escaped my lips as my back arched. Gentle fingers traveled up my spine, tracing the length of it. The demon's fingertips barely grazed my skin.

His hand found my hair and gave a gentle tug on the pinned-back ponytail.

I tilted my head back, exposing my neck. Jax took the opportunity to nip at my neck. I felt my pulse racing and wondered if he could feel it too. Could the demon feel I was on the edge, ready to topple any moment?

"Jax, please," I begged.

"Come for me, little flame," he teased, his free hand wrapping around my waist and reaching down to my center. I could feel his warm body, slick with sweat, pressed against me.

His finger rubbed my clit, making quick work of sending me to pure bliss. I saw stars as I came, the demon king's name toppling from my lips.

He rode out the wave of my orgasm, pumping into me in a feral rhythm. Only moments later, I felt him spill into me.

"Good girl," he whispered.

"Jax," I groaned, still trying to catch my breath.

"Better than dessert," Jax answered. "I could devour every inch of you and still be left unsatisfied, little flame."

I turned to face him, smile spreading across my face.

Jax scooped me into his arms before I could say another word, naked and still slick from the pleasure he had drawn from me. I nuzzled my head into his chest, listening to the pounding of his heart.

One, two, three, four.

I counted the rhythmic beats, listening to his heart slow as he came down from the high of sex.

As he carried me all the way to his chambers, we did not pass by a single palace worker. Somehow, the usual shame I would have felt with my nudity was nowhere to be found. I knew Jax would never subject me to anything he knew would harm me or make me uncomfortable. I trusted him, and that included his decision to leave the dress behind.

Entering his room, he took me straight to his bed. He placed me down in the silk sheets, and I wrapped them around myself, enjoying the cool temperature on my skin.

"Goodnight, little flame," Jax purred, his warm breath brushing my ear as he leaned into me. He pressed a delicate kiss to the top of my head and wrapped his arms tightly around me.

I let myself drift off to the comforting sound of his heartbeat and the rise and fall of his chest.

CHAPTER

TWENTY-THREE

The next morning, I woke up enveloped in the demon king's arms. He held me close, and I could feel the rise and fall of his chest pressed against my back. I didn't want to give up the warmth of his body, but I could tell by the sun poking through the balcony door windows that we had already slept later than anticipated.

My slight movement caused him to stir. A small groan escaped his lips, and I couldn't help but laugh at the pure normalcy of it. I still felt like I was in a fever dream.

I finally found my freedom and escaped the grasp of my controlling father, yet I still couldn't believe it was true. Every time I blinked, I felt like it could all be ripped away from me in a matter of seconds.

"Don't you dare think about leaving this bed," Jax growled.

"Or what?" I challenged.

His arms tightened around me, holding me close,

refusing to let me up. Kisses trailed along side of my neck, and I felt a slight nip at my skin.

"Try, and you'll find out," Jax warned.

"As much as I'd love that, you are still king, and I imagine you have duties to fulfill today," I said, pulling away from the hug. "I'd like to explore the rest of the palace I haven't seen."

Jax stroked his chin, rubbing his fingers over the stubble. It had grown out more than the last time I had seen him. Part of me was tempted to reach out and run my own fingers over it.

"If you give me one hour while you eat breakfast, I believe I can arrange to show you the rest of the palace," he answered.

Excitement built in my chest, and I tried not to show how giddy I was at the prospect of him showing me his home. I had planned to wander on my own, but I welcomed the company of the demon king.

From the moment he had realized I was here, Jax had done everything in his power to make me feel welcomed and special. It was a refreshing change from the restraint I was used to.

"I just need to find Drakor to handle a few things, and then I will come back for you, little flame."

My stomach rumbled, and I quickly grabbed at it, embarrassed. Jax let out a soft chuckle.

"I will have Althea bring you breakfast here. I'll be back before you know it," he said, jumping up from the bed and quickly throwing on an outfit.

I couldn't tear my eyes from his torso as I watched him

button his shirt, covering up his chiseled muscles. I longed to run my hands along his chest, dipping down towards his waistband. It had only been the night before, but already, I craved more. I couldn't get enough of him, like insatiable hunger.

"Try not to miss me too much, little flame," he teased as he walked toward the door and disappeared.

I dragged myself out of the plush bed, missing the warmth of the sheets. I was still naked from the night before. Quickly, I opened the wardrobe that sat near the bed. Rummaging through it, I found a simple black dress. It wasn't as formal as the one I had been wearing to dinner, and its material was more comfortable. I threw it on before heading to the bathroom.

My bare feet crossed the tile, and I found myself staring at my reflection in a mirror. My hair was wild and untamed, and there were the beginnings of bags under my eyes. Even with a full night's sleep, I had not chased away the exhaustion of my journey.

I wanted to pull my hair away from my face, trying to manage the mess of waves that desperately needed to be brushed out. Searching through the bathroom in Jax's room, I found a small spool of thread tucked away in a drawer and ripped off a small piece to use as an elastic for my hair. Before pulling it back, I created small braids on each side of my head. It helped contain a bit of the frizz that had grown after sleeping. I gathered my hair in my hands and tied it back into a ponytail, the two braids running across my head and back into it. Satisfied, I tied a piece of thread around it to keep it in place.

When I finished, I heard knock at the door before it was

pushed open. By the time I made my way back to the bath-room doorway, I found Althea standing with the food.

"I've brought a few options because I was unsure of what you liked," she said shyly.

She smiled at me as she placed the tray on the bed. I hurried over and found a delicious spread of fruit, toast and cheese. Spotting strawberries, I picked one up and took a bite, licking the juice off my lips as I pulled away the top. I let out a slight moan as I swallowed my favorite fruit. Away from pesticides and processed foods of my world, this fruit was unlike anything I had tasted before. It was sweeter and juicier, and I couldn't grab the second one quickly enough.

"Is there anything else I can help you with?" Althea asked.

"I don't-" I paused as my feline slipped out from under-neath the bed.

I almost forgot Mr. Finkel had crawled under during the night to sleep.

"Actually, is it possible you could find him something to eat as well?" I asked, knowing the request was not what she had meant when she offered.

She chuckled. "Of course. I'll be back soon."

With that, she disappeared out of the room once more. I sat on the bed, eating through the tray of breakfast foods, Mr. Finkel hopping up beside me. He brushed against my leg, but I refused to pet him just yet. I knew if I did, I would immediately need to wash my hands. I couldn't control the compulsions, and I was far too hungry to stop eating my way through the platter. A twinge of guilt struck me as the cat gave up, flopping down beside me and purring.

"I promise, I owe you all the cuddles in the world," I whispered to the feline. "I'll make it up to you."

He let out a small meow as if in agreement. Althea found her way back to the room rather quickly with a bowl with what appeared to be cut up fish. By the smell alone, I knew I was correct.

"It isn't the same as your world's food, as I'm quite sure this creature does not live in your oceans, but I promise it is safe for your cat to eat."

She set the bowl on the floor, and immediately, Mr. Finkel hurried over to it, sniffing at it. He must've agreed, because he dug into the food bowl, finishing in a matter of minutes.

"You spoil him like this, and he'll start to like you more than me," I joked.

"Somehow, I don't believe that's true," the witch said back.

We had both finished breakfast, and Althea waited, taking our dishes with her when she left.

I waited patiently for the demon king to return to his room. It wasn't long after that I heard the door crack open again, my heart fluttering in anticipation. It was like a piece of me had returned. Every time I was with Jax, I felt whole again.

"Shall we?" Jax asked, waving a hand.

I strode over to him, taking his hand in my own and letting him lead me from the room.

It wasn't until Jax led us to a spiral staircase off one of the halls that I started to lose track of where I was.

"Where are you taking me?" I asked.

"If I told you, it would ruin the surprise, little flame," he said.

His answer only built anticipation in my chest. I couldn't tell if the rapid beating of my heart was from nerves or excitement. I was willing to venture it was a mix of both.

At the bottom of the steps, there was a door, and Jax held it open like a gentleman. I gave him a quiet thank you as I passed through.

I squinted, adjusting to the bright sun. It was warm, and I was glad I had chosen one of the shorter dresses. A breeze passed, swaying the skirt of my dress, and I held it down with my hands, hoping I hadn't completely exposed myself.

My eyes relaxed, and I realized the worry had been trivial. We were completely alone in a little oasis.

"Welcome to my personal garden," Jax said.

"You have a garden?" I asked.

"I have many, but this one is my personal one. Everything you see, I planted and grew myself. It's where I come to escape when the duties of being king are just a bit too much for me."

Every time I learned something new about the demon king, it made me fall for him a bit more.

I was falling hard and fast, and I wasn't sure I would make it out unscathed.

"And now, I'd like for it to be the same for you. Anytime this world becomes a little too much for you, I want you to have somewhere you feel safe."

The garden was peculiar, mute of color but full of life. Many of the strange plants I'd noticed before grew here. Any color to them was dark enough to be mistaken for black.

Jax let my hand go, allowing me the freedom to take in the garden on my own.

I spotted a flame burning in the corner atop a small column. There was no kindling or fuel keeping it alive. Rather, I could sense the magic that fed into the fire.

"What is that?" I asked.

"A gift," Jax answered. "From an old friend."

"Seri?" I asked hesitantly, not wishing to open an old wound.

He gave me a soft smile. "No, little flame."

I tilted my head, but he'd already moved on. The mystery behind the demon who gifted it would have to wait. I hurried along the path, catching up to the demon king. I almost stumbled over my own feet, halting too fast when a serpent slithered out from a nearby bush.

The creature was about two feet long and entirely black. I met its golden eyes, similar to Jax's, and paused, waiting to see if it would attack.

A warm chuckle pulled my attention away, Jax watching the pair of us with amusement across his face.

"You did that on purpose?" I accused, crossing my arms and regaining my composure.

"I merely called upon one of my serpents. I didn't know it would frighten you."

"It didn't frighten me," I started, but the warmth in my cheeks told a different story.

The snake slithered up the pathway and toward the demon. It wrapped itself up his leg and then arm as Jax reached out to it. I watched as the two stared intensely at each other, not a single word spoken or sound made.

I cleared my throat awkwardly, slowly striding toward them.

"Thank you," Jax said quietly to the creature, bending down allowing it to leave his arm for the ground. It wasted no time, slithering away before I even made it to them.

"What was that?" I asked.

"Part of my job as king," Jax said with a shrug.

"It's your job to terrify me?" I pushed.

"It is my job to know the happenings within the walls of my palace," he retorted. "The serpents keep me updated. They catch the whispers I am unable to hear."

"You can talk to them?" I said, my jaw dropping. Disbelief flashed across my face, and again, I saw amusement in the demon king's features.

"There is a lot you still don't know about me," he offered.

"How?" I asked, confident he knew I meant his ability to communicate with the serpents.

"Through our minds. I can talk to the snakes without uttering a single word," he explained. "Being a serpent demon means having a strong connection to serpent creatures. The bond is magical. It cannot be defined by any laws of nature. I can reach out and feel their presence with my mind. I urge a thought toward them, and they push one right back. There is no better way to put it."

Grabbing my hand, he led me down a path that wove between two beds of flowers. The one to my left was bleak and grey, the flowers themselves low to the ground and almost shriveled.

"This world could use some color," I joked.

"What do you mean? Are the people here not enough to

please you?" The worry that crossed his face sent a pang of guilt running through me.

"No, I didn't mean it like that," I started. "I just miss the color of my world. The orange and reds of autumn, the green grass in the spring, and even the pink flowers planted in my front yard," I recalled, my voice trailing off.

"Soleil..." Jax started, his tone shifting. It was enough to snap me from the daydream.

Following his gaze, I spotted what had caught his attention. A flower sprung up from the ground, its pink petals a stark contrast to the bleak plants of this realm, then another, until a small patch of them stood in our path.

Jax stared at me, his jaw dropping.

"I don't understand. What is that?" I asked, staring in disbelief.

"Magic." The word drifted from his lips like a whimsical promise.

It wasn't possible; I was no witch. But there it was: a beautiful tulip that had not been there only moments before.

"Can you do it again?" he asked, cocking his head.

"I don't even know how I did it the first time," I stuttered, my eyes wide.

He reached up, rubbing the back of his head, lost in thought. I still couldn't comprehend what I had done. I'd created life. Even if it was small, it was still a live flower from my own world, filled with color, unlike the black and grey plants that plagued Eodratera.

"Just close your eyes," Jax coaxed, stepping closer. I obliged his request, curious myself if the magic truly had come from me. "Now, picture the flowers sprouting and growing. Think about how they look when they bloom."

I took a deep breath, inhaling.

One, two, three, four.

Opening my eyes, I found nothing. No more flowers had miraculously sprouted, and the others that had appeared were already wilting.

"Are you sure it wasn't you?" I asked, remembering Jax's mother was a witch. "Could your magic have done this?"

Turning, I almost slammed into his solid chest, forgetting how close he had been. His strong arms wrapped around me, and he placed a kiss to the top of my head.

"No, little flame," he answered. "My magic isn't like that."

Shadows flared around us, consuming us, wrapping us in their embrace.

My muscles tensed, bracing for the shadows to brush against me. I tapped nervously at Jax's chest, as my hands rested on it.

"They won't hurt you," he assured me.

"I know," I answered, unable to help the intrusive thoughts at bay. No matter how hard I fought back, they found every crack and weakness in the walls I had built around my mind.

The shadows rescinded, crawling back to Jax then dissipating all together before I was able to see the sunlight once more.

The reality slammed into me, knocking the breath from my lungs. The magic had come from me. It was the only possibility, yet coming to terms with it felt near impossible.

"Has this happened before?" Jax asked, taking a step back.

I opened my mouth to deny it, but the moment I did, the night in the tunnels with the Nyera came rushing back. The blinding light that had saved me had been myself this whole time. I stared down at my hands, imagining the power flowing through my veins, the magic I could create.

If this power came from me, then-

"I think my mother was a witch," I said slowly, piecing it all together. The apothecary she worked at, Serafeen, her inability to come home... It all made sense. My mind hadn't been ready before to accept all the pieces before me, and now, I was seeing it, like adding the final touch to a painting.

If my father knew what my mother was, he'd plummet deeper into his fears, the existence of witches only confirming everything he worried about. I understood why she stayed away. Maybe her magical was unpredictable, like my own, and she couldn't risk him finding out. His control over me would've increased tenfold, and yet there was still an ache spreading in my heart.

Hurt over her never trusting me enough to know, over the pain that she never stayed long enough to know if I was truly a witch. She had to know what would happen if my father had been the first to witness my magic, and still, she chose to leave me.

"I've always suspected you had witch blood in you," Jax said, snapping me back into reality.

"How?" I asked, my eyes never leaving my palms, as if they may burst into flames.

"I can just sense it," he said, stepping toward me. "You're forgetting I too have witch blood running through my veins."

"And you didn't mention this before?" I asked, glaring at him. My lips drew thin, and I held my tongue from spewing the words that screamed to be let out. I knew my anger with my mother was fueling it, and I refused to take it out on Jax.

"I wasn't completely sure, and you had already been through enough journeying here. I wanted to be confident when I told you."

I nodded, knowing he was correct. If he had thrown this on me on top of the events of the past few days, I may have cracked.

"What do I do now?" I asked, desperate for answers. I wanted to learn everything there was to know about magic and my witch ancestry.

"Now, we find a witch to train you," Jax answered.

TWENTY-FOUR

A few more days passed before Jax found a witch to train me. I spent my time memorizing every corner of the palace and avoiding the glares of the demons within.

"Althea?" I blurted without thinking when I spotted the witch. "You're going to train me?"

She nodded her head. "I may not seem like much, but magic is the one thing I promise I am well versed on," she said.

"I trust you," I said and meant it. Watching her pull items out of her bag, I fidgeted, growing anxious. "We're the same?" I asked, my nerves growing out of control. "Both witches. There aren't types of witches are there?"

"Yes and no. There are covens," she answered, grabbing a pitcher of water from a nearby table in Jax's garden and filling a small bowl she'd brought. To add to her answer, she snapped her fingers, and fire bounced to life at the tips.

Lighting a candle, she took a step back, leaving the two items side by side.

Jax had allowed us full access to his personal gardens to practice and train. My magic was unpredictable, and I had insisted on learning its bounds in a secluded location.

"We'll begin easy," Althea said. "Starting with the other elements. We already know your magic is in touch with the element of earth. Let's find out what else you may be capable of," she said, grinning.

"I'll be able to use other types of magic?" I asked, moving closer to her set-up. Althea motioned for me to sit.

"It depends. Not every witch can. Some only master magic around a certain element while others are able to manipulate more. There are covens with strong ties to powers such as light and shadows."

"Covens. You mentioned that before too," I noted.

"Witches belong to covens; think of them like a large family. Many covens have ties that go back hundreds of years. They tend to have similar magic and settle in areas together," Althea said, but she paused as she coughed into her arm. She continued for a moment before I thought to stand and grab the pitcher of water.

"It's alright," she said, motioning at the pitcher. "It isn't anything that could help."

I sat back down, crossing my legs in front of me.

"Close your eyes," Althea instructed. "We are starting with two elements today. I need you to focus on those. Picture the way the flame flickers on the wick of the candle. Envision how the water looks if I dropped a pebble in it, the ripples that would spread across it. Focus."

My nerves were controlling my every thought and feeling. It was hard to focus when there was still uncertainty behind the powers coursing through me. How far could I take them, if at all? The last time, I had only accidentally grown flowers and couldn't replicate it only moments later.

Taking a deep breath, I counted in my head, repeating the same four numbers I always did.

After a few rounds of counting, I finally felt the anxiety slipping away, like I could finally get a deep breath.

"Good," Althea said. "Now, picture the fire growing. If you had the ability to fuel that fire, how would it look?"

In my mind, the fire grew and swayed with the breeze I could feel running across my skin. Its warmth licked at my face as it swelled. The flame took on a life of its own, and I panicked, letting go of the thought and opening my eyes. In front of me, the flame still sat, wavering on the candle.

"You let go too soon," Althea stated.

"I lost control," I said.

"You never had control," she clarified. "Take a moment to compose yourself, and we will try again."

I tried to refocus myself on training and learning the extent of my magic.

A meow pulled my attention away. I found Mr. Finkel quickly hurrying down the path toward me. The feline paused when it noticed I was with someone else. I smiled, thankful the cat had found me the way it always had.

"Is that your familiar?" Althea asked.

"Familiar?" I asked, tilting my head.

"Many witches have familiars. Pets with unyielding

loyalty to their owners, sometimes manifesting magic of their own to compliment their witch."

"No, Mr. Finkel is just a cat."

As I said it, I didn't believe it. The feline had a way of showing up where he shouldn't be, following me into this realm and now making it into the palace. If that wasn't magic, I didn't know what was.

"Regardless, he's a beautiful little creature," Althea admired, bending to pet him. Mr. Finkel nuzzled into her touch, purring his praise.

After another hour of trying and failing to connect with the flame or bowl of water, I let out a frustrated sigh. I stood, stretching my legs and walking away from the sources of my frustration.

"This is no use," I said. "I'm getting nowhere."

I tried to focus my mind and create the same flower I had before, but nothing came, not even the tiniest sprout. Again, I let out a frustrated grumble.

"This type of magic takes time. It is not something you can just learn to harness overnight," Althea said, crossing her arms and studying me. "The magic you displayed before was a response to a strong emotion. Try to cling to that again. Try to think of a strong memory, one that will help you pull your magic out."

"I've been trying. I've been thinking about the same flower, the ones back in my own world, but nothing seems to work. I tried imagining a growing fire and rippling water, and still, nothing."

"Maybe we need to try a different emotion. If the one you

feel about the flowers around your town isn't strong enough, we need something else."

I tried to think of other memories of home ones that might help bring my power to the surface, but the only thing I could think of when I thought of home was the cage I used to live in. It brought back emotions of frustration and even fear creeping in. I could feel my temperature rising the heat turning my cheeks pink. I clenched my fist as I thought about the new freedom I had here, realizing everything I had missed out on living under my father's tight grip.

I clenched my fists tighter the hotter they became. I felt like my skin was burning.

"Soleil," Althea said cautiously, but I could barely hear her. All I could hear was the rage ringing through my ears and the fury that beat like a drum under my skin, tapping to that same rhythm that brought me comfort.

One, two, three, four.

"Soleil," she said again, a little more forcefully this time.

Snapping back into reality, I glanced at her and saw the concern in her eyes, but she wasn't looking at my face. She was looking down at my hands. I realized why they had felt so hot: flames lit both of my fists ablaze. The two small fires brushed against me, and the more I thought about how angry I had felt, the more they grew. I panicked.

I tried shaking my hands to put the fire out, but it remained. The more I panicked, the worse it became, feeding the flames and giving them life.

"Take a breath, Soleil. You're gonna burn the palace down," Althea said, taking a step toward me.

"If I can't stop it, can you put it out?" I asked, my voice growing higher.

I watched as little embers sparked from my hands, landing on the ground around us, a small fire catching on a nearby fence. Althea put out the flames with her own magic, easily taming them until they were no more than a glow before extinguishing.

"Please help me. I can't make it stop," I begged.

"You need to learn to control it," she said. "I won't always be here to help. You need to contain your magic. If you let it get out of hand like this, you could harm yourself or others. Take a deep breath."

I knew she wouldn't let it come to the palace burning, which helped contain the flames a bit, but still, panic remained, and I couldn't stop. My breath rapidly increased as my heart raced, reality slamming into me.

"I'm trying, but no matter what I do, the feeling just grows stronger," I said.

"Look at me."

I met her gaze and took deep breaths.

One, two, three, four.

With each slow count, I tried to breathe, but it was no use. I was already too far gone. The flames leapt out at Althea, lashing towards her arms with a quick movement. She easily deflected them, containing them for a moment.

I took two steps back, afraid I would hurt her. I knew her magic was stronger than mine, but still, mine was unpredictable. As I dug further into myself, there would be no way back, and my magic would consume me. This power was becoming something that once again had control over me.

Suddenly, strong arms wrapped around me, pulling me back. I felt the breathing behind me. I knew it was him from the smell of pine. He wasn't afraid of my flames; instead, he embraced me.

Jax whispered into my ear, the sound of his voice comforting me, and slowly, I was able to breathe again. "Just like that. Keep breathing."

And I did.

I counted my breath over and over in my head, in for four beats and out for four beats. I watched the flames die down until they were nothing more than little embers crackling in my palms.

Jax hugged me tighter.

"How'd you know that would work?" I asked.

"Because I believe in you," he said, and I heard a hint of shock in his voice.

"I believe that anything you set your mind to is possible, little flame."

As the last of the ember finally died out, I turned to him. His hand gently caressed my cheek, and his thumb brushed over my skin. I blinked away the last of the magic, finding comfort in the demon king.

I heard Althea make her way out of the courtyard, leaving us alone.

"I thought it would consume me," I admitted.

"The more you learn who you are, the more powerful you will become, wielding the flames that run under your skin. You are not meant to be tamed, little flame. You are meant to burn and burn brightly."

I leaned in, pressing a gentle kiss to his lips. "Do you truly believe that?"

"Of course," he whispered.

Before I could say another word, Jax scooped me into his arms, his muscles wrapped around me, holding me tightly to his chest. A small sound of excitement left my lips.

"Where are you bringing me?" I asked, already forgetting about the rage that had filled my heart.

"I'm taking you where you don't have to be afraid of those flames. I'm taking you somewhere you can just be you."

I glanced up at his face for any hint of what he might mean. He carried me through the palace at a brisk pace.

Stalking straight out the front doors to the courtyard, he paused before the large black gate that kept us in.

He spotted one of the palace workers and commanded them to fetch a horse. My eyebrows rose, cocking my head.

"You have horses?" I asked before I could stop myself.

His lips lifted into a smile. "I told you you might be surprised about what you find here."

A clacking sound on the cobblestone pulled my attention to a white creature being led towards us. It was my turn to smile; the beast not at all what I had expected. The creature looked similar to a horse from my own world, but the two horns that grew from its head set it apart. It was all white, except I stared into rich red eyes.

"It's magnificent," I whispered in awe.

"I thought you might like it," Jax admitted.

I walked towards the horse, but before I reached it, I

paused and gave a glance back at Jax. He nodded his encouragement.

I took the last step and raised my hand before I touched its face. It nuzzled into my touch, and a wide smile spread across my lips

"Are we taking this horse?" I asked, glancing back to Jax.

"Of course," Jax said, a devilish grin spreading across his lips. He closed the distance between us, scooping me into his arms and helping me onto the horse.

"We're riding bareback?" I asked, my voice hesitant.

"Is there another way?" Jax asked, cocking his head.

"We have saddles."

He raised a brow, still confused by what I meant.

"Never mind," I chuckled.

"You really are something, little flame," he said, climbing onto the horse.

"Do you have any complaints about us riding together?"

His hand snaked around my waist and rested on my thigh. His thumb circled on the top of my leg, and I leaned back into him, barely able to form a thought.

"No," I choked out.

"I didn't think so," he whispered into my ear, tickling my skin and sending butterflies to my stomach.

One of the palace workers used magic to open the gate. It roared to life and rumbled. The horse began to trot the moment the gates were open.

A meow behind me caught my attention, and I spotted Mr. Finkel trailing behind us.

"I'm alright. Stay here," I ordered of the familiar. The

feline looked like he may protest, but he turned and walked slowly back behind the safety of the palace walls.

"They are very loyal creatures, you know?" Jax said.

"Familiars?"

"Yes. My mother used to have one," Jax explained. "A small black cat, Maela.

We ventured into the city on the back of the horse. I caught a few demons staring at us, gawking as we rode through the city.

"Do you come out often?" I asked

"I try," he admitted. "I want to be a king whose subjects are loyal to him because they want to be. I want to be a king who rules his kingdom with a caring and understanding demeanor," he explained. "I cannot do that sitting on my throne and never venturing out into my own streets."

The way Jax cared for his subjects warmed my heart.

A demon child with green skin and two horns ventured close to the horse. It let out a small giggle as it watched the horse pass with wonder. Seeing these demons react to Jax's presence, I knew he made a good and fair king.

Trotting down the street, we made good time. It only took us twenty minutes to make it to the very outskirts of the city. The streets turned into dirt, and many of the houses and shops faded away. We were in the same land I had traveled to when I first arrived in this realm.

"The journey won't take long," Jax said. "Only about an hour or two ride from here."

That reassurance brought me comfort. I remembered the bargain I struck with Vileer and looked down at the brand marking me. Reading my mind, Jax placed a hand on my arm, covering the mark.

"We'll figure it out. I will figure out a way to get you out of the bargain."

"You know that's not possible," I said. "No one can break a bargain without consequences."

"If there is a way for the bargain to be undone, I will find it," he insisted, and I leaned back into him.

"I know you will," I whispered.

His hand let go of my arm and found its way back to my thigh. Wishing his hand would never move, I let out a soft sound of pleasure.

"Don't tempt me," he said, realizing what I wanted.

"And if I do?" I asked, my core now warm with desire.

"Then who am I to deny you?" he said.

His hand slowly trailed along my thigh, lifting the black skirt of the dress I wore. I felt his fingers run along the edge of my lace undergarments.

Pulling at the lace and slipping under a few times, I tried to adjust so that his hand would reach where I wanted it. He teased me, rubbing lazy circles against my center. Then, he pulled back. I arched in protest, but his hand didn't return.

"We're almost there," Jax said.

We crossed the border marking the beginning of new land, the gray dirt turning into dark sand. In the distance I spotted a volcano.

"It doesn't actively erupt. You are safe here," Jax said, nuzzling into my neck. Somehow, that still didn't bring comfort.

Galloping through the region, I realized why it was named Fuerya. It was different from Gildhor, and everywhere I looked, there were fire elements. It was a quick ride into the main city, and I noticed a large fortress sat in the center of it all. Large black towers rose from the fortress, their tops lined with red, like a torch with a flame.

Riding through the city, I noted there were fires everywhere, which explained how many of the creatures and demons who lived there drew their powers from the flames themselves.

I spotted a fire burning brightly on top of a pillar, staring at it, mesmerized by the way the flames moved. I noticed the center looked as though it had a face. The flames blinked to life, and two black eyes glared at me.

Jax laughed. "Fire demons. They're tricky little bastards. Don't let them fool you. They may be grounded to where their fire is born, but they can still do a lot of damage."

I instinctively backed away from the demon, searching for Jax's familiar comfort once more.

This city was lively much like Gildor. I saw some demons who looked familiar and others who were completely new to me. They hurried through the streets, going about their day, barely acknowledging their king.

"Do they not know you?" I asked, my head swiveling, watching each of the demons.

"They do," Jax noted. "But I frequently visit, so this is a normal day to them."

"Is it not considered rude for them not to acknowledge you?" I asked, realizing people in my own world would never ignore a monarch in this manner.

"No," Jax added. "The customs in this world are not like your own. If I commanded their attention right now, every last demon would stop what they were doing to listen, but it is never expected in a situation like this that they must pause their own busy lives for my arrival. I would never allow that. I expect respect and order within the walls of my own palace, but out here, there is no need for formality."

It struck me as odd, but I didn't push any further. There were still many demon customs for me to come to terms with.

The further we pushed into the city, the more I was able to admire the differences between it and Gildhor. The dark architecture and vibrant reds were striking.

I realized quickly why Jax had brought me to Fuerya.

With the display of flames I had shown, he must've assumed that was the element my own coven had ties to. Could I even have a coven if I didn't grow up with one, or were there rules to being a member?

I spotted a small child juggling three orbs of fire, other children gathering around and laughing. It brought a smile to my face, pushing away the thoughts dragging me down.

We approached the large fortress, stone walls surrounding it. On the top of the walls, guards sat, watching us. The moment they recognized Jax, they gave the signal to open the gates. They drew open, and Jax urged our horse forward with a single click of his heel.

Inside was a courtyard, vast and empty. Only three demons stood inside waiting for us.

A pair of male demons stood on either side of a female demon, both wearing matching uniforms with a red crest. The crest resembled a flame with a dagger stabbed through the fire.

In between them stood the female, tall and petite. Her black dress clung to her frame and trailed to the ground, where her hem turned to a vibrant red.

Her confidence made me feel uneasy, like she could burn me with a single glance. I met her golden eyes as Jax helped me off the horse. As I stepped forward, I realized her skin was a pale shade of red.

The black obsidian tiara on her head confirmed what I suspected: the Princess of Fuerya stood before me, eyeing me with intense suspicion.

Her long, black hair was like my own, her loose curls trailing down her back.

"Silva," Jax said, nodding to the princess.

"Jaxilian." She returned the nod.

"You know it's just Jax," he huffed.

"You know I can't resist," she answered, a smile growing.

She looked to me before turning toward the fortress and shouting behind her, "Welcome to Fuerya."

TWENTY-FIVE

Entering the fortress, I spotted similarities to Jax's Serpentine Palace, adorned with dark embellishments and oil paintings. The faces depicted in the art were none I recognized except the one on the far end.

"Is that you?" I asked Jax as we passed by the picture, following the pair of demons from outside.

"Yes," Jax confirmed.

"And that's-"

"Silva," he added.

The painting showed two children, but the resemblance was easily recognizable. One child was seated on the wooden stool—Silva, her long maroon dress flowing to the floor. Jax stood beside her, a small golden crown atop his dark hair. He not only looked younger, but there was a certain spark in his eye, one I had yet to see in him before now.

We were led down the entry hall, a winding staircase at the end leading up to another floor of the fortress. The demons let us pass, following up behind us. I admired the detailing in the railing of the stairs. It looked like licks of flame sprung to life made from the metal. My hand ran along it, feeling the cool metal as we ascended.

It was a short walk up to the next floor of the palace, and we ventured down a new hall. The demon led us to a door at the end. The door was simple and grey, no indication of what it held behind it.

"I hope you find this to your liking," one demon said, his voice raspy. He pushed open the door, stepping aside to allow us to enter. "If you need anything at all before the ball, please send for one of us."

My brows raised at the mention of the ball. This was the first I'd heard of the event, but Jax hadn't even flinched. I gave a quick glance to him, but he just shrugged.

Stepping inside, I took in all the luxurious details the simple door hid. The bed was not as large as the one in Jax's room, but it was still spacious and lush. After the long journey we had, I envisioned climbing into it and curling up for a nap.

The walls were covered in red paper with a muted black design. It was slightly eclectic for my own taste, but it fit in well here. I breathed in the comforting scent of cinnamon, following it to a small table next to the bed where a candle had been lit.

Moving further inside the room, I slipped off the boots I had been wearing, and my feet found a carpet beneath them, a stark contrast to the cold tiles of Jax's palace. There was no balcony in this room, just two windows well above my own eye level. I noticed the door to my right and assumed it would lead to our own private washroom, but before I could explore, strong arms wrapped around me.

"Ball?" I asked, Jax nuzzling into my neck.

"If I told you, it would've ruined the surprise. It just worked out that your magic leans towards fire. Now that you're here for the event, you can learn all there is to know about fire magic too."

"And if they aren't willing to teach me?" I asked hesitantly. The last ruler I had trusted had forced me into a bargain.

"Trust me, they will. Silva is an old friend and one of my closest subjects," Jax answered, his voice steady. "And even if she wasn't, you just say the word, and I will make anything in this realm happen for you."

I turned around, placing my hands on his chest. His golden eyes overwhelmed me, and I felt dazed glancing into them.

"Anything?" I asked in a sickly-sweet tone.

"Dangerous, little flame," he tsked. "Don't tempt me. We have a ball to get to."

"Fine," I shrugged, stepping back. "Your loss."

I grinned as I walked away, knowing the effect I had on the demon king. His eyes never left me, even for a moment.

"My loss indeed," he murmured.

AFTER AN HOUR, we were almost prepared for the festivities.

Jax had somehow fit a thin, long gown in the satchel he

had packed. I hadn't even noticed the bag strapped to his back when we left Gildhor.

I hadn't noticed much of anything, far too focused on the king himself.

Unfortunately, he had forgotten shoes to go with the gown. I stood barefoot in the form-fitting black gown while Jax fetched a demon outside our door. My toes curled into the carpet, embarrassment creeping in and insecurity freely flowing through my mind. I didn't fit into this setting, formal balls and politics—it wasn't in my nature. Yet, here I found myself, following the king's lead and stepping outside my usual comfort.

Another few minutes of waiting, and I found myself staring down a line up of stilettos and sparkling heels. The sheer number made me laugh.

I opted for the lowest heel I could spot, knowing my lack of practice would land me on my ass otherwise.

"Fucking hell," Jax murmured.

"What?" I asked, snapping my head toward him.

"I want to tear that dress right back off your body," he said, his eyes slowly dragging down my form.

"What's stopping you?" I whispered.

"Politics, little flame," he answered, shaking his head. "It would be rude to be late to this ball."

He still hadn't elaborated much on why exactly we were even attending the ball, and I had a feeling if I pushed again, he'd still shy away from the questions. Instead, I asked something else that had been burning in my mind.

"Aren't we in hell?" I noted.

"What?"

"You said fucking hell. Aren't we technically in hell?" I asked, only now realizing this was the closest a human would get to glimpsing their idea of hell.

"Does this feel like hell to you?" he asked, stroking the stubble on his chin.

"No, more like heaven," I answered, a smile growing across my lips.

The demon grinned, his eyes darkening and settling on my own gaze, then my lips.

"Anywhere you go, little flame, is my own personal heaven."

His words intoxicated me, filling me with more confidence.

I walked over to the bed, sitting to strap my heels around my ankles. They were a simple matte black with a block heel. The straps were thin and wrapped easily around my ankle before I secured them in place. Jax sat beside me, causing the bed to sink, and I automatically leaned in toward him.

"Ready?" he asked.

My legs weakened, not prepared to carry me down to a function where everyone would have their eyes on the human. The thought nauseated me, holding me firmly in place on the bed. My breathing became shaky, and I felt lightheaded.

"Tell me about your mother," Jax said, distracting me from the growing panic in my chest.

"What about her?" I asked, confused. He took my hands in his own, pressing a gentle kiss to the back of one.

"Anything. She must be a witch like you, consider me intrigued," he said softly, his tone already calming me.

"She's brave," I said. It was the first time I had admitted it to someone. Folks around Weeping Vale whispered and gossiped, and it made my heart ache. If only they caught just a snippet of our life and the misery we faced, maybe they'd hold their tongues. Maybe they would have encouraged her to leave.

I had it bad, but my mother had it ten times worse.

The memories had me picking at a loose thread in the comforter of the bed. I kept repeating the motion, hoping it would settle that dread building inside me.

"She left a few years ago," I said. "She was brave, and she left him. Everything he did to me, closing me off in the world, preventing me from living my life, she did even worse. My mother didn't have her own life or friends. She wasn't allowed to see her family. She was barely allowed to make her own decisions. Leaving was the best thing she did for herself."

Jax studied me with a knowing glance, reading my every thought. I knew what he'd ask next before it even left his mouth. It was the same thing everyone wondered, including myself at times.

"Why didn't she take you?" he asked, a saddened tone coating his words. It was what everyone whispered about when she left. She abandoned her daughter—how could she? It was what I wondered on nights where I felt alone or suffocated by my father, and I still didn't have a great answer. I knew that if she could have taken me with her, she would have. Every time I spoke to her on the phone, I wanted to ask, even though I knew our conversations would be brief.

"I think that she needed to find herself before she could

properly care for someone else. I think it broke her to leave me behind, and I think that's why it's so hard for her to talk to me even now. I also think she knew that I would have the strength to also leave him someday. He's my father, but now that I'm an adult, I get to make those choices for myself."

I said the words, and a new confidence built within me. I was confident in my decision to leave my father behind and venture to this new realm, finally picking up the pieces of myself and finding who I was. I think my mother knew this is what I would need to do someday. No one could pick up the pieces for me, and no one could tell me who to be.

"She built me into the person I am now. I hope that someday, I can face my darkness and walk away a better person with control over my own life because of her," I ended firmly.

"I've watched as you've stoked that flame deep inside you. I see you bringing a new light to this world. This kingdom needs a queen who understands struggle, who can allow these demons to prosper the way they deserve. One day, I hope for you to be that queen for them, little flame."

The words overtook me like a wave crashing down.

I was nowhere near worthy to rule a kingdom. I'd only just arrived to this realm, and even after a few days, I still had no idea the secrets and dangers it held. It would take months or even years before I felt worthy of calling this place my new home, never mind ruling over it.

"I-"

"Do not argue that you cannot be queen. I already told you this world follows different rules than your own. I see the flame you've buried deep down, and I know you will learn to let it burn here."

"But I am human," I argued. "They'll never accept me."

"You are part witch, the same as me, and they learned to accept me."

"I doubt they'll see it that way," I said, eyes falling to the ground. Jax's calloused fingers grazed my chin, lifting my gaze back to his.

"Never doubt yourself," he insisted.

"I've barely been here for a day. How do you know you want me to be a queen someday? Doesn't that seem a bit fast?" I asked, my stomach turning at the potential denial I could receive.

"I have thought about you every single day this past year. I finally have you back, Soleil, and I have no plans of losing you again. Regardless of what realm we are in or if you are part human, I want you by my side. Though we have only known each other for a short time, it feels like my heart has known you forever."

I couldn't stop the smile inching across my lips or the pink that spread over my cheeks.

"Now, shall we?" Jax asked, standing and extending a hand to me.

I took the outstretched hand, allowing the king to help me stand. Following him across the room, I focused on each step I took, careful not to waver in my heels. With a deep breath, I tried to focus on allowing myself to relax and enjoy the night.

TWENTY-SIX

Music carried down the hall, the demon king's arm wrapped around my waist. My dress felt tight, and a flash of heat coursed through my body. No matter how many times I repeated encouragements in my mind, nothing fully calmed me. The last corner we turned, the music grew louder. Ahead, I could see the entrance, even with demons lingering outside it.

Beyond the demons, I caught a glimpse of the ballroom. The space opened into a grand room decorated with red and gold, the colors of Fuerya. A large crystal chandelier hung in the center of the ceiling, at least twenty feet above the attendees below it. The polished floors reflected the light shining from the chandelier above. Long banners hung on the far wall, and I spotted the same crest the guards wore on their uniforms.

We paused outside the ballroom, Jax removing his hand from the small of my back and holding his arm out for me to grab. I clung tight, needing the confidence he projected to carry to me.

Walking into the ball, I found all eyes fell on us as Jax lead me into the spacious room. Every demon wanted to catch a glance of the human on their king's arm. Their gazes felt like tiny stings on my skin. I heard a few snickers, but that didn't surprise me, not every demon in the room was expected to trust a human so easily.

It wouldn't matter that I was a witch; they saw an outsider.

My silk gown fell behind me, the train feeling heavier as we made our way across the room. The music picked up, and the further we walked, the more the guests started to ignore us. In the center of the dance floor, Jax turned toward me, holding out a hand.

"May I?" he asked.

My heart skipped a beat realizing he wanted to dance. With no knowledge of how to dance in such a setting, I'd make a fool of myself. I had never been to a formal event, nor would my father have allowed it. I used my thumb to pick at my lace glove, pulling at it rhythmically.

Hesitantly, I held my hand out. Jax took my hand and pulled me close. Leaning in, he whispered, "Don't worry I've got you."

Other demons joined in with their partners, the music playing an upbeat melody, and I found myself moved across the floor and spun in circles. It was a mix of twirling gowns and careful footwork, the demons surrounding us more well-practiced than myself. Each step Jax took was calculated, and he guided me every part of the way.

Without realizing when it happened, I felt a large smile plastered to my face. The sheer giddiness coursing through my body distracted me from the anxiety that had dragged me down before.

Somehow, getting lost in the music with Jax was the cure to my concerns and worries.

"Never stop looking at me like that," Jax suddenly said when I met his gaze.

"Like what?"

"Like you're finally home."

I sucked on my bottom lip, suppressing the maddening grin I knew would grow if I didn't. "And if I am?" I asked.

Jax paused, ignoring the rest of the demons spinning and waltzing around us. Pulling me in close, he dipped me. "This home has always been yours. It just took a little longer to find it." He leaned in, pressing a quick kiss to my lips.

AFTER A FEW MORE SONGS PLAYED AND my feet started to feel sore, the music died down in the room. All the attendees dancing scattered, chatting and drinking the wine placed in abundance around the room. I made to head toward the table where I saw someone of the chalices of wine being poured. Jax quickly grabbed my wrist, halting me.

"Remember what I told you about demon wine?"

"Yes, and I also remember I handled it just fine last time," I said with a grin.

Jax took a step closer, and my heart skipped a beat. His

hand cupped my cheek, his thumb grazing over my skin. He leaned in and whispered, "Is that the way you remember it?"

My cheeks warmed, and I swore his touch stirred the flames boiling under my skin. I wanted him so desperately. I wanted him here and now; the only thing stopping me was the hundred or so attendees of the ball. Every inch of me wanted to drag him from this room and take him in that large soft bed I knew awaited us.

He read my thoughts, and the devilish grin that crossed his lips told me he had similar ideas.

"Easy, little flame. We have business to attend to first," Jax's growled. "And then we can have all the fun you'd like later."

His hand found my waist, holding me tight and pulling me close. He pressed a kiss to my lips before leading me over to the table with the wine.

He poured me a chalice, and I noticed he didn't fill it up as much as his own. Admittedly, I knew it was for the best. Even if I was a witch, my magic didn't know how to cure the effects of wine, and even if it did, I had no control over it yet. I sipped from my glass. This one was even stronger than what Jax had served to me that first night. My lips puckered, the wine sour and burning my throat. I heard small chuckle from Jax's lips next to me.

"You knew it'd be this strong!" I demanded more than asked. I crossed my arms, glaring at him.

"And if I did? What will you do to me, little flame?" His brows raised slightly, and that dark gaze stared down at mine. The flames under my skin only grew, stoked by his playful teasing. I knew that two could play at that game.

I moved close enough that I was chest-to-chest with Jax and could feel his muscles tense, trying to keep himself composed.

"Wicked things, demon." I narrowed my eyes, never letting go of his stare. "Or I might just have to have you right here," I said with a devilish smile as I walked away.

I left him gaping after me and could feel the intensity of his stare as I made my way across the ballroom. I wasn't exactly sure where I was headed, but I knew I needed to put space between me and the demon king before I really did give in to my desires.

The separation had me a little on edge. This wasn't a region or palace I was used to. I could feel the hatred pouring out around me the further I moved into the crowd.

Again, I fiddled with the lace on my glove, the compulsion controlled by a part of my mind I had no control over.

An older demon with pale blue skin stopped me, placing a firm hand on my shoulder. I turned my head to glance at him, waiting for an explanation. What demon would dare place their hands on Jax's partner?

"And who do you think you are? Bewitching our king, placing him under one of your spells," the demon demanded. He spat the words at me, and I could feel his spit hit my face with each word. I cringed, wrinkling my eyebrows.

"He's not under any spell," I started, but the demon's

grip tightened on my shoulder, and I let out a small wince before I could finish my thought.

"I know a witch when I see one," he snarled, and for the first time, I found the courage to meet his gaze. His eyes were vacant, completely white and glossed over. Was he blind? I'd never seen eyes that stared through a person the way his did.

"You lure demons under your spell and use us as your whores to get what you want. I won't let you do that to my king," he said, his voice growing angrier. My fingers tapped at my side, and I could feel my chest tightening.

If I didn't get away from here soon, I never would. I knew the anxiety would take hold of me and never let go.

Before I could answer, I felt a presence step behind me. A small sigh of relief escaped my lips, assuming Jax had finally found me.

It was not Jax who came to my rescue.

"I suggest you take your hands off her unless you want to find that your king leaves you with no hands," Silva said in a steady voice.

Realizing who had stepped in behind me, I cringed into myself, feeling small. I still barely had spoken to the princess, and although Jax had assured me she was a friend, I couldn't help but feel unsettled.

"Princess, this witch-" the demon stuttered.

"I think it's time you leave." She stopped his rambling before he could continue. I spotted two of her guards just beyond the demon moving slowly toward us. The demon following my gaze and quickly removed his hand from my shoulder. He stepped away and scurried off without another word. I caught him giving one last glance toward us before he disappeared out the doors to the ballroom.

"Thank you," I said, turning toward the princess finally.

"It was the least I can do. I will not have Jax making a mess of my citizens by inciting bloodbath and punishing anyone who dare touch you. He knew that many would not like your presence here, and yet, he still brought you," she stated, glancing me over. I still couldn't read her. It was like she had a steel wall built around her and I was pounding on the outside. I was confident others tried before me. Yet, Jax had been successful. The way he spoke of her told me he knew an entirely different side to her.

"You know Jax well?" It was the only thing I could think to say. I wasn't sure if her comment before was meant as an insult or concern.

"We've known each other since we were children; our fathers were good friends. We were forced to spend time together while our parents attended meetings."

I watched the princess' eyes turn distant, like she was recalling a vague memory.

A new presence stepped behind me. I almost sunk as soon as I felt the familiar large frame pressing against my back.

"But she's forgetting all the good parts," Jax said, and I could hear him holding back laughter. "You're forgetting to share how we set the library on fire as children, or how we used to scare the palace workers with your flames and my shadows. I seem to recall that your father's chef almost didn't return to work after one of our antics."

A wild grin grew across the princess' lips. Jax wrapped

his arms around my shoulders, pulling me back into him. The princess cocked her head, watching us in what I knew it was a form of a test. I knew she was trying to gauge just how serious Jax was about bringing me here.

"You never told me that," I accused, turning my chin to glance up at Jax. "And why do I feel like most of these antics were your idea?" I asked, holding the demon's gaze.

He let out soft chuckle. "I seem to remember just the other day when you almost burned down my own palace," he countered. "So it would seem we are more alike than you might've thought, little flame."

"And I'll do it again if you don't behave, demon king," I joked.

I turned back to the princess, who was still watching us.

"I think I like her," she said, finally moving her gaze to Jax's. "I certainly see why you do."

"I knew you would," he said. "You remind me of each other a little," he admitted.

My eyebrows furrowed as I took in his words. I glanced at the princess, trying to figure out how either of us was similar. Our looks were not comparable: she was tall and strong with dark hair, whereas I was short with fiery red locks. The princess was fierce and levelheaded, and I could tell her citizens respected her. I dreamed of having strength like hers, the kind where you build a mental fortress and keep out those trying to tear you down. Maybe if I had been like that, things with my father never would've grown to what they did.

"Jax tells me you need someone to help with your flames," the princess said, interrupting the intrusive thought. My jaw dropped a little. When did Jax had the time to tell the princess about my dilemma? I quickly glanced back at him, but he just shrugged. Every day, the demon king surprised me more. I turned back to the princess.

"Yes," I admitted. Glancing down at my palms, I imagined the wild flames that had almost consumed the garden. I never wanted to lose control over my magic like that again. if someone in this room could help me, then I would happily accept.

"We begin now," the princess said.

I sucked in a breath, glancing wildly between Jax and her. She couldn't be serious. We were at a ball, and the night was still early.

"I assume you are fine to handle this," she said, looking at Jax and motioning to the room.

"It'd be my pleasure," he said, and I saw the princess roll her eyes at the eagerness in his voice.

"Then follow me," she said, beckoning me to trail behind her as she left the room.

CHAPTER
TWENTY-SEVEN

We walked through the halls of the fortress, Silva leading the way. I took quick but careful steps to avoid stepping on the back of her ruby red gown. It was similar to my own: silk and simple, except the straps of the dress were made of a silver material. Each time she caught the light, the material sparkled.

My heart raced, and I could feel the anxiety growing. I hated to cling to Jax and use him as a shield of comfort, but in this unfamiliar territory, it felt like a need more than a want. The relentless thoughts never stopped, and I couldn't cut them off the way I could my own thoughts and ideas.

We ended up walking to the far side of the palace and out into a courtyard. My heels sounded louder on the black stone ground.

The princess led me through to what looked to be a small garden on the other side. It was filled with red and black plants and flowers that matched the region itself.

"How is this possible?" I asked, glancing around in wonder.

Around the plants were rows of flames. The rows alternated between fire and flowers.

"How do they not burn?" I asked, my lips still parted in astonishment.

"These aren't like the flowers you would find in your world, even though their appearance is deceiving," she answered. "These are a special type of plants that only thrive in this region and draw life from the flames kept burning around them. They are much like you and me, needing fire for life and power."

A small ember of hope burned deep in my chest. If these flowers could learn to wield such an unruly element, maybe I could too.

"Where are you taking me?" I asked.

We strolled along the path lined with flowers, and at the end, I spotted a black metal gate. Its twisted metal columns stood only about a foot taller than me. I could tell the metal was old. There were locks attached to it, preventing just anyone from opening it. On top of it sat spikes that, even from a distance, I could tell were sharp. On each side of the gate, a wall extended, twice its height, too high for anyone to climb over.

I cringed as I thought about what would happen if a demon tried.

"You'll see," she answered, striding away from me.

We made it to the end of the walkway and stopped at the gate. The lock on it was sturdy and twisted into an odd, swirled shape, lacking a combination pad or normal keyhole. There was only a small opening at one end of the swirl existed. The princess called to life a small flame in the palm of her hand. She grasped the end of the lock with the opening, letting the flame grow and turning the black metal a glowing red. Within a moment, the lock sprung open, allowing her to push up the gate.

"How? How are you able to do that?" I asked, my eyes widening.

"The lock is spelled to recognize my power and only mine. It knows my flames and will only open for me."

I glanced down at my own hands, wondering what power and magic I was able to wield.

"A witch like yourself created the spell," Silva offered with a knowing glance.

I gave a slight nod, moving toward her.

With the gate open, I followed the princess through, finding a shoreline beyond the gated wall. The walls trapped us in and secluded the small stretch of beach. The sand here was a vibrant red, and tiny pieces slipped under my feet when I tried to navigate it in my heels.

Silva slipped her own shoes off, and I followed her lead, unstrapping the heels and tossing them gently to the side. I slipped off my gloves after placing them on top of the heels. Glancing ahead at the body of water before me, my eyebrows raised. The sight was magnificent, but it was almost out of place. The dark waves lapped against the red shore, the contrast peculiar.

"Everything needs balance, including power. Being

partially surrounded by water helps keep this region in check. It is the same way your magic needs to be kept in check. Your flames will always try to run their own course. If you are going to learn to control it, you'll need to learn that."

Silva called her flames to life, manipulating them. She moved her hands in a circular motion in front of her, the flames swirling in a circle. I watched, mesmerized by the control she had over them. She moved her hands and aimed out toward the sea, the flames following the same path. Her hands guided a steady flow of flames out into the water. The moment they touched the sea, they turned to steam.

The bewildered look on my face never left, watching the display. I tried to gather my thoughts, but I was stunned.

"You can easily do this. It is an easy maneuver. You just must trust yourself and find that balance," she explained, creating another circle of fire. The way the fire bent to her will sent envy coursing through my veins.

I wanted nothing more than to control my magic and embrace who I was. What kind of witch would I be without learning to get a grasp on my magic?

"Will you show me?" I asked, my eyes widening.

Silva nodded.

"Just follow these same motions and envision yourself tugging on that flame deep down, the one that burns the brightest within you. Think about that, and pull it out to the surface," she said. "Let the flame flow through you and guide it in a circle."

I mimicked the same circular motion she had done twice. I let my arms move over and over, counting in my head to steady myself.

One, two, three, four.

I repeated it until I felt confident enough to call on my flames. I let them slowly trickle to the surface, begging to be unleashed fully. I tried to shove it back down and picture the balance she had told me about. The flames sprung to life, moving in a small circle in front of me. I envisioned tracing the outline of a circle with them. A smile grew on my lips as I realized I was wielding fire. I was taming the flames and bending them to my will.

"Now, let's try to move them," she said.

She showed me the motion, stopping the circles and moving her hands out toward the sea like she was pushing the flame away from her. I tried to copy the same motion.

The flames leapt uncontrollably out of the circle but did not head out to sea. Instead, they barreled toward the princess, who quickly deflected them. My cheeks warmed with embarrassment, realizing what an utter failure I was. The more my body warmed from the shame, the more I felt like I'd set myself on fire. The feeling only grew when I glanced down and realized my fists were blazing. The same panic I had felt that day in the courtyard coursed through me.

The fire refused to extinguish, and I lost control. The more I panicked, the more it grew. I shook my hands instinctively.

The flames only caught on the dress I wore. Embers started to spider out across the dress, and soon, the fabric was burning.

The princess looked at me wide eyed and hurried over. She grabbed my hand without a thought for the flames burning them and dragged me into the sea. Freezing cold water hit my skin, and suddenly, I was snapped back into reality. The water doused my flames, and I sunk into it, letting my entire body go under, save for my head.

The princess stayed with me in the frigid sea, watching with intense focus.

"You didn't have to do that for me," I said quietly. I kept my eyes glued to the rippling surface of the water. I couldn't bring myself to look at her.

"Do you remember when Jax mentioned us setting a library on fire?" she asked gently. I nodded, my teeth chattering from the cold water.

"That was because I still didn't have a handle on my magic. My flames were just as unruly as yours when I started to learn how to wield them. Most fire demons take a while to learn how to control them. We learn the moment we're able to comprehend our magic. That's how we're raised. Your world is different. You weren't raised to control magic. I'm not surprised that you're struggling."

She reached out, taking my hand. I hadn't realized I was picking at my fingers repeatedly until she steadied my hands.

"You'll conquer this," she said, her piercing eyes set on me.

I tried to calm the anxiety I felt weighing heavy on my

chest, letting the cold water distract me. Silva let me sit in silence for a few moments before coaxing me from the waves.

After emerging from the water, we kept trying for what felt like another hour, but I barely made any progress. The princess was patient with me, but I could tell she was starting to feel hopeless. The longer we went on, the more evident it became that my power wasn't a simple fix. As much as I tried to find balance, there was only one feeling that consumed me and fueled my fire.

The anxiety that had played me all my life wouldn't release its claws. Panic, nerves, and obsessions all fueled my flames and made them impossible to control. Every attempt only made it worse. I needed calm. I needed confidence, and most importantly, balance.

I had at least learned new techniques and had walked through the motions of controlling my magic, but I still had a long way to go until progress was made. It brought me a small comfort to know everyone in Fuerya went through something similar if they had fire magic. Coming to this region, I had been unsure and doubtful, but now, I was thankful for another friend to walk me through this. In my short time knowing the princess, I felt comforted that she had been so willing to help.

"It will take time. Magic isn't something you learn overnight," Silva said, trying to comfort me. I let out a sigh, dropping my hands to my side. We had been walking through the circular movements again.

"Yes, but is it wrong that I just want to figure it out now? What does that make me?" I asked, feeling defeated.

"I'd say that makes you pretty normal. Witch or not, everyone feels frustrated with magic at some point. I'm not surprised you just want to figure this out. I see the hesitation and holding back every time you call your flames to life. I know what it's like not being able to use your power or feeling like you have to hide it. I am the only female ruler. If I am to survive, I can't show all my cards at once," she said with a sympathetic look.

I understood what she meant. My own world had similar problems with treating women like they were less than others. I'd been fighting to escape the grasp of a man for a long time. My own father had used his control over me to make me feel powerless and weak. No one questioned the way he treated me. I understood exactly what she meant.

"Let's try again," I said, feeling the motivation slowly coming back. I focused and tried to breathe, counting my breaths in my typical rhythmic pattern. With each deep inhale and exhale, I felt myself calming. I envisioned the flames slowly growing to life in the palms of my hands.

I needed to start small before I could grow them large and control them the way the princess could. They grew and grew until I was holding a small fire within my hands.

I settled for that.

Seeing the flames flickering but not growing any larger brought me peace. This was a small step, but a step in the right direction; it would take time, but I knew I could work to grow my magic.

The princess smiled, watching me finally get the hang of calling upon my flames.

"I knew you could do it. It'll just take time. I know the

next time I see you, you'll have mastered it." Her tone shifted to a more hopeful one.

Before I could attempt to take it any further a feeling of panic hit me. I was stunned, the fire extinguishing. I'd been sure I'd mastered my anxiety, that I had everything under control. The more it tugged at my heart, the more unfamiliar it felt. It was like the anxiety was not my own, and the growing feeling of panic came from somewhere else. I felt that same thread leading me to Jax tugging at me. The thread felt taut, like it could snap at any moment. It was like I knew something was wrong without being there.

"We have to go back," I said frantically.

The princess narrowed her eyes, crossing her arms. She tilted her head, studying me.

"You just got the hang of this, so why now? You can't already be doubting yourself. You took such a big step," she said.

I realized she thought I was having doubts and trying to escape the inevitable destruction by flames. I pushed again, trying to make my way across the sand to the gate.

"Something's wrong," I said insistently. "Something's wrong with Jax. Please. We have to go back."

I couldn't tell her exactly what was wrong or why I had the feeling, but in my heart, I knew that going back was right. What was necessary. The princess hesitated, waiting for me to explain, but I didn't have any more words to convince her.

She sighed, finally giving in and following me across the small beach. I had sand stuck to my bare feet and dress, which only fueled the unease I felt. I wanted to wash the feeling from my body. I clenched my fists and tried to push forward, ignoring the nagging compulsion.

I followed Silva as she made her way past me and through the gate, heading back in the direction of the palace we came from. My steps grew in speed as we made her way back to the ballroom. As we approached, the entire atmosphere changed inside the palace. I felt Silva tense next to me, and I knew she could feel it too.

"He's here," she hissed. Before I could ask who she meant, she stormed into the ballroom.

Flames fell off her back as she lit with fury. It was like she wore a cape of fire and embers trailed behind her.

In the center of the ballroom, two figures stood with their backs to us, all the attendees watching. None of the guests moved. I recognized one of the demons as Jax, and my heart sunk as I finally saw the face of the other as I moved closer.

"We've been waiting for you," Vileer drawled. I heard Jax let out a low growl.

"Why are you here? You're not welcome," Silva said.

"I heard you were hosting a ball and was hurt when I never received my invitation. I thought we were beyond petty games," he answered, his voice like scraping stone.

"You know you are never welcome here. Leave," she demanded.

I held my breath, knowing I was the reason he was here. I needed help, and I needed to get away from these people. They already hated me enough. I couldn't allow Vileer to hold any type of power.

I stepped forward. "I'll go with you. Leave them alone."

I swallowed hard, waiting for his answer.

The black suit he had been wearing slowly shifted into a deep purple tunic. I still wasn't used to seeing his illusions. It was hard to tell what was real and what was not when he was around.

A silver crown formed atop his head, and his body had an ethereal glow to it. He looked like a god, a being not meant for this world.

Silence spread across the room and Vileer stared me down, speckles of black creeping into my vision. With all eyes in the room on me and the prospect of having to leave, I wanted to shrivel up into a ball. I tried to breathe through it, but it was useless. The obsession had already taken hold, and there was no getting rid of it.

Shadows crept in from the corners. I heard a hissing sound and found multiple serpents slithering from the edges of the room, surrounding us. Vileer glanced around with a smirk, taking in the king's show of power.

"I'm not here to collect you, not yet. I truly meant what I said. I was hurt by the lack of invitation to this gathering. I wanted to see you and what all the fuss was about. But now that I'm here, I realize this event is no place for me. We'll be seeing each other soon," he said, locking eyes with me before vanishing. The moment he did, Jax's shadows and serpents did as well.

My eyes widened and I searched the room for him, but he was already gone. It was the same magic he used the day he dropped me at the front gates of the Serpentine Palace, an illusion to make himself invisible.

By the way the atmosphere settled and those attending

relaxed, I suspected he'd truly left. He had nothing to gain by standing around if he wasn't there to collect his bargain.

"Why didn't he take me?" I asked, walking to Jax's side.

"He's playing games. It's what he loves to do. He thrives on the chaos of it all," Jax explained.

Dread filled every inch of my body realizing Vileer could continue to play these games until he decided it was time to make good of our bargain. His manipulation was working. Already, it was all that consumed my mind. I needed to find a way to release myself before that day came.

Jax read my mind. "Do you know a way to get her out of this bargain?" he asked, looking to his old friend.

I held out my arm, turning it to expose the crescent moon. The princess gasped, unable to stop herself.

"If you made the bargain, there's no way out of it. Death is the only escape from a bargain like that," she said, dread flashing in her eyes.

"That's what I feared," Jax said, his tone darkening.

I could feel how tense he was just by standing close to him. The thought of Vileer using the bargain was wearing on him. I couldn't tell if it was because he didn't want to lose me, or because he didn't want Vileer to have a way to manipulate the throne. I was too afraid to ask and have that answer destroy me.

"I think this ball is over," the princess said, loud enough for the other attendees to hear.

Demons scattered from the room, leaving by the princess' orders. I turned, finding Jax's hand held out for me.

Passing by Silva, I whispered a soft thanks for everything she had done for me. I knew this wouldn't be the end of our friendship, and I prayed that the next time I saw her, I would finally have control over my magic. I missed Marielle and having a friend around. I saw bits of my own old friend in Silva. Once things settled, I would make an effort to travel to Fuerya once again.

CHAPTER

TWENTY-EIGHT

I followed Jax through the maze of halls until we found our room. Entering, Jax still held my hand and lead us to the bed. He quickly jumped into it, laying back and putting both hands behind his head. He stared at the ceiling, and I wondered where his mind had gone. I crawled into bed beside him, tucking myself into his side. My head settled on his chest, and I felt the rise and fall with each breath he took.

"Why do you smell like the sea?" He suddenly propped himself up, a smile curling his lips.

I almost forgot. "My magic got out of control a few times, and we had to douse me in the sea," I admitted, my cheeks burning bright red.

He placed a gentle kiss on my head. "That just won't do. There's no way I can sleep next to you when you smell like you've been swimming in the sea. I suppose we'll just have to use that large bath I saw," he said in a teasing voice.

Before I could protest, he scooped me into his arms and

250

carried me to the bathing chambers. I found the large tub he had referred to sitting in the far corner of the room. It was white and porcelain, big enough to fit me and the demon king inside. It was circular with two steps leading up to get into it. A small edge had been built around it to hold various bottles of oils and soaps. Jax placed me down and drew the water, and I watched steam rise as the tub filled.

My toes curled standing on the cold tile floor.

"I suppose that's the one thing we can count on here. In the region of fire, there's always heat," I said jokingly, aching to be in the warm water.

A genuine chuckle left Jax. He was already beginning to peel off his clothing, dropping them to the tiled floor. I pulled off the straps of my dress, letting it drop to the floor, only my undergarments remaining.

Jax turned me around so my back was to him. He slowly undid the bra I wore, and as he unclasped it, the garment dropped to the floor. Slowly, pulling back, he knelt, sliding off the lace underwear. He exposed my bare skin, and I felt both his hands cup the cheeks of my ass.

I moaned in response, recognizing his hands were all too close to the place I wished he'd put them instead. I moved to climb the stairs to the bathtub, leaving Jax's on his knees before me. I could feel his hungry gaze follow me up those two steps. I climbed over the edge and into the warm, soothing water.

The moment I sunk into it, I felt all tension in my body slipping away. I turned to find Jax following behind me up the steps. He shed the last layers of clothing, and I tried and shamelessly failed at not letting my eyes wander, following that trail of hair that led straight down to his cock.

I moved over in the tub to make room for his large frame as he sunk under the water. He grabbed a bottle nearby on the ledge and poured a light blue liquid into the water. It immediately bubbled, covering the surface.

Under the water, Jax's hands immediately found my body. He gently guided me to sit in front of him in the tub.

He placed the other bottle down and reached for a new one on the ledge containing an oil. He opened it, placing some in the palm of his hand. Placing the bottle back on the ledge, he turned his attention to me. I felt his strong hands grip my shoulders, and he began to massage. I let out a deep moan, tilting my head back. The squeeze that followed applied pressure to my tense muscles and elicited a new sense of comfort. His hands dipped under the surface of the water and continued to massage my back. His thumbs dug in, working at the knots in my muscles.

I hadn't realized how tense and sore I'd been from two days of training my magic. It hadn't felt like strenuous work in the moment, but I could tell it had taken a toll on my body.

"Do you ever think of home?" Jax asked suddenly.

I thought about my answer. It wasn't as simple as yes or no. I tried not to let my mind wander, knowing I could never go back. Sometimes, I found myself thinking about the parts of it I missed.

"Yes. It hasn't been that long, and the wound of leaving still hurts," I answered. The demon king sighed.

"I'm sorry. I know leaving that world behind could not have been an easy choice," he answered.

"Choosing you has always been an easy choice," I countered.

"I'll find a way to break it," Jax said.

I let my head fall back into his chest.

"The bargain can't be broken except for death," I said. "Even you can't cheat death."

Shadows swirled across the surface, and I felt the king stiffen.

"I meant the tethering of your soul to this realm. I'll find a way so you can visit without worry. I don't want you to have to leave your home behind forever," he said, his voice breaking.

I knew if I turned around, I'd find the same worried look he always had when it came to matters of my happiness. I'd come to memorize every inch of his face, the way his brows furrowed when he was worried or the way his right side of his lips curled up a little more when he smiled.

"You are my home now. I don't need a physical place to feel like home. I just know this is where I'm supposed to be, and I know I'm supposed to be with you," I admitted.

I was too frightened to turn around. I didn't know what reaction he'd have, and I couldn't picture the look on his face.

"You are my home as well, little flame," he answered, his voice soft. I felt his strong arms wrap around my naked body, his head nuzzling into my neck and his teeth nipping at my exposed skin. "Now, relax and let me soak in this moment of peace with you before we return to reality tomorrow."

THE NEXT MORNING, I found myself wrapped in the king's arms. We had been far too exhausted to focus on anything besides sleep after our bath together. The temptation to roll over and press my lips to his consumed me as I breathed in his scent and sank into the warmth of his body.

Jax was the first to move instead. I let out a sound of protest, but he quieted it with a quick kiss. Sweetness coated my lips, and I could still feel the way they delicately brushed my own when he pulled away.

The demon disappeared into the bathroom, and I wrapped myself in the comforter of the bed, wishing for another few minutes of sleep. I thought about the multiple times I had overslept or missed my alarm over the years. My father would turn beet red with anger after realizing I hadn't left the house on time. If I wasn't punctual, I wasn't to his standards. The thought drained me, and I could feel my face pale.

I tried to shove it aside.

A few minutes passed before Jax reappeared. I frowned, realizing something was different. He was still the same demon king, but something was off.

"You shaved?" I asked, noticing the lack of stubble across his chin.

"Do you not like it?" Jax asked, wrinkles creasing his forehead. His hand slid behind his head, scratching his dark hair.

"I do. It's just-" I paused, tilting my head. "Unexpected."

He laughed. "You didn't expect demons to shave?" he asked.

"It just seems so human," I offered. "I hadn't thought about it."

"And you thought you were human your whole life, but you are actually a witch," he countered.

"I suppose you're right," I chuckled. "Nothing is how it seems."

The illusions woven by Vileer at the ball had proven the sentiment the night prior. Nothing in this world was how it seemed. Plants could kill someone in a second, illusions brought demon's nightmares to life, and creatures of my dreams turned out to be real.

I slid out of the comfort of the bed and found a new set of clothing waiting for me on a nearby table. It was a simple set of riding pants and a white blouse.

"Silva?" I asked, eyeing the new outfit.

"Who else?" Jax asked, grinning.

I tried to hide my smile but failed, appreciating my newfound friendship with the princess. I knew it meant a great deal to Jax to have us become acquainted. The pair had become close over the years, and she was an important piece of his life. If I was in Eodratera to stay, then it was important to make an effort to know the demons closest to Jax.

That included Drakor.

The moment we returned, I would try harder to get to know the demon who Jax trusted fully. After hearing Jax's story about Seri, I knew it meant more than he was saying for me to give Drakor a chance. He wasn't just a loyal subject; he had become almost the only family Jax had left.

"Tell me about your mother," I suddenly blurted. I knew

she lived in the realm, but Jax had been secretive about her from the moment I arrived.

"It's better if I don't," he answered darkly. His back was to me, and I watched his shoulders stiffen.

"I'm sorry. It was foolish-"

"It wasn't, little flame. I just can't, or I risk her safety," he said, turning to face me. The sincere concern in his eyes and defeated sigh he let out made my heart ache for him. To have a parent who loved you but couldn't be with you was a pain I knew too well.

I twisted a ring on my finger, waiting for him to continue.

"If I could, I would tell you everything about her, but these walls have ears. You saw the illusion magic Vileer has. If anyone was to use similar magic, they could easily spy and learn secrets I have held close to my heart for years. Anyone can change their appearance or pretend to be something they aren't, and that isn't a risk I am willing to take. She is the last living relative I have left. Vileer knows this, knows I would do anything to protect her, including giving up my crown. It is the reason I work so hard to keep my palace free from traitors and spies."

I nodded slowly, listening to every word he said. The tumultuous politics of Eodratera made it impossible to feel secure on the throne. Power decided everything, and one show of weakness could lead to Jax's downfall.

The clothing Silva left for me fit perfectly, and I quietly slipped on a pair of boots sitting beside the table. With the laces tied, the shoes were snug.

"I'm sorry," I whispered under my breath.

"For what?" Jax asked, grabbing a leather jacket behind the chair pushed against the table. Instead of wrapping it around himself, he wrapped it around me.

"For pushing about your mother. I didn't think before asking," I admitted, keeping my eyes glued to the floor, my loose red curls hanging in front of my shoulders.

"I love that you want to know more about her, and it breaks my heart that I can't share that part of my life with you, but I promise—someday, I will tell you everything. For now, do you trust me?" he asked.

"Of course I trust you," I answered without hesitation.

"Good. Now, let's go home, little flame," he said, gathering our belongings and ushering me out of the room.

TWENTY-NINE

Another week came and went when we arrived back to Gildhor. Jax had disappeared most of the time dealing with the politics of the realm and the aftermath of Vileer showing up to the ball. The palace was still trying to root out traitors and spies, ensuring Vileer had no advantage over the crown. I could feel the tension hanging in the air each day. The guards worked day and night, questioning anyone who acted out of the ordinary.

Seven days passed before I was finally able to spend significant time with the king again. We sat at the same dining table as the first night, Drakor and Althea seated as well. Jax had called us together for a meal, an opportunity for me to become closer with his two most trusted subjects.

"Vileer will not show his face here. He likes to play games, but he cannot be that bold," Drakor insisted.

"You didn't see the look on his face. He took pleasure in watching how the bargain made Soleil writhe. He knows the power he holds over me now. We cannot stop him from coming to fulfill the bargain, or we risk Soleil's life," Jax explained for the hundredth time.

I was growing tired of hearing them play over the bargain that weighed on me. Althea picked at a slab of meat on her plate, pretending to be uninterested in the conversation, but I could tell she was soaking in every word.

"And you are sure there is no way out of it? Have you checked the old scrolls in the library or spoken with your mother?" Drakor prodded.

Jax's gaze snapped to the demon, and the dark gleam in his eyes had me sinking further into my seat. I felt invisible listening to them argue over my own fate.

"I have read every last scroll in that library, and there is nothing. You know I cannot discuss this matter with my mother," Jax growled.

I tapped my fingers against the table. Each time they connected with the wood, I felt a bit of my anxiety fade. It was all I could do to stop myself from screaming. I was slowly losing my composure, and the more they droned on about me, the more I wanted to shout back. Arguing was doing no good, though, and the more time we wasted wondering about impossible solutions, the less time I had to savor with Jax.

"Enough," I huffed under my breath, rolling my eyes. "I'm sitting right here."

"Sorry," Drakor said softly, and I returned a grateful smile.

His demeanor shifted, and I watched him squirm in his seat after expecting some snide comment. I was genuinely trying with him, and each day, I could feel myself warming to his presence. Again, I caught that shadow of darkness flicker across his eyes.

He quickly looked away.

"You are just lucky Vileer didn't decide to invoke the bargain that day," Drakor said to Jax. "At least you bought yourself more time before he comes."

"I am lucky Soleil came back when she did. I was ready to go to war in that ballroom. The sight of her was the only thing that contained my shadows and serpents."

Jax leaned forward with his elbows on the table. He folded his hands and turned to me.

"How did you know to come back?" he asked, tilting his head. It was the first we had discussed what had happened. I hadn't told him about the urge to return to him or the foreign anxiety that plagued me, but suddenly, the words were pouring from my lips.

Everyone sat quietly as I explained. Feelings that weren't my own plagued me, the thread I constantly felt tugging me back to the king, the feeling like my own body was acting against me and pushing me in his direction. The entire possibility sounded like the tales of mad men. It reminded me of the way my father used to ramble about the dangers of the world and monsters who walked our streets.

When I finished, Jax just stared at me, and I felt like I may combust.

"I think your magic is fated," Althea said, breaking the silence. Both of our heads whipped to look at her.

"What?" Jax asked.

She coughed into her sleeve before clearing her throat to

continue. I reached for a pitcher of water nearest to me, but she held up a hand and shook her head.

"Your magic is intertwined. It is rare, but it does happen to witches. Since you both are half-blooded witches, I suppose it is possible. Your magic will always call to each other, will always find each other," Althea explained.

"Is that why I always felt that thread leading me back to him?" I asked, sitting forward in my chair.

The stronger my magic became and the more I learned to control it, the stronger the tug on that thread felt. I'd noticed it more and more the longer I stayed in Eodratera. I remained silent, waiting for the answers I sought.

I wished Jax would say something to let me know what he was thinking. It was hard to tell if he was upset by the news. I wouldn't have wanted my magic tethered to me either.

"Yes, the two of you are destined to be together. A magical bond like this cannot be broken. Your magics are a perfect complement to each other, the same way the pair of you are."

"Like soulmates?" I asked, my voice raising a bit higher.

"You could say that," she confirmed.

"Does the demon community accept this sort of bond?" Jax asked, finally speaking. I saw his brow raise as he waited for an answer.

"It would be hard for any of them, including the other rulers, to argue against it. I suppose they may not like it, but they cannot change the laws of magic," Althea explained.

Jax's golden eyes settled on me, and I felt the intense

heat of his gaze. My cheeks turned a shade of pink, and I let my eyes fall back to my plate of food I had barely picked at.

"I'll leave you two," Althea said, rising from her seat and turning to exit the room, realizing we needed space. Drakor followed closely behind, and the door shut behind them.

I stood from my chair, walking over to Jax, waiting in silence, watching the demon king.

Jax was quiet, his eyes glued to the floor. I took a hesitant step forward, afraid he would push me away. I wasn't sure my heart could handle the denial. I came all this way to find him, and if he turned me away now, I would finally shatter. It would be the final straw. I knew there'd be no coming back from the heartache.

"Please, say something," I said, my voice a measly whisper. I barely had the strength to get the words out.

Jax's eyes lifted and settled on me. He pushed back his chair, standing, and took a step, closing the distance between us. I held my breath as I waited, my mind racing and my anxiety growing. I felt my fingers moving like a puppet master was controlling them. I couldn't stop myself, and the tapping began, over and over, awaiting the answer.

"I do not need magic to tell me my heart is yours," he said. My stomach exploded in little butterflies as I realized the weight of his words. He was giving himself fully to me, admitting what I had prayed to be true.

"My heart is only full of you, little flame," he breathed.

Jax pinned me against the door, the wood shuddering against our weight. I ground my hips against him, my core aching. I wanted more.

I demanded more.

Jax held out a hand and let little swirls of his magic form. Shadows danced in his palm. Instinctively, I held out my own hand. Little embers immediately formed and grew into a small fire.

The flame leapt for Jax's hand, and I closed my palm quickly, extinguishing the fire.

"No, let it happen," Jax said, using his free hand to open my own once more.

I let my fingers unclench and tried again. The flame grew and leaned toward Jax, and I watched breathlessly as my flame intertwined with his shadows. The pair danced and swirled, moving in sync. Our magic balanced and worked in harmony. I stared at the display, stunned.

Jax closed his hand slowly, the shadows disappearing, and found my gaze. I let my fire go out and placed a hand on his chest, running down his torso toward his waistline.

My hands reached for his belt, fumbling with it and finally guiding it from his pants, allowing me access, exposing his large cock. He was already hard and waiting for me.

Pounding sounded against the door, and I startled. I moved away from the door just in time for another thunderous knock to sound.

"Ignore them," Jax said, kissing me. My body arched into his touch, and a slight moan escaped my lips. I wanted more.

Another knock.

A low growl left Jax as his eyes narrowed on the door.

"I will tear them limb from limb for interrupting us," he said through bared teeth. "What is so important you would disrupt your king?" he demanded, flinging the door open without a single regard for the clothing he'd lost. I hurried to fix the strap of my top, pulling it back up to my shoulder.

"I—" the demon hesitated, sinking into himself. "I'm sorry, Your Majesty. We found a traitor," he explained, lowering his head and refusing to lift his eyes to Jax.

"Where?" was all Jax asked.

"They are awaiting your orders and keeping the prisoner in the dungeons," he answered. "She isn't talking."

"You are dismissed. Tell my guards to bring the traitor to the throne room, and I will be there soon," he said.

CHAPTER

THIRTY

I could feel the tension in the air as Jax paced. His distress was pouring out of him, filling the bedroom, suffocating us. I wrapped the comforter around me at the edge of the bed, holding the blanket like a shield. I kept my own anxieties barricaded, preventing them from adding fuel to the king's fire.

It was an impossible choice. The demon had given him no other option, but I had seen the moment of hesitation, the second where Jax paused.

Immediately after the guard left, Jax stormed back to his chambers. I followed, trying to keep up, waiting for him to say something, but it never came. Since moment we'd stepped into the room, he hadn't stopped pacing.

I sat patiently on the bed, hoping he would talk to me. There were no words to comfort him in a choice with such drastic consequences.

The palace was strict with traitors and spies; there was

no room for forgiveness. If Jax wished to protect his people, the sentence for such a crime was death.

There had not been a single execution committed for any of Vileer's spies. They always slipped free before they were caught, and never once had the palace come this close to capturing one.

"I can't do it," Jax said. "I can't kill her. How can I kill someone for following orders? What if she has a family?" His palms were held out as he continued to pace. His eyes never left them, like he already had blood on his hands.

"You are protecting your people," I offered quietly. There wasn't a single thing I could say that would make him feel any more secure in his decision.

"I have to protect them and this realm from him," Jax said, growing antsier.

I knew he meant Vileer, the one demon who could destroy all seven regions.

"I'll be here regardless of the choice you make," I said, trying to comfort him.

"But there is no choice," Jax countered. "I am damned no matter what. I have to get information from this spy, and I cannot let them return to Vileer. The choice is already made."

His own father had been taken from him too soon by a spy who went unnoticed behind palace walls. If Jax didn't put an end to the threat, it could be anyone's life next—Drakor, himself, myself, the list went on.

I stood, and the comforter fell behind me. With Jax before me, I grabbed his hand and pressed a kiss to it.

"I will be here every step of it," I promised.

"You will stay here," he said, his eyes darkening. "You will not leave this room until I return."

I opened my mouth to argue, but he stopped me.

"I can't have you there, Soleil. It's too risky, having the spy know about you and see you here. I don't want to give Vileer any more reason to come for the bargain. If I can't do it, and the spy escapes with their life tonight, I do not want them to know about you."

I nodded frustrated, but I knew his heart was in the right place. I wanted to be there in that moment for him. Nothing he did would ever sway how I felt about him, and I needed him to realize that. I knew part of his hesitation was fear that I would see him as some monster.

"I'll be back soon," he said, walking out of the chambers and leaving me to reel through my own thoughts and anxieties.

I COULD HEAR the tortured screams from Jax's room as they rang through the palace from the throne room. Part of me wanted to jump out of bed and find the source of the tortured yells, but the other part of me was afraid. I was afraid of what I might find, afraid of what I might witness.

Jax asked me to stay, and I promised I would; if I wandered the halls, I'd be breaking that promise. I hated to disappoint him.

Screams rang out again through the halls, and curiosity got the better of me. Pushing back the covers, I jumped out of bed and made my way to the door. It easily pushed open, and I stepped slowly into the hall.

Another yell; the demon's cries were hard for me to listen to. I wished it didn't need to be this way. I knew Jax was just trying to keep his kingdom and his subjects safe, but it felt wrong to torture information from this person. I knew that if there had been another way, he would've chosen it, but without this information, without knowing who this demon was loyal to, the people within these walls would never be safe.

I saw the door was cracked, and I pressed against the cold wall to peek my head in slowly. My heart thundered in my chest, and I had to glance around to ensure it wasn't truly loud enough for someone to hear.

Looking through the crack, my vision was obscured a bit, but I could still make out the scene. On their knees, blood splattered on the floor, the prisoner let out a defeated cough. I spotted two large serpents in front of the demon, one on each side of Jax. His obsidian crown was tilted on his head, his fists clenched, and I could see the look of pain in his eyes.

"Tell us who sent you, who gave you the order to not be near the gates," Jax said.

"I will never help you, half breed," the demon choked, her words strained.

"You already admitted you were told to ensure the gates were cleared the day he brought her here. How did he communicate with you? We already know it's Vileer; all I need you to do is confirm it. Are you willing to give your life for someone who will not save you? He knew what your punishment would be if you were caught."

I held my breath, waiting for the demon to answer.

Just as quickly the serpent lunged, its fangs bared, it bit into the demon's skin, drawing more blood and then recoiling. The other serpent circled the demon, lunging for her back and sinking its fangs in. Another loud cry rang out from the demon as she fell forward, her hands slamming into the ground. The demon was on all fours, and I could see her heaving, her breaths shaky. Blood dripped from multiple wounds, covering her body. I tried to open the door a little more to get a better view, but it was hard without alerting the rest of the room to my presence.

"You knew the rules when you took an oath to work in this palace," Jax said. "You knew what consequences for being a traitor. I cannot have traitors within my walls, and I cannot have traitors within this room." The demon lifted her head to meet Jax's gaze.

"When the time is right, he will take everything you love," she growled, her dark hair now slick with blood. Before another word could be uttered, Jax flicked his wrist again.

One of the serpents lunged at the demon, sinking its fangs into her neck before it pulled back, taking a patch of the demon's skin with it. The demon fell forward, dead before she even hit the floor. I stumbled in shock, losing my balance and pushing the door open.

The agony on Jax's face broke my heart.

I could see he so desperately didn't want me to see that side of him. I opened my mouth, but nothing came out. The demon still lay dead on the floor.

One, two, three, four.

I started counting in my head. It was the only response that made sense to me. Glancing down at my hands, I felt as though the blood was on my own hands. I suddenly felt the urge to wash my hands, to rid myself of the spilled blood I had witnessed.

"Clean this up," Jax demanded of one of his subjects standing nearby.

He went to take a step toward me, but I backed away. I wasn't afraid of the demon king, and I knew this is what needed to be done, but still, instinct took over, and I needed to distance myself.

Another demon rushed to me. I barely had time to react before Drakor ushered me away.

"Let's get you back to your room," he said gently.

"Thank you," I whispered, afraid my voice would break.

I never should've left the room like Jax warned. If I hadn't, I never would have created the mess I found myself in. My stomach sunk knowing the disappointment Jax would carry.

Drakor brought me back to my room, and I waited for what felt like forever for the demon king to return.

I LISTENED to the crackling fire, my eyes growing heavy the longer I waited for Jax to return. Sleep wanted to claim me, but I fought it. I'd started a fire using my own magic. It was small, but it was a start.

I needed to be awake when he finally returned. He'd need

me. I could tell by the way this task seemed to weigh on him, made his shoulders physically cave in.

When I returned to the room, I had washed my hands repeatedly until the thought of the demon's dead body no longer plagued my mind.

It took another hour before I heard the faint footsteps approaching. Sitting up, I waited for the sound of the door creaking open.

"Jax?" I called out, afraid that I'd been wrong when he didn't immediately appear.

A second later, his large frame appeared from the short hall. He walked slowly to the bed and sat beside me, his head falling into his hands. His entire body looked defeated. His shoulders sunk inward, and I could feel his tension.

"I'm sorry," I said before he could say anything. "I never should have left the room."

"No, I'm sorry," Jax answered, shaking his head. "I did the one thing I swore I would never do after hearing your past. I took away your freedom. I had no right to demand you stay here," Jax said.

"You were trying to protect me," I said.

"I was being selfish," he answered. His head lifted, and his golden eyes found mine. "You have freedom here. Do not let anyone take that from you again, not even me."

I nodded slowly, and we sat in silence for a few minutes, neither of us wanting to discuss what had occurred in the throne room.

"Are you alright?" Jax asked, breaking the silence.

"I'm terrified," I admitted. "Most the demons want to see me dead and would gladly do the deed themselves." I shuddered at the thought, remembering the first demon I'd encountered and imagining the others dwelling in the shadowy corners of the kingdom. "And now, there are spies who want you dead as well, and they are loyal to the one person I owe a bargain to. I am terrified every day that he will show up to claim it."

"Come here, little flame," he said, drawing me in close.

His sheets swallowed us as I nestled against him. His heart pounded in my ear, and his strong arms held me close.

"I won't let any harm come to you," he whispered. "You are safe here."

At those words, I settled into the bed with the king. Mr. Finkel hopped up, seemingly appearing from thin air. The three of us cuddled in together under the soft comforter as I let sleep consume me.

CHAPTER

THIRTY-ONE

The more time I spent with Althea, the less I noticed her nagging cough. I swore, each day, she seemed to grow stronger, the magic she was teaching me more powerful. I'd noticed the cough since our first lesson but had never wanted to pry.

It was already an hour into our lesson, and not once had it bothered her.

"Keep that form," she scolded as I dropped my arms.

I swore in another life she must've been a doting mother; the way she spoke and instructed me reminded me of my own.

"My arms are killing me," I complained, shaking them out before lifting them again.

"Do you think your flames care if you're sore? The moment you show weakness, they will seize control."

She was right. I hated feeling weak, yet the way my muscles were shaking made me question whether it was all worth it.

"Again," she said, raising her own hands to match my stance.

She moved her hands in a circular motion like Silva had taught me. Instead of fire, her magic formed into a vortex of air. It was the first time I had witnessed her call upon the element. I'd seen her tame my flames during our lessons and grow vegetation with the flick of a hand, but I'd never seen her manipulate water or use any type of other magic.

A breeze blew strands of my hair away from my face, and I scowled as I spotted Althea directing some of the air toward me.

"Focus," she chided.

I settled into my stance, spreading my feet slightly and raising my hands. I let my mind focus on the magic flowing through me and called it to the surface. The familiarity of my magic was becoming more apparent each time I practiced. It was second nature for me to summon my flames.

I still had little control over the other elements and my fire was unruly, but it was progress I never expected I would see.

Althea set up targets in the private courtyard we were training in. Each target was made of metal and shaped into circles. They reminded me of the targets an archer would shoot arrows at, except instead of arrows, I was using flames and any other magic I could muster.

The first target I aimed at, I missed. The tips of my fingers tingled with anticipation of the next ball of fire I'd throw. Each one felt powerful but unruly. Even with control over my flames, my manipulation of the flames was still limited.

I cursed under my breath when I missed the target a

fourth time. The continual failure started to poke holes in my confidence.

"I'm never going to get this," I growled, letting my flames go out.

"You will; you just need to be patient," Althea encouraged me, again sounding like a caring mother.

"My mother should've been the one teaching me this," I said in a moment of pure anger.

I knew the words and frustration were misplaced.

One, two, three, four.

I counted the targets in my head, switching my gaze between each one. The repetitive act brought me no more comfort, and I tried to stop myself but couldn't. Each time I did, it felt like my chest may explode. The intense pressure and crippling anxiety forced me to continue.

"Soleil," Althea said, seeing the mental decline.

"I just can't move past it," I admitted. "I want to so badly, and somehow, I can't."

"No one expects you to," she said gently.

I collapsed to my knees, the weight of expectations I had held for myself crashing down on me. The expectation to learn magic, to be a perfect daughter, to fit into a world filled with demons who wished me dead...it was all too much.

"Your mother may have had her reasons for leaving. There are many forces of magic we cannot control, even as witches," Althea offered.

"Still, I don't understand why she never told me," I argued. It was like a war was being waged in my head.

One moment, I felt I finally understood and could truly forgive her, and the next, that small little voice inside crept back in, making me doubt everything. Why hadn't she just explained? Why didn't she bring me along? If she went back to her coven, did she not want me there?

Every insecurity and piece of self-doubt tore me apart from the inside out.

"Enough of that," Althea scolded. "I can see where you're headed, and it's not a place you want to go."

I sighed, pushing everything aside once again. It didn't matter how; my soul was stuck in this realm. This wasn't a place I ever imagined my mother would search for me. Maybe Serafeen would tell her. Maybe someday she'd come, but for now, that felt like a distant dream.

Althea wrapped her arms around me, holding me tightly. The gesture calmed my breathing, and finally, the numbers stopped playing on a loop in my head.

I stood back up, determined to do it for myself.

I knew I could hit the targets. I would stand there all day if I had to.

I brushed off the pants I was wearing, and when I couldn't get a spot out, I wished I could change into a new pair. The focus on the stain slowed me from re-focusing. I drew in a deep breath and tried to channel the feeling and fixation into my magic.

The spot could wait. I knew nothing would happen if I didn't change, but it didn't make it any easier.

My hands extended in front of me, and flames sprang to life, covering them entirely.

Footsteps sounded behind me, and I lost focus on my flames, letting them die out and finding Drakor behind me, arms crossed. He was studying us, and I scowled at him, not enjoying the way he was judging my progress. Over the weeks I'd spent in the palace, I'd come to tolerate Drakor.

One could even consider us friends, but I was still wary of him.

"Can I help you?" I asked, trying to sound as annoyed as possible.

"Can I not observe?" he asked, darkness flashing behind his eyes.

"Not if you aren't here to train," I shot back. I had yet to figure out what type of demon he was, and he hadn't once shown his own magic.

"I already told you: that's not something you want," he said, eyes narrowing. "I am not like your king, and I am certainly not like you, witch."

Somehow, the word witch felt like an insult when he said it. Fire rose inside me, and my fists turned to flames. I threw a ball of fire in his direction without warning, but at the last second, he side-stepped the attack. I threw another, watching as it tumbled past him.

"You will have to do better than that," he stated, barely acknowledging the two offenses I had sent his way. The nonchalant attitude infuriated me more.

One, two, three, four.

I sent continual flames in his direction, all of which he dodged. He was pushing me, forcing me to show my magic and my limits. Even with that knowledge, I continued. He moved quickly through the garden, and I followed closely behind him. Each opening I saw, I took the chance to send more flames in his direction.

None hit their target.

I growled, throwing them at a faster rate. Althea watched in disbelief, hands on her hips. Even with the disproving look on her face, she didn't intervene. This was my battle to fight.

Drakor and I had been back and forth in our attitudes toward each other. One moment, I felt he was trying to win me over, and the next, he wanted to spar with me. I didn't know what to believe anymore. Was he only tolerating my presence for Jax?

The dark hues of the plants surrounding us were a contrast to the vibrant energy pulsing through me. The air felt heavy, the tension building around us.

Flames erupted from my hands the faster I threw attacks at Drakor, casting an eerie glow throughout the garden.

Drakor was a blur of motion, moving impossibly fast and with precision. His steps predicted my attacks before I even knew where I'd aim. The game was becoming old, and I wanted to be done with it.

I felt toyed with.

"Enough," I shouted. "I thought you were supposed to be my ally in this place, someone I could trust."

"I am," he shrugged, dodging another attack.

"Then why provoke me?"

Drakor stayed silent, still pushing further into the garden.

Frustration bubbled in my chest with each missed attack. I gritted my teeth and pushed more power to the surface.

This time, instead of fire growing in my palms, the ground around us shook. I saw hesitation flash in Drakor's eyes before he trained his face again. A bead of sweat dripped down his dark brown skin, and I knew he was growing tired of my attacks.

I raised my hands and, in one motion, created vines from the ground. They grew impossibly fast, wrapping around Drakor.

He squirmed against them, but they grew tighter against his black t-shirt, his torso covered by vines snaking up his legs.

I stifled a laugh, afraid it would break my concentration.

"Release me," he demanded.

"No, not until you answer my questions," I shouted back. I was only feet away but remained firmly planted where I was.

I wanted answers to why he had provoked me and what game he was playing at.

That same darkness as always flashed in his eyes before the entire garden sunk into night.

My hands dropped to my side, and I glanced wildly around, unable to see. I was paralyzed; whether physically or in fear, I couldn't tell.

I shifted anxiously, waiting for someone to attack or end the nightmare.

It was only for a second, but I was consumed by complete darkness. A cold chill ran down my spine, and stress built up inside me. The feeling lasted for the blink of an eye, and then it was gone, along with the darkness.

When it receded, Drakor was no longer tangled in the vines. Instead, he was standing inches from me with his hand extended.

"Come with me," he said.

"Why?" I asked, not ready to take his hand.

"The King requested you," he explained.

My heart jumped at the mention of Jax. I'd barely seen him all day, and both my body and magic craved him. After using so much of my magic, I needed to be near him. His alone could replenish mine.

"And you needed to spar with me for that?" I asked skeptically, frowning.

"No, not necessarily," he answered, his own smile dipping. "But I felt it necessary."

I tilted my head, raising an expectant brow at him and waiting for him to elaborate.

He sighed. "The other rulers are here," he continued.

My heart sunk.

"And I wasn't about to take you straight to them without knowing if you could handle yourself in their presence. Believe it or not, I always have your protection in mind."

His eyes hit the ground, avoiding my gaze.

"I will not let the future queen die at their hands," he finished before hurrying off, leaving me to follow.

I had no time to process what that last bit meant.

CHAPTER

THIRTY-TWO

The meeting was being held in a room I had never been to, which required Drakor to escort me. I was shocked when Jax requested my presence for it, but I wasn't going to turn him down. All the other rulers had been summoned to the palace, and this was my chance to gain a glimpse into the rest of Eodratera.

I'd hurried to our shared room and changed out of my training outfit. Peeling back the layers stuck to my skin with sweat, I noticed I had burned small holes into the material in a few places. The wardrobe was still filled with exquisite dresses I had barely touched, a veritable rainbow of blacks, greys, and maroons.

I reached for a muted silver, almost grey dress. The neckline was lined with tiny black gems. The straps were thin and slid easily up to rest on my shoulders. The dress fell to the floor, stopping at the perfect length. Hair clung to my face from sweat, and I rushed to the bathroom to fix it.

"Hurry up in there," Drakor shouted from the hall,

waiting to escort me. He'd warned me of our limited time, but I doubted the king wished for me to show up a mess to this meeting.

"I'm hurrying," I muttered under my breath.

I splashed water on my face to wash away any remaining sweat. My hair the clung to my face before it was slicked back with water and I tied my hair back into a bun.

I noticed the fire had been left crackling, and I used my magic to extinguish it. Satisfaction flashed across my features before I turned to find Drakor.

We walked the halls together, and my nerves only grew in my stomach. I had a chance to talk to Drakor and finally put any unease between us aside. The idea of admitting my own faults only soured my stomach more.

"What are they like?" I asked, trying to make small talk.

"The other leaders?" he asked. I nodded and let him continue. "Each of them is different, a representative of their region. You've already met Silva and seen her fiery side, I am sure. The remaining rulers are similar, each fighting to keep their power."

"Have you met them all before?" I asked.

"Unfortunately," he answered, and I didn't push.

"Will Vileer be there?" I forced myself to ask.

"No," Drakor answered firmly. "Jax would never willingly invite him here and put you at risk like that."

The pounding of my heart slowed. At least that was one less problem to worry about for the day. It wasn't the end of my growing list of issues, but it was a start.

The mood inside the palace felt colder. The workers we passed were silent, keeping their heads down and barely acknowledging us. My head followed each of them when they passed. After the fourth, my heart race picked up.

"Seri would've loved you," Drakor said, breaking the silence.

"Huh?" I glanced to him.

"You're stubborn like him, strong-willed. I think you would've made good friends."

No one wanted to be compared to someone's last love, but somehow, I knew Drakor only meant well by the comment. This was his brother, and immense sadness filled me imaging the loss they'd faced.

"I wish I could've met him," I said with a warm smile. "I can tell Jax held a lot of love for him."

"They were inseparable until Vileer," Drakor growled.

I watched the sadness on his face shift into anger. I wanted to know what happened, but it felt intrusive to pry.

"He was attacked by Vileer's men on a trip to a village in this region. They killed him to appease their own ruler," Drakor snarled.

"How-"

"It's what I would want to know too," Drakor explained after reading my thoughts.

"He will pay someday," I said, anger boiling in my own chest. "He will pay, and he will never use this bargain." My hand ran along the tattooed mark on my arm.

"I won't let him take you from Jax," Drakor promised. "I cannot watch him lose the one he loves again."

I hadn't realized we made it to the meeting room until Drakor completely froze.

Outside the door to the meeting room, Jax waited for

me. He was dressed in finery, his crown of serpents placed on his head. Drakor bowed his head in respect, and Jax nodded.

"My flame," he said, greeting me.

Drakor shifted uncomfortably before clearing his throat.

"I'll be inside," he said quietly and hurried off.

"Are you ever going to tell me what you are?" I asked as he passed me, unable to shake the feeling of darkness from the garden still.

"Maybe someday," he answered.

Jax waited to speak for Drakor to disappear behind the wooden door behind him. I took his hand, noticing the worried look on his face.

"What is it?" I asked.

"There's something I need to ask you before we go in there," he answered.

Nausea took over, and I bit the inside of my cheek to hold back a wave of sickness. The unknown plus the unease on Jax's face brought me no comfort.

"Yes?" I asked, giving his hand a light squeeze for reassurance.

"I want you to rule by my side in this kingdom."

A laugh almost escaped me before I realized how serious he was. I was no ruler. I'd barely been able to fight for myself. What made him think I could fight for his people, be the one to protect them?

"I—"

"Before you deny me, please hear me out," Jax said. "You have been here for a few months, and already, the demons within the walls of this palace have warmed to the idea of you being here. You walk freely through the halls unbothered, and there are no longer threats to your life."

It was true. Since I had arrived, Jax, Drakor, and Althea had worked tirelessly to convince the palace staff to accept my presence. It hadn't taken long, and after a few months, even Kasius started treating me with respect.

"If the Serpentine Palace can see you for who you are, so can the rest of Eodratera. I am no fool; I know it will take time, but they will come to love you the way I do. There is no one else meant to rule by my side."

"You're just saying this because of our magic," I said, my cheeks turning red.

"No, little flame. Our magic makes our rule that much stronger, but it is not your magic that would make you the ruler this kingdom needs. It is your kindness and compassion for others, and most of all, it is your determination and bravery. I can only aspire to rule with the same traits. Please, little flame, I know this is a lot to take in, but I would love if you walked into that room by my side. The choice is yours. You can walk away now, and I will love you no less, or you can take my hand and trust me."

I paused, watching him reach out his hand. My eyes were glued to his calloused palm, my mind reeling. Everything inside me shouted to run, to turn and never look back. Being a ruler and leading a kingdom were not skills I had. I'd barely escaped the confines of my bedroom; I wouldn't know what was best for an entire realm.

There was another part of me, the one that embraced my magic and took the leap of tethering my soul to Eodratera, that fought away the insecurities. If I could push myself to accomplish so much in such a short time, why couldn't I push myself to do this one thing? It would take time for me to learn and convince the realm, but the tough work would be worth it in the end.

I didn't say a single word to Jax. Instead, I took his hand with a firm nod.

He pushed open the wooden door before leading me inside.

The meeting room was spacious enough, holding a large circular table, four other rulers seated around it. An empty seat remained where Vileer's place would've been. Drakor remained in the corner, watchful.

"Why are we here?" a short demon with skin as dark as night asked. His brows were furrowed, and his face appeared to be stuck in perpetual frown. I recognized him as Prince Svelk, ruler of the region of darkness, Drazmin.

"You are here because I summoned you," Jax said, his voice dangerous.

I knew this was the side of him he had worried about me seeing, strong and unyielding to hold onto his throne. These demons were not like the ones I met before; they were not palace workers or demons in the city.

I could feel the power pouring off each of them in waves.

"You are here because I would like you all to pledge loyalty to a new queen," Jax started.

I felt the hair on my skin stand up; no matter how hard I tried to convince myself I could do this, the thought that this was a terrible idea plagued me. These demons would never accept me as one of their own.

"I have found my queen,' he stated, and I felt every pair of eyes in the room fall on me.

One of the demons bared his razor fangs, his skin a pale blue, and I could only guess he was Prince Emris from Auneer, the region of water.

Jax had told me varying stories of each of the regions and the families who ran them, all types of demons who drew their powers from certain aspects of their lands.

"And you expect us to just accept a human into our realm, to take her as our queen?" the demon sneered at me. His golden eyes were similar to Jax, but his rich brown skin told me he was a different type of demon.

Prince Xavi was the only ruler I had not named at the table, the prince of the shifter region.

"I expect you to honor your ruler's decision and show respect to your new queen," Jax growled.

"So you have married," Prince Emris added.

"No," Jax said. "We will wed before the end of the moon cycle, and I expect each of you to accept our rule."

Jax held each of the rulers' gazes. Silva's eyes flashed to me, and I swore I spotted sympathy. She understood what it was like to be the only female in a room of males questioning her capabilities. I tried to give her a quick smile to show my appreciation.

A deep chuckle escaped Prince Svelk. My eyes settled on him, watching him stand from his seat as his hands slammed on the wooden table.

"I will not bow to a human," he growled, and darkness flashed across his eyes. It was so fast, I doubted for a moment that I'd even seen it.

It was the same darkness I'd caught in Drakor's eyes on multiple occasions. My gaze immediately caught his, and I saw the subtle shake of his head telling me we would have this discussion later.

"Sit down," Jax growled at the prince.

He remained standing, his eyes set on Jax, neither willing to back down. "Just because you found some human whore to fuck, does not mean the rest of us should have to tolerate her being here."

I heard Silva's gasp, the other two demon princes tensing at the table. There was no trace of the demon king I had spent months with. His body had gone rigid, his eyes filled with rage.

"You so much as utter another word about Soleil, and I will ensure a slow and painful death."

The demon paused for a moment, weighing his options before sitting. I saw his distaste for humans in his eyes, but I could tell he feared Jax more.

"I'm a witch," I added quietly. "I'm not human. I'm a witch."

Jax turned, his face stunned, like he had forgotten I was there. It quickly shifted into pride. I was standing up for myself. Already, I was trying to act like a queen.

"I do not need the demon king to make my threats for me," I said, stepping forward. "If I hear you so much as utter another word of disgust toward humans, I will give my flames a taste of that tongue of yours," I threatened.

The moment the words left my mouth, I could feel myself cowering back into myself. My stomach turned, and I knew if he argued, there would be no counter I could come up with.

It was the smallest piece of bravery I could muster, but I had to try. They would never learn to respect me if I didn't.

I caught the smile on Silva's face before she hid it.

"Does anyone else disagree with my decision?" Jax questioned.

Not a single demon spoke.

"Then it is done," he answered. "Now, bow to your future queen."

Each of their heads fell into makeshift bows. I glanced to Jax and found an amused grin. I narrowed my eyes at him, but I couldn't help the smile growing on my face. He took my hand, pulling me in closer. Queen was never a title I thought I would hear about myself. Yet, standing beside Jax, it felt like everything was falling into place.

CHAPTER

THIRTY-THREE

Months passed, and my fondness for the demon and his court only grew. Exploring every inch of the palace brought me a feeling of contentment I'd never known. This much freedom was intoxicating.

Some days, Jax was busier than others. The other regions were constantly at unease, and having a human in his court hadn't helped. Even though each demon had bowed to me that day, they still were wary of me becoming their queen. Word spread fast about my new position in the palace, and the curious stares and whispers never became less unsettling.

There had been no coronation or ceremony, but Jax had promised when I was ready, we could hold a similar event. Even with his offer for me to rule by his side, he let me take my time. It was a big shift in my life, and I didn't want to rush into it. I knew the anxiety and compulsions would only grow worse if I did.

Instead, I took it day by day, learning all I could about Eodratera and magic, preparing myself to fully step into the role.

I was walking the halls of the Serpentine Palace when a snake slithered its way by me. I barely flinched, all too used to the serpents that freely roamed the palace. I'd caught Mr. Finkel toying with the creatures on multiple occasions.

It was like the thought had summoned the feline as the calico familiar ran by me.

"Eh, eh," I scolded the cat.

The familiar paused, glancing back as if he hadn't seen me before.

"Come back here," I hissed, and the cat glanced between me and the serpentine before choosing to obey.

"Queen," a deep voice behind me called out.

I turned, finding Drakor hurrying to catch up. He was dressed fully in black, and his presence sent a chill running across my skin.

It had been months, and I still barely had answers from him. The first week following the meeting, he avoided me. The past few months, he'd been dodging my questions. He even began to join my training sessions more often, but I never saw his power again.

This would be different. I wanted answers, and I was finally ready to hold my ground.

"Mind if I join your session with Althea today?" he asked, knowing I would head toward the garden soon.

"Fine," I drawled. "But only if you answer one thing." I batted my eyelashes at him and put on a sickly-sweet smile.

He rolled his eyes. "Not this again."

"Tell me about Drazmin. You are from the region of darkness. What type of demon are you? What is it like there?" I asked.

"That was two questions."

This time, I rolled my eyes.

"Fine," he said. "Only because I do not see the harm in sharing."

If only he had come to that conclusion earlier. I huffed.

"Drazmin is a region of nightmares. It is cast into darkness for more hours than not of the day. The demons there breed a magic that is not to be taken lightly. It is dark and chaos, unruly. You have caught glimpses of my magic. Even as it stirs inside me, it aches to be set free. Sometimes, it almost makes it to the surface before I contain it," he explained.

"So your eyes?" I asked, and he nodded.

"Are you satisfied?" he asked.

"I supposed," I answered.

I let him follow me to the garden, where we met Althea for training. Again, I noticed her cough was no longer nagging her as much. It was still present but not as debilitating.

"I've set up new targets today," Althea explained. "We will work on controlling the direction of your magic."

I glanced around, realizing the targets were in new spots. My chest felt tight as I counted the targets.

One, two, three, four.

I kept counting them, over and over. Each time, the cycle

didn't feel right. The new placements set off an alarm bell in my own mind. The counting continued, and I came no closer to feeling the usual relief when I routinely counted through the targets.

I started to feel panicked.

"Are you ready, Soleil?" Althea asked.

I couldn't answer. I felt paralyzed, trapped in the compulsion. I continued to glance between each target, counting them. It was never-ending, and I felt like I couldn't breathe any longer.

My legs shook, the black dots filling my vision.

My anxiety took control of me, and I lowered myself to the ground. I placed my head in my hands, trying not to look at the targets.

"I can't," I barely managed to get out before hyperventilating, my breathing rapid and shaky.

"Soleil?" Drakor asked, but I couldn't answer.

I heard him hurry off and felt Althea's presence next to me.

"It's okay, child," she said. It was strange; although I didn't know her age, the witch did not feel much older than I was.

Two more minutes passed, and I heard footsteps rushing toward me.

"I got this," Jax said, and I heard Althea and Drakor walk off.

I still had my head in my hands and found it almost impossible to lift it. When I did, I found golden eyes watching me.

"What happened?" Jax asked. His presence alone helped chase the feeling away. I could feel myself settling.

"The targets were moved," I admitted.

Jax cocked his head, patiently waiting.

"I can't help it. Sometimes, I have to count things. These compulsions just happen, and when they do, I can't stop them."

My face felt like it was on fire. Shame crept through me, and I wanted to hide behind one of the nearby trees.

"Why can't I stop?" I asked him. "Why can't I make the thoughts go away? Why am I like this?" Tears swelled in my eyes. "I feel broken. I wasn't always like this," I admitted as they slipped down my cheeks.

Jax wiped them away with his thumb. "Never broken," he said.

"Then what?" I asked. I could feel my heart breaking. I couldn't take it anymore: the repetitiveness, the anxiety creeping in, the feeling of being out of control of my own body.

I struggled to calm myself. I could feel my body trembling, and Jax pulled me closer.

"You are not broken. This is not your fault," he said.

Every word felt so distant; I couldn't get out of my own head. Over and over, I just kept thinking I wasn't enough. I would never be enough. I was damaged and ruined.

"Look at me," Jax said, but his arms remained around me. He wouldn't force me. I knew it was my choice. Everything was my choice when I was with him.

I glanced at him and wanted to look away, to avert my

eyes to the bedsheets. I didn't want him to see just how shattered I felt inside.

"You are not what he did to you. The way he controlled you and made you feel like nothing. The way he kept you in a cage, pushed you to your breaking point. Your mind found a way to get through it. It found a way to comfort you when no one else did. You found a way to survive the crushing weight of manipulation. I don't care if he didn't leave physical scars on you. Just wishing the memories away is not enough. It will take time, but I will be here for you. I will be by your side every step of the way, no matter how hard it is. It may never fully get better. I don't think something like this ever fully goes away, but we will find a way to make it more manageable. You are not broken. You are stronger because of what you went through," he said as he held me. "I will never let anyone hurt you again."

I felt the threat in his promise. I knew that if anyone laid a single finger on me, they would walk away without a hand.

"I knew it was supposed to be you," I said.

"What do you mean?"

"That entire year, I clung to a small thread of hope that led me straight to you when I was ready to give up. I tugged on that thread, and I begged it to show me the answer. I found you, and I will forever be thankful for that," I whispered.

"Your Majesties," a palace worker sheepishly said from behind us. I had almost forgotten we were sitting in the middle of the garden where anyone could see us.

"Not now," Jax growled, pulling me close protectively.

"I'm sorry, but it is urgent."

"What is it?" Jax snapped, and I placed my hand on his arm, trying to signal the interruption was alright.

"He's here," the worker said, and I heard the fear laced in their words. My stomach dropped.

"Who?" Jax demanded, but I already knew.

"Vileer."

THIRTY-FOUR

My heart felt like it stopped when I saw the demon enter the throne room. How he had made it past the guards and walls was still a mystery. He'd appeared in the palace's entryway, demanding to see the demon king.

Jax's muscles tensed, gripping the arms of his throne. Three serpents circled us, one slithering close to where I stood beside the throne.

"I've come to collect what's mine," Vileer stated, his black crown tilted, his eyes narrowing on me. The friendly face of the stranger was nowhere to be found. Instead, the prince of illusions eyed me like he had won a prize.

My stomach sunk, and I could feel my balance swaying.

Jax stood and took a protective step forward, putting himself between Vileer and me. I heard the low snarl that escaped his lips.

"You will not lay a single hand on her. She goes

nowhere," he commanded, and I could feel the presence of his magic filling the room, snaking through every inch of it.

"But that's not what was promised," Vileer said, throwing his arms open. "I happily held up my end of the bargain. Now, it's time for her to keep hers."

"I am still your king," Jax growled. "You'd do best to learn your place."

"Your loss, then," he shrugged.

"What do you mean?" I asked, stepping beside Jax.

My magic had been improving over the weeks of practice. I knew I was no match for Vileer, but I also knew I didn't want to hide behind Jax. This was my problem to solve. I'd been naive enough to trust a demon, so now, I would find a way out.

"I warned you, Soleil. Break the bargain, and your life will be forfeit," he said, setting his gaze on me.

The way his eyes bore into my soul ripped little shreds of my being from me. I could feel that confidence peeling away faster than I could bolster it up.

"And the throne is rightfully mine. You're nothing but a bastard," Vileer sneered, his purple eyes narrowing. " Nothing more than the human scum your mother was."

"She was a witch," Jax bit out.

"Those inbreeds might as well be human. They choose to live in that world," Vileer spat back.

I remained deathly still, afraid even the slightest movement would remind the pair of my presence. I could see the heat in Jax's eyes from where I stood.

Nervously, I tugged at my side, picking at a loose thread in my skirt. Tightness formed in my chest that threatened to squeeze the life for me. I could feel my knees trembling and prayed they wouldn't buckle beneath me.

One of the serpents near my feet lunged, but Jax immediately called it back. I saw Vileer flinch, but only slightly. He regained his composure faster than most could probably register.

"You are not welcome here, and I advise you leave," Jax said in a low tone.

I spotted movement in the back of the room and watched as Althea and Drakor shuffled in, tucking themselves into a corner.

"I've come to collect what is mine. I want to make good on our bargain," Vileer repeated, glancing around Jax at me. I swallow hard.

It was like the tattoo on my arm was burning a hole through my skin. I could barely bring myself to look at it, my cheeks heating with shame. The consequences of my choices were finally catching up to me.

"No," Jax said firmly.

His serpents circled me protectively, slithering on the ground beneath my feet. When I first arrived, their presence had unnerved me, but now, I'd come to find it a comfort.

I startled as the cool scales of a snake brushed against my leg, and I glanced down to find one of them climbing my limb, wrapping itself around me. It continued to circle my body until it was perched on my shoulders like a protective scarf, wrapped around my upper arm to secure itself. I could hear the slight hiss it let out as it made eye contact with the prince.

The serpents had become protective of me the longer I lived here in the palace.

"Pick a different bargain. Ask for anything else," Jax said, and I knew it was a mistake.

He had shown Vileer exactly what he wanted to see. He knew exactly how much the demon king cared for me, and he would never allow me to walk away after witnessing it firsthand.

I realized his mistake the instant the words left his mouth.

"I'll go with you," I said, surprising myself. I didn't want any harm to come to the rest of the demons, and I knew this was my mistake to fix.

Dark golden eyes stared up at me, and I could see the pleading look behind them.

"You leave them alone," I said, my heart feeling like it was ripping in two. I tried desperately to keep the tears in my eyes from falling but couldn't.

"Leave them alone, and I will come with you," I demanded.

I stepped down from the dais, holding out one arm and bending over to the dais steps, urging the serpent to slither from me to its master. It moved down my arm and back to the throne with Jax.

"Don't do this. Don't go with him," Jax pleaded.

"We both know what happens if I don't. Death is the only way out of a bargain. I have to go," I said sadly.

"I know. I just hate that I can't change that."

"It's not forever," I promised, turning back to Vileer.

He was tapping his foot impatiently. Each time his foot

hit the ground, I counted in that same rhythmic pattern. I looked back to Jax once more.

"I'll find you," he whispered. "And I will bring you home."

"I know you will. I can hold on that long. Whatever he does, I will be there when you finally come for me."

A weight on my shoulders made it feel like my feet were stuck in place. I didn't want to leave the demon king, but I didn't want to lose my life. There was no way around it, no tricks to be used.

I turned before I changed my mind and before my nerves made it worse. Walking over to Vileer, I sneered at him.

"Let's go," he said, his mouth curling into a cruel grin.

He grasped my arm tightly, and the moment he touched my skin, I heard chaos break out through the room. I knew he'd cast an illusion over us and that we'd disappeared. He pulled me from the room faster than my feet could keep up, and I almost tripped over myself trying to follow him. He knew the faster he got us out of the palace, the less likely it was that Jax would fight him.

I knew Jax would never risk my life, and that was why he let me go so easily. I couldn't guarantee I would live if we'd stayed.

We hurried down the palace halls. I tried to take in every last detail. Filled with decor that brought back happy memories, it reminded me of all the days I'd had with Jax before Vileer came. I tried to think about that thread of hope. I pushed a little magic out to it, but we were moving too fast, and my concentration was shaky.

I still didn't understand exactly how it worked, but somehow, my magic always find his.

Jax always had a way to find me, no matter where Vileer took me, and that was something the prince didn't know. He could use his magic. The bargain was only to take me. Once it was fulfilled, Jax could come for me.

Vileer had to know that, and I was willing to bet he would take me to a secluded location Jax didn't know about. It would be foolish to take me to his own palace or fortress. He would be asking for war upon his doorstep.

A horse was waiting for us outside the palace. It was completely black, its red eyes staring down at us menacingly.

The moment Vileer dropped our illusion, he hurried up the horse and forced me to join him.

A chill ran down my spine as his arms wrapped around me and grabbed the reins. I hated being close to him. I could smell the scent of alcohol clinging to his skin.

I heard a meow and turned to find my familiar watching me from the courtyard. The sad look in the feline's eyes told me it understood what was happening. I gave a small acknowledgment to the cat and watched as it ran back inside, likely to find the demon king.

I tried to get one last glance at the palace as we trotted off, but Vileer's body blocked me.

Throughout the journey to his land, I kept trying to reach out to my magic. It was harder than I expected, and although I could feel that slight thread there, I didn't understand how to tug on it, how to let him know I was at the other end.

Tired of using magic, my eyelids grew heavy. I knew

when we cross the border anything around me could be an illusion. I let myself slip into the sleep my eyes desperately begged for. I would need all my strength.

PART FOUR
ENCHANTED

CHAPTER

THIRTY-FIVE

Three days had passed, or maybe it was four—time was blending together in my little cell, and I was starting to lose hope. The first day or two, I had been sure Jax would come, that he would rescue me. I had fulfilled the bargain, had gone willingly, but now, I wanted to escape. I wasn't sure how much more my body could withstand.

My magic was still unruly and unpredictable, and every time I tried to call on it, it was nowhere to be found. Every time he inflicted pain on me, burning me, poking me with his dagger or torturing my mind with his illusions, I took a step closer to wanting to give up.

Maybe my magic had abandoned me, or maybe it was all one large illusion. I was losing track of reality and nightmares, blending together, becoming harder to differentiate

The pain was too much to bear, and I was slowly losing my sanity. I had nothing to hold onto, no comfort to keep me alive in the cell Vileer kept me in. If he wanted to hurt Jax, then he was doing a good job.

Even if Jax did come for me, I would be a shell of the person I once was. I had taken major strides in repairing my mental health after finally walking away from my father's abusive grasp, and now, I found myself losing every piece I had glued back together.

There was no telling if I'd ever be able to pick them up again.

My small cell had concrete walls with only a single door leading in and out. The door was kept locked with no handle on the inside. For all I knew, the cell could be an illusion. I had no way of knowing what was real and what was not. The cold, hard ground I laid on was the only jolt of reality that let me know I was still alive.

I heard footsteps echoing from outside of the cell, like there was a long, straight hallway beyond the door. I had never been allowed to see what was beyond it; Vileer slithered through the crack of the door each time he visited.

The lock click had me backing into the furthest corner of the cell. I knew what was coming. It would be another session of Vileer or one of his men torturing me for no gain. I had nothing to offer them, no knowledge or power, yet they still tortured me, just because it would hurt.

The demon king had held this kingdom together by his own power and empathy; now, a single witch could risk it all.

Part of me wished he wouldn't come. I knew what he stood to lose. Vileer overthrowing his rule would turn the realm into something so horrid, I wouldn't let my mind imagine it. What would that leave for me?

The door pushed open, and I wrapped my arms around my legs, pulling them close to my body. The perpetual silence that usually comforted me in this cell vanished. Viller stepped in with a chuckle that felt like it echoed across the walls.

"What? So easily broken?" Vileer asked.

His demon appearance was ghastly enough that I kept my eyes to the floor. No longer did the human form stand before me. Instead, he allowed himself to show his true form.

The first time I had seen it, I wanted to shut my eyes as tight as I could. He had grey skin with black flecks spread across the surface. It was leathery, with boils that popped up across his appendages. His eyes were two narrow slits, the center glowing a vibrant yellow. When he spoke, his tongue snaked out of his mouth, a split in the center with a serpent appearance.

His hands reached toward me, razor-sharp claws running over my skin.

He stood in front of me and grabbed my chin, forcing my gaze up to his face. I tried to look anywhere but his eyes, but he held firm.

"How you witches always fall," he said. "Each one of you is the same: lackluster, your magic insufficient compared to my own. Your mother was the same."

My heart and breathing stopped. I squeezed my eyes shut, counting in my head, trying to breathe normally again. He was lying. It was another form of torture.

I winced when one of his claws cut into my cheek and

forced my eyes open again. I felt the cold drop of blood run down my face onto his finger. He brought it to his mouth and licked it, a malicious smile coating his lips.

"You think I lie?" he asked. "I can show you."

He waved his hand, and the cell melted into a new scene. I was no longer the one crouched in the corner. A woman who looked eerily similar to me was curled into a ball. Vileer entered the cell, stalking over to the woman.

When he reached down to pull her up, my stomach dropped. He used impossible strength to hold my mother up by the collar of her shirt, limp and barely conscious. Without hesitation, he plunged a claw-like finger into her chest.

I watched helplessly as the life drained from her body. He dropped her to the floor, and she didn't move.

"Please, Mom," I whimpered. "Please get up."

I knew it was an illusion, but still, I couldn't help the bile rising in my throat.

The room shifted again, and I was face-to-face with Vileer.

"Knowing that the demon king cannot save you, knowing that you are now mine and not his, brings me almost enough satisfaction," he drawled.

Something in me broke. It had been broken for a long time, but this was the first time I had admitted it to myself. Hope was gone, and I knew Vileer would never allow me to leave the confines of this cell.

"I think today, we will see what I can do to your precious little mind," Vileer said. "How far can I push it until there is nothing left of the little witch Jax loved?"

He took a step back, looking me over, his hands on his

hips. I met his eyes, and a shiver ran down my spine. I braced myself for the illusion I knew would come. Suddenly, the walls faded from the blank grey to a dark night sky.

The illusion quickly grew, and I was back in the familiar throne room where I first found Jax. He sat on the throne, but his head hung. I could see the blood trailing down his body, and I tried screaming out to him. My voice refused to work; I couldn't get anything out. I tried to call to him, but the longer I did, the more my throat burned with a ghastly fire.

Vileer stepped into the room from behind the throne, stalking across the dais. Lifting Jax's head by his hair, Vileer grinned as he exposed the limp king's neck. Jax's eyes were shut, and I could see his shallow breathing.

My heart ached. No matter how many times I told myself this was only an illusion, it felt more and more real each time.

I tapped at my side, trying to comfort and wake myself from the nightmare. My eyes remained glued to the throne; no matter how hard I tried to shut them, I couldn't.

Vileer whipped out a sharp blade, and I watched as he ran it across the demon's neck, letting go of his hair. Jax's head dropped, lifeless.

Agony tore me apart as I watched his last breath leave his mouth. No longer did the demon sit on the throne. Jax toppled over, his body hitting the ground. Vileer moved around Jax to sit on the throne, kicking his feet up on the back of the limp king.

Anger swelled inside me, and I tried to step forward, but I couldn't move. I was always stuck in place, watching his illusions. The more rage filled me, the more I imagined bursting into flames. I wanted to explode, to consume the room with pure wrath.

"You bitch," Vileer snapped.

The illusion disappeared, and I was back in my plain cell. My eyes adjusted, and standing a few steps from me, Vileer stood, cradling his hand, painted in a vibrant red.

"You burned me," he snapped. "You still think you have a chance of leaving? It would seem I have not broken your spirit enough yet."

A shudder ran down my spine, and I could see the wheels turning behind his eyes as he thought of every way to break me. I hadn't meant for my flames to come to the surface. With every illusion he showed me, every image he forced me to watch of Jax dying, I became more furious. I could not let myself break completely.

I knew I was close, but I grasped that thread, hoping I would find a way out.

"Why are you doing this?" I asked, my voice burning from days without water.

"I'm a demon; it's who I am."

"Please, let me go," I begged.

"You will find no sympathy here. The only thing I desire is your pain and misery because I know it is what will finally bring Jax to his knees. I've waited years for this opportunity, and no human or witch will stand between me and the throne that is rightfully mine."

He moved quickly, slashing across my face with his razor-sharp fingers.

My tortured scream echoed through the otherwise empty

cell. I could feel my face dripping blood, the dried liquid on my face creating a layer across my skin.

Vileer's heartless laugh filled my ears.

My head whipped back as he pulled my hair, forcing me to stare up at him. It was hard to see through the tears welling in my eyes.

I didn't know how much longer I could hold on. When would it finally end?

Death sounded like an empty promise as he pushed me to the brink and then brought me back again.

I knew it was my fault for making the bargain.

My scream pierced the silence as Vileer raked his finger down my neck and shoulder blade. Agony spread across my shoulder, searing pain coursing through my body.

"Scream all you want, witch. Your king isn't coming for you."

Another scorching jab hit my exposed ribs, and my vision went white. I screamed out again, unable to hold the pain in. I could feel myself slipping out of consciousness. If Jax didn't come soon or I didn't find a way out, I didn't know if I could hold on much longer.

My world swirled, and I fell to the floor, watching Vileer walk away before my vision completely faded to black.

I woke to chaos.

I could hear screams ringing through the fortress. I never saw the outside when Vileer dragged me to his lands; he cast an illusion over the location when we approached. I couldn't be sure any of the the landscape I'd witnessed was real.

Loud clangs echoed through the halls outside my cell. I heard shouting before footsteps hurried toward my cell. My back pressed into the wall, my feet pushing me across the floor into the furthest corner. I prayed whoever was hurrying through the halls would pass me.

Agonizing screams and shouts made their way to me, and my heart raced. Was this going to be the end? Would my suffering finally be over?

If Jax had come, would he find me before Vileer got to me? If the king had arrived, there was no way the prince would let me go. He wanted to inflict pain on Jax; killing me was an easy way to do it.

The handle outside my door rattled, and I braced myself.

A loud clang hit the door before it was slowly pulled open. I hugged my knees tight, hoping rescue had come.

When the door opened, I found the last demon I expected to see staring down at me.

"Come with me," Silva said gently, holding out a hand.

I hurried to my feet, accepting her help. She had traded her usual gowns for simple black pants and a tight black shirt that clung to her curves. Her dark hair was pulled back, and a small drop of blood ran down her face from a cut near her hairline.

"Don't worry about it," she said, catching my gaze.

"Why are you here?" I asked.

She pulled me through a long hall lined with other cells, all the doors were open to and they remained empty.

"Where are we?" I added.

"You are in the region Imoni, and I am here because Jax needed help," she said.

"Jax is here?" I rasped, my throat still burning.

"Yes, searching for you. He hasn't stopped searching for you these past two weeks."

Two weeks?

I had been trapped for two weeks, not the few days I originally thought. The illusions were endless, and my mind could never keep track.

"I thought it had only been days," I whispered.

Silva flashed a look of sympathy toward me.

"That's what he does. Vileer plays with your mind until you no longer know reality."

We reached a staircase, and Silva pulled me along at a brisk pace up the stairs.

I quickly realized I had been held in the basement of the fortress. The moment we emerged from the stairs, I found a window at the top that let in a dim red glow from the moon outside.

Shouts carried from down the hall, and Silva glanced around before deciding to go left.

"We need to find Jax, and I need to let him know you're alright. He was searching for Vileer, convinced you would be with him."

My heart sunk realizing what that meant. If Jax had already found Vileer, there would be no escaping the battle that would follow. He had invaded Vileer's region and come to take the prize the prince held.

My heart raced, my feet moving faster. I had to find Jax before it was too late.

CHAPTER

THIRTY-SIX

We searched the ground floor of the fortress with little success. Each hall was either a dead end or full of demons fighting. I recognized many of the guards from the Serpentine Palace and a few fire demons as they battled with magic and swords, unaware of our presence.

"Why did you come?" I asked.

"I told you: Jax needed help," Silva said before swearing under her breath at another empty hall.

"But why did you agree? Why would you come for me?" I asked.

My body was growing more tired the longer we searched. My shoulder ached from the wound Vileer left, and my eyes felt heavy.

"I haven't seen Jax this happy in a while. You bring out the best in him, and that is what I want for this kingdom. If saving your ass means we receive the king we deserve, then I will always agree," she explained.

We hit another dead end, and she paused.

"Plus, I really didn't wish you dead. It's rare I find demons or witches I can tolerate."

My cheeks warmed, and I felt a sense of gratefulness for the princess. I was thankful I had found another friend in the grim realm. I knew I wouldn't survive on my own.

Shouts rang out from behind us, and a loud bang shook the fortress. Sprinting to find the commotion, we found a set of stairs leading to the second floor and followed them up. At the top, doors were thrown open, revealing a spacious room.

It looked like a makeshift throne room.

On one side, I spotted Jax, dressed in his dark pants and white shirt. He wasn't wearing his crown, and two serpents were posted protectively at his side.

On the other side, Vileer stood, no illusion over his appearance. My mouth fell open in horror seeing the pair dripping in sweat, eyes locked, ready to tear each other apart.

"Jax," I said, walking in.

His head whipped in my direction, and I saw his eyes soften.

"Soleil," he murmured. "I thought you were dead. He said-"

"He lied," I said firmly.

"You're not..." He paused. "You're not an illusion?"

'I'm real," I promised. Before I could run to Jax, I watched his eyes turn vacant.

With his loss of concentration, he opened himself to be vulnerable to Vileer's illusions. His magic wasn't fast enough to protect him, and he was trapped in his own mind. I knew the agony his illusions could cause.

"Jax?" I shouted. "Jax, please!"

It was no use. Once he was trapped in the illusion, only Vileer could release him unless he freed himself.

"Let him go," I demanded.

"No," Vileer chuckled. "He played right into my hand, coming for you. Why would I let that go now?"

"You don't want to do this, please," I begged. I knew I sounded desperate, but it was the only thing I could do. My magic felt drained, and I couldn't let his risk be for nothing.

"Oh, but I do," he drawled. "This is everything I wanted."

"Let him go," Silva demanded.

"Or what, princess?"

Flames burst to life in her palms, and I instinctively backed away. She didn't hesitate when she attacked, throwing flame after flame in Vileer's direction. He used his illusions to hide his true position and consistently shift the appearance of the room.

One moment, there were columns along the walls, and the next, they lined the middle of the room, allowing him coverage to hide behind. It continued in this manner for what felt like an eternity.

I hurried to Jax, hoping I could snap him out of the trance. From the moment I made it to his side, I knew it was no use. I tried shaking him, calling out to him, but nothing worked. The look on his face was a mixture of horror and vacancy. His skin felt clammy, the serpents beneath him distraught.

Silva cried out, and I turned to watch her hunch over,

clutching her stomach. She stumbled backward, and I clocked a dagger plunged into her abdomen. Vileer stood only feet away, watching with a pleased grin on his face.

He stalked toward her, and I called on my magic, hoping it was enough. Fire appeared in my palm, and I hurled it in his direction. The attack was enough to turn his attention away from the princess.

"No, Soleil," Silva cried out.

"Go," I said softly to her. My words were barely audible, but she understood.

"No. I won't leave you both," she answered.

"Please," I begged. "Find Drakor."

I knew if she could find him, we would stand a chance. Alone, I couldn't move Jax, but with his help, if we made it far enough from Vileer, maybe he would wake from the spell he was under.

"You're a fool," Vileer hissed. "You're magic is no match for me."

I knew he was right, but I stood my ground. I wouldn't be weak, not in this moment. My entire life had been spent locked away; I would die before he dragged me back to that cell. I would give my life protecting Jax.

Silva hesitated to leave, but I nodded. Holding the dagger in her gut, she hurried out of the room, her blood trailing behind her on the ground.

It made my stomach turn to see her in pain.

I focused my attention back to Vileer. He had his eyes set on me, and I knew the illusion would be coming soon. I couldn't let him close enough to harm me, and if I kept him moving, maybe he wouldn't be able to focus on his illusions.

Flames erupted in my palms again, and I forced myself to call on as much power as I could manage. I continued to throw attacks his way, forcing him to dodge them. We moved around the room in a vicious dance, and Vileer was able to conjure smaller illusions.

He built shields and shifted reality so my attacks missed him.

I let out a frustrated growl when one ball of fire narrowly missed him.

I made a grave mistake, pushing Vileer toward the side of the room where Jax stood. The moment he set his eyes on the king, I felt terror take hold of me. Jax was out of my reach, and Vileer knew that.

He hurried over to the king and pulled out a second dagger, holding it to Jax's throat. I held my breath, raising my hands.

"I wouldn't do that," Vileer drawled. "You risk burning him—do you think for a second you are faster than me?"

He was right; I couldn't risk harming Jax with my own magic.

Fire was not the only element I had conjured. I reached deep into myself, pulling on that spark of magic and forcing it to the surface. I pictured the green vines, the way they grew rapidly, spreading where they pleased.

With one last push, the magic flowed from me into the ground. In the blink of an eye, vines shot up around Vileer, tangling him. They wrapped around his torso, and he slashed at them with the knife.

I rushed toward Jax, but I was too late.

Vileer plunged the dagger into Jax's stomach after breaking one arm free from the vines.

"No!" My scream broke through the darkness filling the room, every inch of me consumed with agony. I watched as Jax fell to his knees, clutching the hole in his abdomen.

My vision went red, and my entire body burned with rage. I barely noticed the flames filling my palms as I set my steely gaze on Vileer.

He'd pay for this egregious mistake.

Embers trailed me as I stalked toward him, his sniveling face faltering. The confidence I'd seen him cling to was slowly depleting, my power finally awoken, ready for pure vengeance.

Fire erupted across the room, and I poured all my energy into the showing of my power. Vileer stood no chance. His illusions broke, the room changing back to how we'd originally found it.

He tried to back his power into shielding himself, but he was too late. The immense heat of the flames consumed him, tearing through his magic down to his very soul.

I rushed to Jax, without another glance to where Vileer stood before.

"You found me," I whispered, cradling his head. I heard Drakor join us but continued to hold Jax's gaze.

"Of course I came. I'm done running, done hiding from my problems. I have something far too important to protect now," he said.

I didn't move, my heart racing, a lump forming in my throat.

"You, little flame," he continued. "It will always be you."

THIRTY-SEVEN

It took days at the palace before I was able to leave my bed again. Each night, I was plagued with nightmares of my torture, and every morning when I woke, I felt too weak to face reality. Jax had healed quickly from his wound, and news had arrived that Silva made a full recovery.

I had almost broken. My mind wanted me to give in, to give up. How could I look Eodratera in the eyes and promise to protect them as their queen if I could barely protect myself?

Mr. Finkel remained glued to my side, refusing to let me out of his sight again. Even when I walked to the bathroom, he still followed. I could sense the anxiety the familiar had after almost losing me. I knew his small well of magic was tied to my own.

A quiet knock sounded on the door. I rolled over, pulling the covers with me. Jax had sent palace workers periodically throughout the day, but each time they left food or offered to bring me anything, I always politely turned down their offers.

"May I?" I heard Althea's soft voice carry through the room.

I didn't answer. I didn't have the energy to. The only person I had spoken to in days was Jax.

He had been kind and patient with me while I healed. I wasn't ready to talk about the torture.

I heard Althea without seeing her. She shuffled through the room and sat on the empty space in the bed. I didn't move, hoping she would soon give up and leave.

"You cannot stay in here forever," she said. "Someday, you will have to face what happened."

I made a small noise that sounded like a grumble. I just wanted her to leave.

"Soleil, I know this hurts, and I know it feels like you will never move past this, but you are so much stronger than this," she said, trying to comfort me.

"You speak like my mother used to," I observed. It was the first thing I had said in days to someone. I wasn't sure why my mind had wandered to my mother, but she was the first person who had popped into my thoughts. My heart hurt thinking about her.

"Because I am one," she said, reaching over to me, her hand running through my hair.

I sat up.

Fiddling with the edge of the sheets I ran my thumb along it repetitively for comfort.

"What?" I asked, unsure if I had misheard her.

"With Vileer dead, there is no reason to hide anymore," she explained.

"You're Jax's mother?" I asked, my eyes widening as the realization fell into place.

She looked too young to have a child Jax's age, yet she was a witch, and I wasn't sure what her magic fully entailed.

She nodded slowly, letting out a slight cough into her elbow. Lifting her hand, she flicked her wrist, and a haze fell over her body, shrouding her from view. It only lasted a moment, but in that time, her appearance changed completely.

Her long hair was now a shining silver, and the corners of her blue eyes had little wrinkles that webbed out.

"More believable?" she asked in an amused tone.

"But how?" I asked, stunned.

"Witches can cast simple illusions. Mine has been draining my magic for some time now."

I nodded, trying to follow along. "You've been here the entire time, hiding in plain sight? How? Why?" I knew she was hiding from Vileer, but I didn't understand why she didn't run far away from the Serpentine Palace.

"I needed to remain near Jax. Each year, he insisted on crossing the line between realms, and I needed to be here to go with him."

"But why was he crossing into my world?" I asked. I knew Jax had dreams of some day living in the human world, but I never understood why. He seemed to love the demons he ruled over.

"He was searching for a way for us to both live in the human realm," she said with a sigh. "He knew I'd never leave him here alone. This place would eat away at his kind-hearted soul if he had no one."

She placed a gentle hand on my shoulder, her long, wrinkled fingers curling around it. "I'm glad he has you, Soleil. When I am gone someday, at least I know he still has you."

"What do you mean *gone*?" I asked, my worry growing.

"I'm ill. It's part of the reason Jax couldn't come back this year. I've been very sick, too weak to travel between realms. Even with the lines blurred, it exerts a lot of energy. With the war and conflict brewing, Jax wouldn't leave me here unguarded, even with my identity secret."

As she finished a few coughs escaped her lips.

"But what are you ill with? Can it be cured?" My hope was shattering as she gave me a small, sympathetic smile.

"I'm dying of a lonely heart. Magic is great, but it always has a price. Witches, for example, are more powerful together in their covens. I've been separated from mine for far too long. My magic's price is slowly killing me, suffocating me while I endure this alone."

"But you could go back to the human realm and live with your coven."

I reached up to my shoulder, placing my hand on top of hers, giving it a squeeze.

"What kind of life would that be? I could never see my son. He's the greatest thing to come of this life; I could never leave him behind. I'd rather die with the happy memories."

My mouth dropped open, words failing to form.

"What about your coven? They're just going to let this happen?" I asked, wishing I knew more about how covens even worked.

"Some have set off about the world in search of an answer, but none have come back with any." She shrugged, her smile dipping slightly.

"Please. He needs you," I tried.

"No. He thinks he does, but I know he'll be okay. He has you. Please, Soleil, promise me you'll be there for him."

"But—" Tears lined the rim of my eyes.

"Please," she begged, her voice cracking.

"I promise," I said as she pulled me into a hug.

This close, I could hear the slight wheeze in every breath she took. My chest felt heavy knowing nothing could cure her ailment. I thought she had been getting better, but it turned out, she was still very ill.

Something clicked in my head as I slowly pulled back.

"I think this is why my mother left," I blurted. "My father mentioned he thought she'd been smoking again, her cough coming back. She just left us one night without any explanation. She told me she'd come back for me when I was ready," I said.

I'd never understood until now. She didn't want this world thrusted onto me. My mother had wanted me to find my own way into it. Pride swelled in my chest, a grin curling my lips as I realized that time had finally come.

"I'd say you're finally ready to accept who you are," Althea said, smiling gently. "Your mother was a kind soul, and I know she would be proud to learn you've truly found yourself."

"You knew my mother?" I asked, trying not to let my hope rise, protecting myself from the disappointment I anticipated.

"I did," she said warmly.

"How?" The question flew from my lips.

She gave a slight chuckle. "She was a part of my coven. I've visited her in Weeping Vale many times. Her apothecary is a haven for all witches."

"Do you know where she is? Why she left?" I asked, speaking faster now as my heart beat harder.

Her smile faltered. "As you guessed, she grew sick from being away from our sisters too long. She longed to have a life where she could just be your mother. Unfortunately, magic had other demands. She knew a time would come when you'd finally learn who you were, and she'd be able to be with you again," Althea explained.

"Did my father know?" I asked.

She nodded slowly. "I never met him, but your mother spoke of him a few times. He never fully wrapped his head around the idea of magic, of our worlds."

Everything made sense—the struggle to control me, to keep me under his watchful eye. Fear was a powerful motivator, and my father was afraid he'd lose me to magic the way he had his wife. All his struggle to gain control, and he'd only pushed me toward it. A small ache in my heart grieved the father I would never see again, the one who had held tightly to his daughter but lost her to his one fear anyway.

Althea must've seen my guilt on my face, because she said, "You cannot fight fate. You were always meant to be this person, and no matter what, even your father could not stop that from happening. He knew this day would come, and instead of embracing it, he tried to fight a pointless battle."

Her gentle hand found my shoulder, holding tight for a moment.

I nodded, knowing her words held truth. "Thank you," I said, grateful she had opened up to me and thankful I finally felt like life was worth living once more.

"How did you travel freely between worlds?" I asked. "I thought your soul must be tethered to this world to remain here."

I tilted my head, confused on how she had found a way around the magic.

"No, Soleil. The only thing binding you to this world was your bargain. You are free now. You have the option to go back home if you wish. I am confident the witch who sent you here knew you needed to find your way yourself. It is why she lied to you about being tethered to the world. She knew once you discovered your magic, you could easily go home."

Home.

I repeated the word three more times in my head. I hadn't thought about home in a long time, but I found myself missing it deeply. If I wanted, I could leave and find my mother.

I needed to find the demon king before making my choice. I had spent days in bed, and I was finally ready to face what happened. I needed Jax to know the love I held for him for rescuing me, but I also needed him to see the pain and suffering I felt from it all. My mind wandered, wondering if maybe going back home wasn't a bad idea at all.

THIRTY-EIGHT

After my conversation with Althea, I knew I needed to find Jax.

The knowledge that I could go back to my own world weighed heavy on me. I could stay and be the queen this world wanted, or I could run away once more. I had run as fast and far as I could when I finally escaped the grasp of my father. Could I do that to Jax?

The thought felt like someone took a cleaver to my heart.

I left our room and found my way to the throne room as quickly as I could. Outside the doors, I could hear Jax talking. I knew that, throughout the day, he often had duties to attend to, including meetings and hearings in the throne room.

Guilt ate away ate me, unwilling to interrupt the dealings. Instead, I planted myself firmly outside the doors, waiting my turn.

Seconds turned to minutes, and soon, an hour was approaching. My back was against the wall beside the door, and I tried to listen to the conversation inside. The voices were too muffled to make out any words. I sighed, feeling hopeless the longer I waited.

Anxious and unable to sit still any longer, I pushed off the wall. I paced back and forth in the hall outside the throne room.

One, two, three, four.

I paused and turned around to pace four steps in the other direction.

The door to the throne room opened, and I froze. Drakor stepped out, his brows raised when he spotted me.

"What are you doing here?" he asked and quickly added, "I am glad to see you are feeling better."

His cheeks warmed with red tones, his eyes falling to the ground.

"I-" My hands trembled while I tried to form a reason. "I need to speak with Jax."

"He's, uh-" Drakor started, glancing toward the door. "He's in the middle of something."

Disappointment and anxiety washed over me. If I didn't speak with him now, I would lose my nerve. It took everything in me to even admit it to Drakor. He must've seen the desperation written on my face.

"It can wait. Come with me," he insisted, turning back toward the door.

The doors flew open when we passed through, and all eyes inside the room fell on us. I felt myself retreating, hiding behind a façade. If these demons knew the war being waged inside my mind, they'd never want me to be their queen.

Jax and the serpents beside him caught sight of me the moment I stepped inside.

"Leave," Jax ordered.

"But the budget," a short and stout demon with pale skin complained.

"His Majesty ordered you to leave," Kasius, who was standing at the base of the dais, said.

Kasius escorted the demon and the other palace workers from the throne room. I swore I caught a look of relief on Kasius' face as he passed by, seeing me for the first time in days. I tried to force a smile onto my face, but it didn't feel genuine. Everything inside me still felt broken.

The room cleared, and I made my way to the foot of the dais. Jax remained seated and motioned for me to join him with a warm smile. I remained frozen beneath him.

"What's wrong, little flame?" he asked.

"I-" The words felt stuck in the back of my throat. I swallowed hard and took a deep breath. "I don't know if I can stay here," I admitted.

Jax's face fell, but he tried to regain his composure quickly. He adjusted his black leather jacket as he sat forward on the throne. From this angle, I could see his dark snake tattoo running up his neck and the way his pulse raced beside it.

"I thought your soul was tethered to this world?" Jax questioned, but I could see he was already putting the pieces together.

"Althea said with the bargain broken, I have the magic to be able to come and go as I please in this realm. All I have to do is learn how to control it. The bargain was the only magic tethering me here. Serafeen knew by sending me here, I would always have a way back once I figured my magic out. That old witch may be irritable, but she is not heartless," I finished.

Jax stroked the stubble growing on his chin.

"I just need to figure things out. Everything with Vileer is still burned into my mind. If there is a chance my mother is out there and I can find her, how do I turn that down?" I asked.

"I cannot make you stay, Soleil, but just know that you will always have a home here."

He dropped his knee and knelt in front of the throne. My eyes widened standing before him.

"Regardless of my title and crown, you are the only one worthy of bringing this kingdom to its knees. So hear me when I say that the choice is yours, but I will spend every day protecting your eternally pure soul from the darkness of this world."

"I-" My words failed me, speechless in front of the man still knelt before me. His head hung down, and butterflies flew in my stomach seeing the king of demons, ruler of Eodratera, giving himself and his crown fully to me.

"I need time," I finally said, catching the sadness in his eyes. I hated disappointing Jax, but I knew I needed to heal before I could give myself entirely to another person—and a kingdom.

"Take all the time you need, little flame," he said, rising from the ground and striding from the room. "I'll be here when you're ready," he called back.

I felt more confused than when I had entered the room. I

thought I had known exactly what I wanted, but seeing Jax offer himself to me, kneeling in front of me, vulnerable, made me question everything. The serpents hurried quickly out behind him.

I climbed the steps to the throne, my feet moving on their own. The last time I'd sat in it was the day I arrived.

I ran my hand along the arm of the throne, the material cool to touch. Something inside me urged me to sit. No one was around, and I knew it was harmless. Turning around, I sank into the seat.

The large chair consumed me, my legs barely long enough to reach the ground. I crossed my legs, staring out into the throne room. Light poured in through the windows, illuminating the space. Even with no one present, it felt warm and welcoming.

I sat there for a few minutes, letting my mind wander. I imagined the life I could have as queen if I chose to stay, and when I did, I felt an undeniable warmth filling my chest.

CHAPTER
THIRTY-NINE

It was the following day, and I still hadn't made my decision. I knew if I chose to stay, I could still leave later on, but somehow, it felt like I needed to decide now. If I stayed, only to leave months or years in the future, it wouldn't be fair to the demon king or Eodratera. They needed a queen they could rely on.

The one thing pulling me to the human world was my mother.

I knew she was out there, and I wanted to find her, if only to tell her I understood. She couldn't stay with my father. Her magic wouldn't allow it, and he would never accept her magic.

She had fallen ill with cursed magic and needed her coven. If she had stayed, she would've faded away to nothing. Forcing me to leave wasn't an option. I had never known magic, and my life was rooted in Weeping Vale at the time. It would have been cruel to uproot me with no warning and force me into a life I had never been aware I belonged to.

I understood, and I craved being able to finally tell her that.

I wandered aimlessly through the palace, avoiding Jax. I had crawled into bed well past him falling asleep and left early, before he woke. I needed to make a decision before I could face him again.

Without thinking, I found myself in the garden where I normally trained, the targets still set up in various corners of the courtyard.

I needed release, to be able to channel my emotions into something I could control. I stood a few yards away from one of the targets and called on my magic. The flames grew until I shaped them into an orb, throwing the ball of fire with as much strength as I could spare.

It connected with the metal, harmlessly extinguishing.

Satisfaction built in my chest. It had taken weeks, but I finally had enough control to connect with a target. The burst of energy I had shown in Vileer's fortress had awoken some part of me. I think I always knew I was holding back, but now, there was no denying it.

I threw a few more balls of flame and moved to the second target.

The second was raised above a bush of grey flowers, the bush itself covered in thorns. It was similar to a rose bush, but far more deadly. I recalled Althea's advice to steer clear of the plant, the thorns containing poison deadly enough to take down even the strongest of demons.

I summoned my magic, warmth flaring around me, their heat licking against my face.

I throw the flames toward the second target, barely

hitting the bottom half. The flames dispersed, but a few embers trickled down from the target when they did.

The bush below burst into flames, and before I could extinguish the fire, the bush was completely consumed and turned to ash.

My jaw dropped, and I stood frozen, horrified by what I had done. With the flames gone, I tried to focus on my other elemental magic. I moved my hands in a rising motion, keeping my eyes on the pile of ash. Instead of the grim, deadly bush, new plants sprouted—tulips full of color and life.

In the middle of the dark and colorless garden, they looked out of place.

I backed away, still staring at them. The color was beautiful, a piece of home in Eodratera. The world was dark and deadly, but in Jax's little oasis, there was now color.

A grin spread on my face, and I raised my hands again. In the empty spaces around the garden, more flowers and plants grew. I made sure not to harm or damage anything Jax had planted, only adding my own touch to the garden. Jax had stated this could be a place for me to come and escape, and this made it truly feel like mine now.

A movement through the garden caught my attention, and I noticed Mr. Finkel chasing one of the smaller serpents. The cat paused, taking notice of me before bounding over, his tail raised high.

"Do you like it too?" I asked.

He gave a short meow in response. I watched with wide eyes as he trailed through a patch of soil, little flower buds popping up everywhere he stepped. It was the first I had seen his magic firsthand.

The garden bloomed to life with color. I walked along the paths, admiring the extent of my magic. I spotted daisies, roses, and marigolds. Vines grew up the bases of the targets, adding a pop of green to the garden. Sprouts of grass peeked up through the soil that had been empty before.

"It's beautiful," a voice behind me said, startling me.

I turned, finding Jax watching me. The king looked delighted, a genuine smile reaching his eyes.

"I hope you don't mind," I said, all too aware it was too late if he did.

"I never mind," he assured me. "Now, it is truly ours to share."

His words sent a shot of guilt through me. I still hadn't given him the answer he deserved, and here I was, changing his garden.

I turned away, glancing around the garden. Pride filled me seeing the beauty my magic brought. This was my little piece of home in Eodratera, and I had created it myself.

I knew in that moment what my decision would be.

"I'm staying," I said firmly.

"What?' Jax asked, approaching my side. He took my hand and squeezed lightly.

"I want to stay," I repeated.

Eodratera was slowly becoming my home. It had been months, and already, I felt more like I belonged here than I had anywhere in the world.

It pained me to turn away from the opportunity to find my mother, but I knew someday, I would see her again. She had rejoined her coven and made a life forh herself. She built her life in the human world, and now, I built a life for myself here. I understood how it felt to give up everything and start from scratch. I couldn't leave behind everything I had worked so hard for.

"Is it selfish if I say I'm glad?" Jax asked.

"No," I said, glancing up at him.

His golden eyes stared back, and he smiled. "I think this calls for celebration," he said, a mischievous look crossing his face.

"Oh really? What kind?" I asked.

He didn't answer, sweeping me off my feet and kissing me.

We spun in a circle before he put me down, kissing me deeper, his hands trailing lower to my ass. He gave a gently squeeze before breaking away, scooping me into his arms as I instinctively clung to his neck. I knew we'd be heading back to the bedroom.

Once the demon king had his eyes set on something, there was no stopping him. In that moment, I just wanted to be fully his.

WITH JAX'S strong arms wrapped around me as he carried me down the hall, I felt safe in his embrace. I let myself savor the feeling before we arrived to the bedroom.

He threw the door open, hunger in his eyes. Butterflies

fluttered in my stomach, and my core warmed, seeing the desire when his golden eyes fell to me.

The room was dimly lit, the curtains shut to cover the window and glass balcony doors. I used my flames to light the fireplace.

My breath hitched when Jax set me on the bed. He pulled off his shirt faster than I was able to slide myself back, and I spotted the pink scar where magic had healed his stab wound. I kicked off the shoes I was wearing while Jax climbed onto the bed, gently pushing me back.

His hands wandered down my body, exploring every curve until he found the skirt of my dress.

"Hold this," he said, pushing up the fabric.

His mouth trailed up my thigh, and he nipped at the skin.

I winced out a noise of pain and pleasure.

"I warned you once, little flame: I am anything but gentle," he said. "If you don't like, anything stop me. Are you sure you want this?" he confirmed.

"Yes," I said, tipping my head back and spreading my legs for him.

His mouth trailed higher and found my center. My grip on my dress tightened the moment he moved my underwear aside and his tongue met my center. He licked in slow, teasing circles, the wet friction against my clit making me moan his name. I needed more, and I tried to move my hips to demand it.

I weaved one of my hands through Jax's dark hair, but before I could grip the strands, he grabbed my wrist and pinned my hand to my side.

"You will be patient while I have my way with you," he growled in a low voice. The demand only made my desire worse, and I could feel my clit throbbing, aching for more than he was giving me.

He backed away and climbed over me. I pulled my dress higher and over my head. I hadn't worn a bra, so my breasts were bare and exposed, my nipples hardening the moment the air hit them. Jax bent his head down, kissing my breasts and toying with my nipples.

With Jax on top, I was at his mercy. He was in control, and all I could do was beg for more.

I grabbed his chin, ignoring his earlier warning and bringing his face closer. I smashed my lips to his, kissing him deeply, refusing to hold back.

His tongue slipped past my lips, and I let out a sound of pleasure, his fingers trailing down and finding my center. They slid in easily, and my back arched at the rapid pace they moved.

"Always wet for me," he groaned, his breathing rapid.

"Jax." His name was enough for him to know what I needed.

My hands fumbled with his pants, and he helped me pull them off.

His cock was hard and ready, and I couldn't help but grin, knowing it was a reaction to *my* body. I helped guide him to my opening, and he slid inside me with ease. I cursed under my breath, the length of him pumping in and out of me.

"Jax." I repeated the only word I seemed able to utter between waves of pleasure.

"Say it again. I want my name on your lips when you fall apart for me," he whispered.

"Jax," I moaned louder. "Fuck."

The words fell out of my mouth as he thrusted hard and fast into me.

"Filthy," he responded. "Kiss me with that filthy mouth of yours."

I obliged his request, savoring every last bit of it. His hand found its way into my hair and gave a light tug. The pain mixed with pleasure was euphoric.

He pulled back and out of me before flipping me over. I propped myself onto my hands and knees.

He ran his hand through my hair again and pulled, my head tipping back slightly. His other hand grabbed my ass as he thrusted into me once more. The sound of him pounding into me rang through the room, only sending me closer to the edge.

My cries of pleasure became more frequent and louder.

"Look at you. So perfect. Every inch of you mine," Jax observed.

I knew I was close to toppling over the edge. Each pump of Jax's cock threatened to destroy me, and I craved the release.

I could tell the demon king was close, his hips picking up pace as his breath came harder. His hand gripped my ass tighter, and I felt the sting of his fingers digging into my skin.

I reached down with one hand, keeping myself propped with the other as I rub my clit. I refused to be at the mercy of someone else when all I craved was release.

"Let me see you pleasure yourself, little flame," Jax said, catching sight of the movement.

My breaths became pants as my fingers moved quicker. I couldn't hold on any longer, and all my muscles clenched as an orgasm ripped through me. I rode through the pleasure, letting Jax pump into me with primal desire.

His hips continued to slap hard against me until I finally felt his cock jerk as he spilled into me.

I waited until he fully pulled out to flip over and fall onto my back. I was still trying to catch my breath, and the demon king laid down next to me.

He glanced over to me and cupped my chin in his hands.

"I love you, little flame," he whispered. "I love you across every realm and universe, until time is no longer."

"I love you too," I whispered.

CHAPTER

FORTY

Jax and I had spent the rest of the day in bed, finding new ways to pleasure and tease each other. Our only duty was to each other, allowing ourselves the release we had been seeking. Realizing it had been weeks without training, I rolled over and turned to Jax.

"Will I be training with Althea today?" I asked, knowing our usual morning sessions needed to resume if I was ever going to step into being queen.

"Actually, I had another idea for today," Jax said, leaning in and kissing my lips.

"Huh?" I managed to get out before kissing him deeper.

"I have someone I'd like you to see," he said, and I didn't miss the way his eyes lit with blissful wonder.

Jax threw off the covers, and cold air raked against my skin. He sat up, quickly climbing from the bed and throwing on the first clothing he found.

The wardrobe doors opened easily for him as he started sorting through my dresses.

I sent a ball of flame tumbling for the fireplace, lighting the cold wood remaining in it. If he wanted me to leave the bed, then I needed warmth. I wrapped my arms around my bare skin, covering my hardened nipples. I slid out of the bed and stood next to Jax, who had pulled out a short black dress with a dark orange design.

Looking closer, I saw they were little orange stars.

I pulled the dress over my head and found it fit perfectly.

There was no time to adjust my hair or find food before Jax eagerly led me out of the room, but I managed to slide on black slippers before he led me out.

The mood within the palace felt light. I knew immediately what direction we were heading in. The halls of the palace were becoming second nature to me.

Jax led me to the throne room, grasping my hand tight.

"Where are you taking me?" I asked with a giggle. The thrill of the surprise sent butterflies to my stomach.

"You'll see," he said, squeezing my hand and picking up our pace.

I'd never seen Jax this giddy.

I heard the hiss of a serpent and found one following beside me: a black python that almost seemed to nod its head at me in encouragement.

We finally made it outside the throne room, and Jax turned to me, taking my face in his hands and kissing me, softly at first, then harder.

"What has got into you?" I asked laughing.

"I need you to know that I love you, little flame," he started.

My heart felt like it would burst at the words.

"I love you, and I would do anything to see you happy. I sent Althea to the human world these past few days, and late last night, she returned. One of my serpents let me know the moment I woke this morning."

I had been sleeping soundly enough to not realize one of his serpents visited early in the morning.

Jax turned and pushed the doors to the throne room open, and I stepped inside, only to be quickly halted in my tracks.

My knees gave out, and I dropped to the floor. I could feel my shoulders heave as the sobs came. In the center of the room, sheepishly watching me, stood my mother.

She walked over to me, kneeling down to my level. I brought my hands to my face, feverishly wiping at the tears streaming down my face. It had been years since I had seen her, and now, she was in Eodratera.

"How-"

"Althea found me. She explained everything. Why you hadn't answered my calls, where you had been, and that I could choose to join you here. It has been a long time since I have been here," she admitted.

"You've been to Eodratera before?" I asked, my eyes widening and my mouth falling open slightly.

"As a little girl, I visited with my own mother."

"Gigi has been here?" I asked, my voice raising in pure disbelief.

My mother laughed, a sweet, genuine sound that was like music to my ears.

"Yes, Gigi has been many places. She is a witch just like us."

"And you all hid this from me?" I asked, starting to stand. I dusted off my skirt as my mother rose.

"I'm sorry," she said, her gaze falling to the ground. Sadness filled her eyes, and I could see the regret written on her face.

"I understand," I said, placing a hand on her arm. "I understand why you didn't tell me, and I understand why you left."

"It pained me more than anything in the world, but I would never force you into this life of magic. If you remained unaware the rest of your life, then you would never fully become a witch, and you would never know the dangers of the world. I wanted to protect you, wanted the choice to always be yours. I'm sorry I stayed away," she said. "And I am sorry I left you with him."

I knew she meant my father. She'd been through his manipulation and control herself; I couldn't blame her for needing to leave, for doing what was best for her own health, physically and mentally.

"I forgive you," I said and truly meant it.

She smiled. Beyond her, I caught sight of Althea watching us, pure happiness written on her face.

"I am here to stay in Eodratera," my mother stated, and my eyes flew back to her.

"But what about your sickness?" I asked, worry spreading across my features.

She stepped closer, studying my features. "You are enough. You are my family, my coven. I do not need more than you and Althea," she said.

Turning, I almost forgot in those few seconds that Althea

stood nearby. She was still smiling, the little wrinkles by her eyes adding to her happy glow.

My mother wrapped her arms around me, pulling me close in a tight embrace. It was everything I had wished for over the years. Finally, I had her back.

I pulled back for a moment to glance to Althea and wave her over. She strode quickly to us, joining our tight embrace. I heard a meow and found Mr. Finkel at my feet, rubbing at our ankles.

"This truly is enough," Althea echoed as she embraced us.

FORTY-ONE

After a few days, when I finally felt completely myself again, Jax called a meeting.

We gathered in the same room as the last one, and I recognized Silva, Emris, Svelk, and Xavi. Again, there was one seat that remained open. Drakor stood post in the corner, and I caught his lip curling up in a quick smile when his eyes met mine.

"I will only say this once: our queen has taught me that ruling is about more than just dominating with an iron fist. I do not wish to continue a reign of death and destruction. I want each of you to aid me in my rule, to work with me, not against me. I am offering a chance at continued peace. Those who accept will have a say in how this realm is ruled," he said, extending his arms as if to embrace those seated at the table. His eyes grew dark. "But those who do not, those who choose to oppose me and threaten my family, will meet the same fate as Vileer," he growled, throwing a golden ring onto the table.

I held in my gasp as I spotted the crescent moon symbol on the ring. I hadn't known Jax had taken the ring after the ordeal in the region of illusions.

Each of the princes and the princesses seated at the table kept their eyes on him, weighing his threat, calculating the risks.

Jax's gaze fell specifically onto Prince Svelk, the one who had given him the most grief at the last meeting. I held my breath, waiting for the demon to make his decision.

One by one, they stood and bowed their heads to Jax, including Prince Svelk. The sign of respect solidified their choices. I joined them in bowing my head in Jax's direction.

He lifted my chin, tipping my gaze back to his.

"We are equals," he said firmly.

I was left speechless. I hadn't been born into this life, and I didn't claw my way to power the way the others had. One fateful Halloween had led me to this.

"You are queen, and we will rule this kingdom together or not at all," Jax added.

"I vow to protect Eodratera with my life," I promised, and each of the other rulers raised their gazes to me. I watched each demon's face shift into some form of acceptance.

They'd seen me survive Vileer and the dangers thrown at me by the realm. Somehow, I had earned their respect, and I would do everything in my power to keep it.

I nodded to each of them.

The meeting was cut short for the celebrations planned for the evening. The rulers had been invited—not only to extend an invite of peace, but also to finally solidify my acceptance of my position as queen.

Jax remained behind to discuss a few more matters while Drakor escorted me back to the room to change before the event.

Walking back, I realized how thankful I had become for the demon. The start to our friendship had been treacherous, but I had come to love Drakor the way Jax did. He was part of our little family, and I appreciated everything he had done for me.

"Thank you," I said to him, needing him to know how I felt.

"For what?" he asked.

"For never giving up on me. For continuing to protect me and look out for me, even when I didn't make it easy," I admitted.

"I will forever protect you and Jax. It is not only my duty, but my honor," he said.

"And for that, I shall be eternally grateful," I said, pausing.

Drakor stopped in the middle of the hall and turned to me. I threw my arms around him, taking him by surprise as I hugged him.

He hesitated before wrapping his own arms around me.

"Also, you aren't as terrifying as you'd like people to think," I teased.

"Don't test me, witch," he retorted, and we both laughed.

"I wish Seri could be here to see everything this place has become," he admitted. "He would've loved it."

"He will always be a part of this palace," I assured him. "Even if he is gone, he will never be forgotten, and his love for the king and this realm will always be known," I promised.

Drakor nodded, and I swore I caught a glimpse of a tear lining his eye before he turned away.

We made it back to the bedroom, where Drakor departed. I entered the room and found my familiar sleeping on the bed, my dress laid out beside the cat.

It was a long, black velvet dress, the sleeves sheer with minuscule sparkles sewn in.

I easily changed into the dress, waiting for the king of demons to return. I found a tiara waiting for me in the bathroom and used the mirror to pin it securely in my hair. The black gems in the tiara matched my dress as my red hair fell in neat curls over my shoulders.

I heard the door open and found the demon king waiting in the room.

"There you are," he said, a mischievous grin spreading across his lips. "I've been waiting for this moment."

He took my hand, leading me to the balcony doors. Pushing them open, he stood aside to let me step out. The balcony overlooked the front courtyard of the palace.

I looked down when I heard gasps and cheers ringing through the air. Below, I found hundreds of demons eager to catch a glimpse of their queen. The courtyard was decorated with blacks and orange, and I spotted a few pumpkins spread across the space as I turned confused to Jax.

"Did you forget?" he asked.

"Forget what?" I asked, tilting my head.

"It's Halloween," he said, smiling. He moved closer,

wrapping his arms around my waist and kissing my neck. I smiled, realizing it had been exactly a year since I arrived.

He'd decorated for the holiday, knowing what it meant to me: the start of my freedom, myjourney. Halloween would always hold a special place in my heart.

Standing on that balcony, I pictured a new world, one filled with magic and life, a balance against the darkness, one where the demons who roamed the streets knew greys and blacks but also color. I let my magic trickle from my palm, tiny embers floating in the wind.

I could feel the warmth of Jax's muscular body pressing against me.

"I love you, little flame," Jax breathed. "Every part of me wishes I could have that year we spent apart back, but I suppose I'll settle for every year to come instead."

I smiled up at him. "You rescued me when I was lost, when I had nothing to live for anymore," I admitted. His gentle touch brushed my face, and I angled my head to rest against his hand. "You made me feel a little more alive, gave me a reason to fight. I will continue to fight my personal demons every day."

That brought a smile to his face.

"And as for this demon?" he asked, raising a brow.

"Come, my king," I said playfully. "The night is still young, and we have a whole year to make up for," I said with a mischievous grin.

My heart raced, butterflies fluttering in my stomach as I anticipated the long night of pleasure ahead of me.

"But first, we have guests to greet," I added.

"My queen," he whispered. "I could never deny your wishes."

His golden eyes found mine, and I held his gaze for a moment.

I'd spend a lifetime lost in those eyes, a lifetime ruling by Jax's side, where I belonged.

The End

Acknowledgments

There are so many wonderful people who made this book possible and I am going to try my very best to address them all here.

First and always, to my wonderful husband, this book never would have been written without all of your help with our baby and making sure I had time to sit down and write. I love you endlessly.

To my baby bean, thank you for attending all of my book events and giving me endless newborn snuggles while I wrote this story.

To my best friend, Ky Venn, this journey has been a wild ride and there is no one else I would want to take on new bookish adventures with than you. Thank you for listening to my endless rants, keeping me motivated, and supporting me no matter what. I love you!

To my amazing alpha reader, Allyn Hamrick, thank you for believing in this story and making me feel so seen. Writing Soleil to face the same OCD struggles as myself was terrifying and your endless love and support has pushed me to share her story with the world.

To my beta readers, thank you for giving this story a chance and for your feedback. This story is better because of your suggestions and support.

To my editor, Alexa (The Fiction Fix), thank you for being the best editor a girl could ask for. Anyone who adds a Monty Python GIF during edits is a 10/10 editor in my opinion.

To my other writing besties, S. Frasher, Kate Korsak, and Kyla Shinder, thank you for all of the advice, writing sprints, and support you have shown me.

To my sisters, Leah and Rory, thank you for always being my biggest supporters and making me feel much cooler than I actually am.

To my parents, Tammie and Patrick, thank you for believing in me and never once questioning if writing was the right path for me. And thank you for instilling a love and appreciation for Halloween into me. I will forever be a spooky season girl now.

To my in-laws, this was the first year of being married into your family and the never-ending love you have shown my books and writing makes me feel so welcomed into your family.

To all of my readers, I would be nothing without you! It is because of your continued support for my books that I am able to do what I love.

ABOUT THE AUTHOR

MK Ahearn grew up in Massachusetts as one of three sisters. She now lives in Maryland with her husband, son, and their three cats. She received her bachelor of arts in international relations and a master of professional studies in homeland security. When not writing or studying she can be found planning her next travel adventure.

Discover more by MK Ahearn on Amazon.